Book #1

[redacted]

08/Jan/2023

Chasing the Staff

(revised edition)

by

Deron Rennick

Deron Rennick

Images associated with this book are stock images provided by prettysleepy1 (user_id:2855492) and prettysleepy (user_id:2973588) on PixaBay.com.

(Print Version: November 4, 2022)

ISBN: 978-1-7387406-1-1

•

Deron Rennick Books

Dedication

To my friend and writer,
Peg Ainsley,
who continued to believe in me
even when I no longer
believed in myself.

TABLE OF CONTENTS

New Ranidae

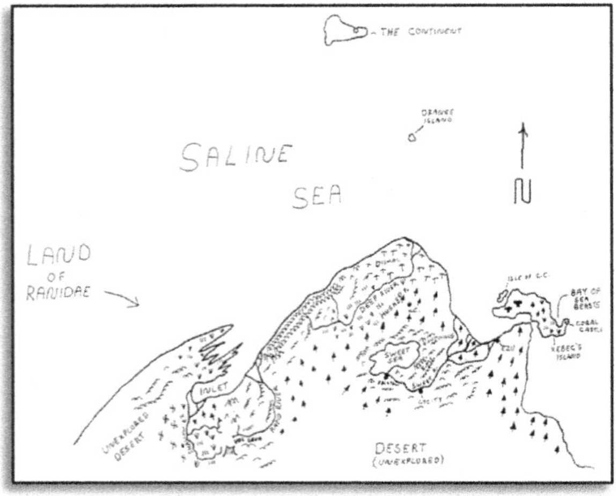
THE CONTINENT
SALINE SEA
N
LAND OF RANIDAE
INLET
SWEET SEA
BAY OF SEA BEASTS
CORAL CASTLE
KEBEC'S ISLAND
UNEXPLORED DESERT
DESERT (UNEXPLORED)

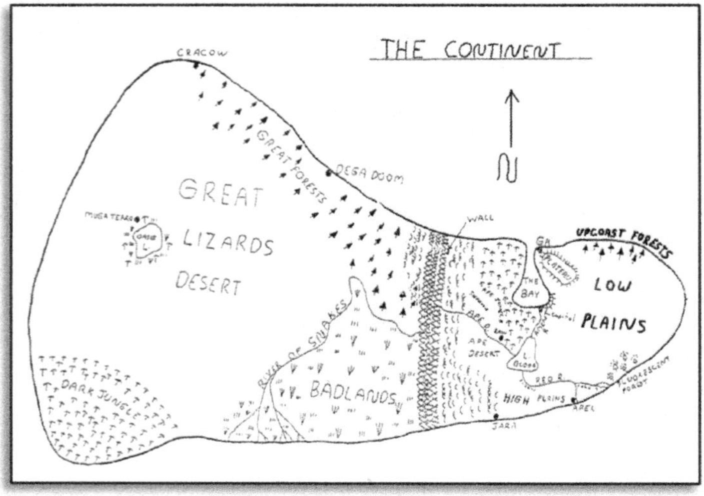
THE CONTINENT
N
CRACOW
GREAT FORESTS
DEGA DOOM
GREAT LIZARDS DESERT
WALL
UPCOAST FORESTS
GA
PLATEAU
THE BAY
LOW PLAINS
APE DESERT
RIVER OF SNAKES
BADLANDS
DARK JUNGLE
HIGH PLAINS
RED R.
APEL
JARA

Taleteller

"Well, hello, hello, hello, hi, hi, hi. It is truly a pleasure to meet you. That is, assuming that we have never met before? After all, this is by no means my first trip to your beautiful blue globe. Oh no. No. No. Uh-uh. Noper. But constant travel across both space and time can really sauté one's senses. Can so. Can too. For certain. For sure. Please don't throw a flaming asteroid if I should remember you but I do not.

"Oh my. I've neglected to formally introduce myself. Tsk. Tsk. This certainly will not do. Noper. It will not do at all.

"Ahem. Introducing the well-aged, well-travelled, invisible, intelligent and most learned, Taleteller Of This Book!

"Actually, my full name is Me. And, of course, if I am Me, then that makes you, You. Together we're just Me and You. Ha! Hmmm...? You know, if I had a chin I'd rub it. Would too. Would so. For certain. For sure.

"So. So. So. So. Just what in the name of creepy constellations is a taleteller doing roaming about your planet Earth, you ask. What? You didn't ask? Then pretend ya did! I'll have you know that I skipped out on this millennia's Convention of The Disorder of Galactic Gossips just to be here with you in this one-star solar system! The convention is taking place two galaxies away and only occurs but once in every thousand of your Earth years. Personally, I'm not at all interested in hearing buzz of who actually got lost in a charted galaxy or who singed themselves by flying too close to a star. Boring. Could happen to anybody. I'd much rather taletell to you. Please don't close this book on me just yet.

"Now, where was I? Oh yes. There are actually two reasons why I am here. First, whenever I'm feeling a little cooped up in the cosmos and fancy a good giggle, I often lighten my mood by

traveling here to watch you humans manage your planet. In fact, amongst we space travellers, human jokes have become quite popular at comet-rides and other intergalactic social functions. For example, have you heard about Earth's new human dolls? Just wind them up and they foolishly waste irreplaceable resources! Ha! Ha! Ha! Ha! Hmmmm...? Not funny, eh? Oh well, I guess you'd have to be a seasoned time tripper to get that one.

"But alas, I am also here to entertain and intrigue you. Am too. Am so. Besides, what I now observe going down on your home planet somehow just doesn't seem all that funny anymore. In fact, in the future I think I'll only venture to Earth in the past. But enough about Me. Let us get on with the tale.

"Our tale mostly takes place in the Land of Ranidae, which lies due south across The Saline Sea from The Continent. If we have met before, I may have already taletelled to you of past events there. And if not, no matter. What does matter to this tale is that The Continent does indeed exist and that it sustains The Fluorescent Forest, where an aged and surly sapkeeper named Snarly Grouchwhiner dwells.

"But more about that cranky old curmudgeon later. What really matters most if you are to understand and enjoy this tale is that you must know The Legend of The Demon Chaser.

"You see, millions of zillions of kilahillions of.... well, a very long time ago anyway, even before your own planet had cooled, a pair of wicked Demons roamed about the infinite expanse of boundless space. Sworn enemies of anything that is beautiful, the demons set out to undo all of the beauty that the deity, Seed, had forged over all of eternity; beginning with the complete destruction of your own young and still maturing Universe. None know for certain why the demons began with your Universe, or why they hated beauty so much; although one theory has it that they were simply jealous of Seed's creative powers, as well as also being quite envious of those other two most powerful of deities, Destiny and Morgue.

"Together, the resentful Demons began wreaking havoc all across your Universe. They used their combined powers to bend gravity and divert comets from their proper paths; sending them

crashing into newly thriving globes, and thereby causing widespread devastation and extinguishing many of Seed's finest creations. Entire atmospheres were stripped away. Wowza! Big bangs up there, eh? Talk about dee-struck-chin!

"According to legend, Seed became enraged and created a Demon Chaser to seek out and destroy the wicked pair. To properly carry out its task, the Demon Chaser was granted a staff. Not just any old staff, however. Oh no. Not at all, at all.

"Created by Seed herself and forged from only the purest of white gold, this staff grants its bearer the powers of a sixth sense. Also, at the bearer's will it can shoot forth a beam of blazing light so intense that it can actually melt stone; and, of course, slay demons. Apparently, the staff's powers can only be unpowered in the depths of the Saline Sea. Seed forged it so because the sly demons were partial to salty water and known to lurk well beneath the wetrollers. Thus, should they somehow defeat the Demon Chaser in combat and seize the staff, eventually the unsuspecting pair would accidently unpower the awesome weapon themselves.

"Still, should the staff ever fall into the wrong hands, all creatures would suddenly find themselves in a right fine mess indeed. For certain. For sure. Will too. Will so.

"Anyway, the Demon Chaser eventually found the wicked pair skulking about amongst some white skysheep off the rocky coast of the Land of Ranidae; high above the Isle of Countless Caverns, to be more precise. And that is exactly where they engaged in battle for an entire era. Plus an entire second era. Then most of yet a third... Whew, I'm getting exhausted just telling you about it.

"Finally, The Demon Chaser, aided by the staff, was able to slay both Demons. However, the price it paid proved to be its very own being. Fatally wounded, it plummeted downward until its fall was broken by the Isle's rocky skin, where it soon came to meet Morgue.

"But not before it had managed to drag its own battered form deep down into one of the Isle's countless caverns; whereupon, after holing up in a small cave, it sealed the mouth

with molten rock. Rock which eventually cooled to form a thick slab of solid granite, thereby securing the staff for all of eternity. But then again, all of eternity can be a very, very, very long time…

"Why then is the staff still unfound, you ask? That is a most excellent question. Most, most excellent.

"Three reasons come to mind. First, legend also dictates that whoever possesses the staff shall grow increasingly mad over time. Only the Demon Chaser itself, for whom the staff was originally forged, was immune to such sapping of sense.

"Second, the Isle of Countless Caverns is most aptly named, with each cavern appearing much the same as all of the others.

"And finally, I give you the third and perhaps most important reason of all. Hardly a creature, mortal or otherwise, actually believes in the legend to begin with. And of those very few who do believe in it, virtually none are deranged enough that they would ever dare to actually seek out the staff.

"That is, virtually none but one…"

1
Xebec

(Pronounced Chebek)

Ruler Xebec peered west from the tower of his pink limestone castle, which dominated both the valley and its shoreline from its place atop a steep plateau at the extreme eastern end of his island.

A dim sorcerer by choice, Xebec's appearance can only be described as glumdreary, with a dour demeanor and a sullen stare. It was even said that he never looked at others, but that he stared straight through them. None could claim to have ever seen him smile, or even hint at a smile. And what passed for his laugh was vocal grating at its worst.

Patience had never been one of Xebec's better blessings, and one more sleepless night was not going to change him. Day once again ruled the sky as he paced back and forth across the tower's brattice, pausing at long intervals to peer as far west across the valley as his eyes could see. Straining his sights even further west, he viewed beyond the Bay of Sea Beasts towards the distant coastline. The sky was empty of skysheep, and the sun's light glistened atop the sea's rolling skin.

Vapors of breath rolled out from between his lips. His mind was filled with but a single thought; as it had been for many *cycles*, ever since he had first switched from clean magic to dim sorcery. He was drawn to his choice by an unquenchable thirst for power, not unlike an unfed finner unto bait. And, as with most who desire power above all else, Xebec was now unable to alter the course of his own fate even if he had so wanted to.

He was now a prisoner of his own greed and ambition; completely void of empathy, compassion or love of others. Loneliness was his one true friend, and he was content that it should remain so. All that mattered was getting whatever he coveted. And what Xebec coveted beyond anything else was to possess The Staff of The Demon Chaser, and thereby rule over all of everything.

He often stayed awake for all of Night's rule. Pacing, always pacing. Deeply entranced in thought, until dawn shattered the spell and his mind moved on to other matters. But his primary obsession never fully went away. It was always there, picking at his mind. Ruler Xebec was a sorcerer possessed by himself.

BOOM!! BOOM!! BOOM!!

The echo of the pounding upon his bedchamber door always annoyed Xebec. Of course, virtually everything annoyed Xebec. He entered the realm of deepest dreams annoyed, and awakened back into the realm of reality annoyed. Rain most certainly annoyed him. Sunshine also annoyed him. Both Day and Night equally annoyed him. Skysheep. Wetrollers. Wind. Calm. They all annoyed him. In fact, most everything annoyed him.

BOOM!! BOOM!!

"Enter!" Xebec shrilled.

Slowly, the door creaked open, exposing one of the many boorleez that served and feared Ruler Xebec. Boorleez are burly, bald characters with short and skinny legs, hairy torsos, and thick arms that reach down to touch the ground. They mostly move about by arm-swinging upon their hard knuckles. Whatever traits the boorleez may lack in smarts can be offset by their honesty and loyalty, as well as by their kind nature.

Yet even the brooleez' wanting wit fares far above that of their adopted pets, the kooky critters. Scaly creatures with droopy jowls and long tongues which roll out from between their pointy teeth, the kooky critters have webbed claws for swamp dwelling, as well as transparent lids that can cover their bulging yellow eyes. And they always stink like yuck.

"What!?" Xebec snapped.

"Ruler Xebec…" The boorlee meekly responded. "Flying cooer comes with tag from Isle. Cooer's tag dooz be blue, so sez boorleez dooz find melty wall thingy."

"They have found the melted wall? Gaffwit, are you absolutely positive?"

"Um, dooz ye sez?" The boorlee was clearly baffled.

"I mean, are you sure?"

"Uh-huh. Dooz be sure," Gaffwit replied with a nod.

Desire sparked in Xebec's eyes. *'Could it be true?'* he wondered. *'I must leave at once and find out for myself.'*

"Gaffwit, have my griffin saddled for flight. Now."

"Me dooz, Ruler Xebec." The boorlee turned and arm-swung from the bedchamber; forgetting, as always, to shut the door behind him.

For once, Xebec was undaunted about the door being left open. "Can it be true?" he muttered aloud, snatching his black cloak and matching skullcap from their wall pegs. "Have the boorleez really found the melted wall? Is it possible? Or, did they attach the wrong-coloured tag by mistake? Again."

Xebec scooped a baggy sack from the floor, slung it over his shoulder, and exited the bedchamber. For the first time ever, he too forgot to close the door behind himself.

With the haste and energy of someone less than half his age, the old sorcerer bounded down a spiraled stairwell and passed through a narrow archway, before slipper-sliding into a spacious vaulted chamber. Next, he strided with purpose down the long, winding corridor that descended in stages to the courtyard. He was indifferent to the corridor's many grim wall paintings, the meanings of which are known only to magicians and sorcerers.

His loyal griffin eagerly awaited him in the courtyard. It was truly a magnificent beast, with the silver body and claws of a sabre-tooth, and the golden wings and head of an eagle. Xebec had forged it himself and breathed it into being by way of dim sorcery. Many attempts had failed before he had finally met with success. Subsequent efforts to produce a mate for the beast had always met with failure. Still, the sorcerer was somewhat satisfied, having under his control a metallic beast capable of streaking across the sky with him saddled upon its back.

Avoiding speech, Xebec motioned for some boorleez to move aside. Paying them no further mind, he seized the saddle pommel with one wrinkled hand, while slipping a foot into the stirrup. He next threw a leg across the griffin's back and drew himself upright into the saddle. Gripping tight the reins, he commanded the magnificent beast into flight. "Griffin, fly North by West!"

Even at streak speed, almost a full phase of the moon would pass before they reached the Isle of Countless Caverns; which reached up from the wetrollers off the western tip of Xebec's Island, and whose peaks sought to scratch the sky.

Xebec grinned as they passed over the white ribbon of sand that parted the growth of the valley from the wetrollers of The Bay of Sea Beasts. Below them, a pod of blue spouters plowed through the sea, breathing spray up into the wind.

Xebec thought, *'Soon, even you giants of the sea shall obey me.'*

Night came and retreated and came and retreated before they reached the far shore; yet they rested not. Beasts forged of precious metal were quite immune to fatigue, and its creator was himself accustomed to napping only half of his own body at any one time during long flights. Thus, one wary eye could keep a constant watch for the other, while one hand always gripped tight the reins.

No, there would be no stops on this trip, at least not until they reached the Isle; even if such required rising high above flocks of stormy skysheep to avoid a drenching.

The marshlands along the shore eventually gave way to Fern Forest. Covering fully one third of Xebec's Island, the forest sprawled out below them like a breathing green beast. Its lush and leafy skin was only broken by the shimmering aquaveins that nourished it. Flocks of flappers honked and chirped and cawed as they crissed and crossed above its endless form. Despite their being concealed from on high, the forest's inner body was home to countless creatures.

Xebec thought, *'Soon, every creature of every forest shall obey me.'*

Day and Night fought many battles before the griffin cleared the far edge of Fern Forest. Upon once again passing over marshland, the beast straddled the northernmost edge of The Baobabs, where the treefolk grow so large that you can even get lost in their trunks, and where the sun's rays seldom strike soil. The Baobabs are indeed a most mysterious place, where peepers peek from the shadows and shrill cries will shiver your skin.

Even Xebec himself had never dared venture into that creepy place. Nor had he any desire to do so unless he possessed the staff. A familiar thought brought a rare smile to his face. *'Soon, I shall fear neither plant nor beast – for they all shall fear me.'*

After what seemed like forever and then some to the impatient sorcerer, they at last cleared the final ribbon of white sand that divided soil from sea, and there they veered due west.

Not far distant loomed the bleak outline of the Isle of Countless Caverns, its grey peaks stabbing holes through the ring of steaming mist which always choked the Isle's base. Always. Be it day or night, warm season or cool, be there white skysheep or stormy skysheep, skytwinklers or blackness, the steaming mist never waned. Drawing too near to it would blister one's skin. Flying in amongst it would boil the flesh off one's bones.

Even though the metallic griffin would be unharmed by such steam, it nevertheless rose well above the mist to protect its sorcerer. Past visits had conditioned it so that Xebec need not even utter commands. The loyal beast instinctively avoided the hazard and flew directly for the Isle's highest peaks.

Rising above them all was Scald Summit, with her lake of magma glowing orange inside her cratered crown. In the past, she had breathed smoke and ash high up into the sky, and spilled lava down her sides. When moody, she could still cause the entire isle to quake.

Like the lingering mist, Scald Summit never slept. Always, she hissed and crackled and breathed smoke; an ominous warning to intruders: "CHALLENGE ME NOT!!"

Xebec wondered if the staff could even tame her? *'Imagine being master over a volcano?'* he mused.

But for now, the griffin heeded Scald Summit's warning'; maintaining a safe distance from her crater, and flapping towards that of her sister, Slumber Summit, whose cratered apex was cooled, bumpy and hard. Slumber never uttered a sound, not even a gaseous yawn; for, unlike her sister, she had slept peacefully for many ages. Of most importance, however, Slumber's belly offered safer passage down into Scald's, as both sister's were connected below their peaks and thus shared many tunnels.

Several boorleez stood stooped within Slumber's crater, supporting their huge, hairy torsos upon their hard knuckles. Near them lazed some kooky critters with their long tongues lapping their scales.

As the griffin touched claws to surface, the biggest boorlee arm-swung up to Xebec. "Ruler Xebec, we dooz find melty wall thingy."

"Show me," Xebec demanded. "And have my griffin washed clean with vinegar and then polished."

The biggest boorlee motioned with his huge hands and all of the other boorleez frantically took to their tasks. They were, however, not at all aided by the kooky critters; the kooky critters being much too tardy of wit to ever risk helping with such tricky chores.

Xebec glanced about the crater. "Where?"

"Ye spozed takes blue path..."

"Don't just tell me," Xebec snapped. "Show me!"

The big boorlee bit his tongue, and then turned and swift-swung his way across the crater's bumpy surface. Lest he should be scolded. *Or worse...?*

Slightly shy of the crater's face, the big boorlee and Xebec entered a cage which had been built of sturdy chutes. A hemp rope was knotted to a metal ring atop the cage, from which it stretched straight upward until it reached the boom of a hoist. Many anxious faces with bald heads peered down at them.

Somewhere beyond the crater's lip, unseen hands commenced cranking a winch and the cage slowly began to rise. It swayed and spun as the rope slid through the spinning pulleys, lifting the cage upwards.

Xebec stewed in serious silence. Could the boorleez have actually found the melted wall? Was it possible after all these cycles of seeking? Or, did he once again travel the entire breadth of his island for failure?

Failure. The very word gnashed his teeth. Quickly, he erased all thought of failure from his mind and patted the baggy sack. Could its contents crack through the wall? Could anything?

"I shall succeed," Xebec muttered as the boom swung about and cleared the lip. Then he stepped from the cage without acknowledging the presence of others.

The big boorlee arm-swung his way over to a huge slab of stone with a blue arrow painted onto it. Aiming down the steep and rugged incline, the arrow pointed to a boulder far below. A second blue arrow on the boulder indicated a slight change of direction, pointing to yet another boulder and arrow. And so on. All quite necessary to keep one from becoming hopelessly lost in the confusing maze of crevasses, chasms, crags and caverns; each of which appeared much like the last.

Even so, some boorleez had already vanished trying to find Ruler Xebec's prize. *Unless, of course, they had simply snuck away to freedom?* And some of the boulders and slabs had arrows crossed out, indicating that the first arrows may have been painted in error? Hardly a surprise with boorleez.

Plus there were the caves. More caves than a hundred scholars could count in a hundred cycles. Home to silkspinners and blackwings, the caves served as gaping mouths for the tunnels that led down into both mountains' bowels: a labyrinth of pits and caverns, many of which served as crypts for a long extinct genus of ogres. A place where stone swirls twist up from floor to ceiling, and where drips echo like skybangers. A drab and dankly place, where the dampness chills breath and shivers skin. A place where no breeze ever blows. A place where no breathing being should ever dare to be.

This was the mythical domain of the Kymeera; ferocious, hooved monsters with maned heads and dragons' tails, which were drawn to the smell of flesh.

Together, Xebec and the big boorlee zigged and zagged their way down from the summit, guided by the blue arrows. They struggled to maintain their balance whenever the pitch of the hazardous trail steepened, or narrowed to a squeeze. As it so often did.

Occasionally, they were forced by circumstance to straddle bottomless rifts, or tippytoe along narrow ledges to avoid falling into an abyss.

Being accustomed to arm-swinging, the big boorlee in particular found such moment's breath-bating at best. Although mindful that just one errant step of his unskilled feet could mean an early meeting with Morgue, he was likewise wary of the testy sorcerer barking at his back.

Their trek eventually led them to the gaping mouth of a tunnel. A pair of boorleez and a kooky critter stooped sentry outside, while the flame from a torch flickered from within. Secured in a metal bracket, the torch bent its light in a silent rhythm for a troop of dancing wall shadows.

Xebec ignored all gestures of greeting and made directly for the torch. Snatching it from the bracket, he then gestured for the big boorlee to lead on.

Despite some heat from the flame, a chilly breeze still nipped at their skin. That is, until they rounded the tunnel's first bend. Then the wind bated its blow, and all became still and silent and very cold. Blue crystals coated the tunnel walls.

"Lead on," Xebec prodded, seemingly indifferent to the drop in temperature.

As the pair descended deeper into the mountains' insides, the stillness grew and grew and grew... Until they could almost hear themselves shivering in sync with their chattering teeth.

Xebec refused to rest. Drawing fresh torches from strategically placed brackets, he pressed onward. Down and around and down and around they went, until the temperature rapidly began to rise.

The big boorlee finally braved a question. "Ruler Xebec, dooz cum tunnel be so hot now?"

"Because we have descended deep into Scald Summit's belly, where molten magma flows freely through her veins." Xebec explained.

"Huh? Dooz ye sez?"

Xebec was annoyed, yet simplified his explanation. "This mountain's belly is so hot that it even melts stone. See how the wall crystals are sweating."

It was true. Little droplets glistened upon the tunnel walls and ceiling. The tunnel floor had become slushy with puddles. Breath had ceased blowing in vapor, and frosted ears and digits burned from their thawing. Only the stillness remained.

After much time spent huffing and puffing and sweating like snorthogs, they rounded a bend and sighted an orange glow far off in the distance, beyond a steep incline.

Xebec quickened his pace. His breath was hot and laboured, and sweat soaked his garments. Both legs stretched in step as he hastened to exit the sweltering tunnel. He could feel its walls closing in about him. Squeezing him. Trying to trap him like a snack in a serpent.

Suddenly he was free. Huffing and puffing, he stood on the narrow tongue of a path just beyond the tunnel's inner mouth, gawking at the strange spectacle before him.

He had entered a cavern unlike anything he had ever imagined. The grotto itself seemed fully awake and aware. Its moist walls were flush in colour. Blushing fibre pillars twisted upward to support a fleshy ceiling. Down below, meaty matting covered most of the cavern floor, except for where there were spit-pools filled with sticky saliva.

Freaky flowers with flushy petals and feeted roots stood beside the pools. They blinked up at the intruders. Xebec was quite certain that some even moved.

"Did you see that?" Xebec asked, pointing past some flowers. "Something just submerged itself into that spit-pool. See how the surface is still rippled."

"Bad thingy dooz hides in pools," the boorlee stated with angst.

"What sort of bad thing?"

The nervous boorlee merely shrugged his broad shoulders.

Xebec would have pressed the issue, except that he spied the upper rungs of a rope ladder that had been tied to a pillar and dropped over the ledge. Grabbing hold of the ladder, he carefully began his climb down to the cavern floor.

"Wait until I am clear before you follow me," he ordered, already concerned about his clumsy guide falling and snagging him along for the crunch.

Xebec soon felt the meaty matting beneath his feet. Releasing his hold on the ladder, he beckoned for the big boorlee to follow. He then turned to once again inspect the immense cavern. The freaky flowers had now vanished, yet all of the spit-pools were unrippled at the surface? *'Where did they go?'* he wondered. *'They were just...'*

"Ooops!"

Xebec reacted just in the nik of a quick to avoid being squashed beneath sixty stone of falling boorlee.

Destiny still smiled upon the big boorlee, however, as the cavern floor's meaty matting and his own thick skull absorbed most of the impact. Therefore, although dazed and dizzy, the burly klutz avoided any serious injury.

Xebec glared in disgust at the boorlee, who had somehow managed to pull himself upright onto his knuckles and stretch a silly smile. Briefly. Until both of his eyes spun blank into his brow and he pitched forward to enter the realm of deepest dreams.

"Dung," Xebec cussed, "Now, how shall I find the others?"

He slowly scanned the cavern, noting that its moist walls were broken by a multitude of recesses and caves, and that no other boorleez were anywhere about?

"Hmmppff," he grumbled, dipping a wrinkled hand into his cloak.

Retrieving a tiny glass vial from an inner pocket, he quickly popped the cork. Quick as a blink, a ghostly haze spewed forth from captivity and swirled about the sorcerer.

Xebec raised both arms high as he chanted:

"OH, DIM SORCERY, PLEASE ABET WITH THIS SPELL…

INSPIRE THIS HOUNDHAZE TO SERVE ME QUITE WELL…

MY GUIDE IS WITH DREAMS, FROM THE LADDER HE FELL…

LET IT SNIFF OUT THE SPOT WHERE MY BOORLEEZ DO DWELL…"

The hazy apparition ceased swirling and shaped itself into a long sniffer. It then began to drift across the cavern. Gently. Effortlessly. As if pushed along by a gentle breeze; *yet the cavern's aura was still?*

Only the sound of sniffing stole the silence as the houndhaze floated slightly atop the meaty matting, expertly tracking a scent. Slowly at first. "Snff. Snff. Snff," Then it began swiftly increasing its speed. "Snff-snff-snff-snff…"

Xebec panted and cussed as his aging limbs struggled to keep the houndhaze in sight. For what seemed like forever, he chased after it. He followed it through fleshy tunnels and around tight bends; all the while winding in and out of fibre pillars and about sticky spit-pools. Twice he ducked under bushy arches with fleshy pores that stank of sweat.

Eventually, the meaty matting ended and the fleshy tunnels were once more of solid stone. Undaunted by the change, Xebec kept on after the hound haze; following it across mucous covered ledges and over lichen crusted boulders. Through tunnels and caverns. And on and on and on…

Xebec cared not that his panting breathers might burst. He wanted his prize! Then, just when he could chase it no further, the houndhaze vanished. Its task fulfilled, the hazy apparition was at last free to hide and haunt on its own.

Using each other as pillows, about a dozen boorleez snoozed atop the cavern floor in a pile of lumpy fur that breathed up and down as one. Some kooky critters were dozing nearby. Xebec's stare, however, was not upon any of them. He saw only the oval granite slab that had been carefully melted into the cavern wall near to all of the snoozing – *sentries?*

Unlike the rest of the cavern, this section of wall was smooth with a faint glow to it; almost as if had been poured as a liquid, and then cooled and polished with care. One could even feel an energy emanating from the sealed chamber behind it.

Even though he was still panting, Xebec staggered up to the glowing slab and pressed both palms against its smooth surface. A most welcome warmth rushed up his arms and into his weary body. He had finally found what he had sought after for far too long. Too tired to cheer, he merely smiled and pressed his cheeks tight against the surface. *'My prize. At long last I have found you.'*

"Ruler Xebec…?"

The sorcerer turned about to encounter many burly shapes stirring about him.

"Boorleez dooz good thing, huh?" one boorlee asked, clearly looking for praise.

"Tools!" Xebec demanded. "Have you the drilling tools?"

"Dooz gots tools," several voices responded together.

"And have you any buckets?"

"Dooz gots buckets," replied the burly bunch.

"Good. Go and fill them with saliva from the spit-pools while I mark out the wall for drilling."

All eyes wided at Xebec.

"Why are you all staring at me?"

"Beez big monster lurks in pools," replied one shaky boorlee.

"A big monster?" Xebec inquired skeptically.

"We dooz heared monster roar," explained another.

"Ohhh, you did, did you?" Xebec's tone revealed much cynicism.

Every boorlee nodded their head.

Xebec smirked sarcastic as he parted his arms. "And exactly where is this BIG monster?"

His question was met with lowered eyes and shrugging shoulders. The kooky critters quietly skulked away, determined to avoid Xebec's wrath.

"Well?" Xebec pressed.

One brave boorlee finally dared step forward. "Boorleez heared hooves clopping, Ruler Xebec. Dooz be scared..."

Xebec's tone went beyond taunting. "Ohhh, hooves clopping."

"And a splash..." added another.

"Ohhh, and a splash?"

"Uh-huh," replied the boorleez, all nodding in unison.

"Phooey!" Xebec scoffed, reaching inside his sack. "The only monster you lot shall encounter down here is Me! Now, do as I say... Move it!!"

Panic erupted as the boorleez scrambled to do the irate sorcerer's bidding. All feared the monster, but they feared Xebec even more. None amongst them wanted to risk a scolding. *Or worse...?*

Xebec scowled and produced a wooden peg from the sack. His plan to break through the granite slab was quite simple, yet clever.

The pegs were to be thoroughly soaked in saliva from the spit-pools. Meanwhile, he would keep the boorleez busy drilling holes into a portion of the slab. Trial and error on granite faces had proved it best not to space the pegs beyond two hands apart. Therefore, he himself would mark out the exact points of drilling, knowing all too well the wanting math skills of boorleez.

After all of the necessary holes had been drilled, the soggy pegs were to be pounded into them like plugs. Prior experiments had proved that sinkwood does indeed soften and shrink when wetted. It also hardens and expands when dried.

Xebec's gamble was that the heat and energy from the slab would dry out the soggy sinkwood quite quickly, and that the ensuing pressure produced from the expanding pegs would break apart the granite. This, he reasoned, should enable the boorleez to break out chunks of the slab with sledges and picks. All that would be required was a hole just big enough for him to slip through and the staff would be his!

Xebec produced a stick of chalk from his cloak pocket and began using his own hands to measure out spacing in the center of the slab. He ever so carefully plotted each X into its exact and proper place.

Soon, the boorleez returned with full buckets.

"What, not eaten by monsters?" Xebec teased as he spilled the sack's contents into the buckets. "Good that you weren't. More to share in the work. And do put your backs into it. I want to hear those drilling bits buzz. We will neither nap nor nourish until our deed here is done."

Several boorleez fetched some hefty iron augers from a battered old tool chest and immediately set to work cranking the drilling bits into a spin.

Boring into hard stone in such heat proved to be a most arduous task indeed, and soon every boorlee was puffing for breath. Beads of sweat danced atop their thick skulls. Backs ached with each twist of the tools as forearms were worked numb. Strong fingers became blistered and sore. A fine dust stung into their eyes and caused them to choke.

The hardy beasts toiled on and on, even making a game of their labours. They competed to see which team could bore out a hole to the maximum depth first, with the winners of each heat being rewarded with a vigorous volley of knuckle noogies upon their thick skulls. Awarding knuckle noogies was a strange and confusing ritual that never ceased to puzzle Xebec, yet it seemed to be serious stuff to the boorleez.

Xebec thought, *'Oh well, at least it keeps them willing and working.'*

After ample drilling, the boorleez finally managed to bore out enough holes that Xebec instructed some of them to begin pounding in the soggy pegs. The dull clack of mallets meeting sinkwood began to echo off the cavern walls.

Save for the knuckle noogie rituals, the boorleez' toil continued uninterrupted until all of the wetted pegs were pounded into place. Only then did the pushy sorcerer permit the weary and dusty bunch to nourish on fruit and nuts. And, of course, the ever-important desserts.

While the famished boorleez gorged themselves, Xebec commenced with a chant:

"MAGICAL SINKWOOD, BACKWARDS YOU ARE…

WHEN WET YOU SHRINK UP, THEN DRY LARGER BY FAR…

THE BOORLEEZ FIRST DRILLED, THEN IN YOU DID GO…

WE WILL REST WHILE YOU DRY, THEN THIS ROCK SLAB WILL…

BLOW!!"

Having finished with stuffing their bellies, the boorleez next arm-swung over to a far corner of the cavern. There they proceeded to use each other's bloated bellies for pillows as they cuddled up into a lumpy pile of fur that breathed up and down as one.

Shortly thereafter, the pegs began to dry out and expand. One tiny crack, thin as a thread, started to slowly sneak its way across the granite slab. Zigging and zagging. Seeking.

A second crack appeared. Quickly followed by a third. More and more cracks appeared until an entire network of thin cracks crissed and crossed the slab like a silkspinner's web. In quick time, the distinct popping sound of expanding pegs busting up granite grew so loud that it even awakened the boorleez.

Xebec was beside himself with a rare aura of joy. Perplexed boorleez exchanged quizzical glances as the smiling sorcerer swaggered over to the tool chest and attempted to retrieve one of several sledges. However, it proved to be much too heavy for his frail frame to budge.

Smiling, and seemingly still in a cheery tone, Xebec requested, "Could one of you fine boorleez perhaps assist me with this sledge?"

More quizzical glances were exchanged. Somebody whispered, "Me thinks Ruler Xebec dooz be boink? Why him dooz be nice to boorleez, huh?"

"I'm waiting." The cheer was waning from Xebec's tone and the aura of joy was fast fading from his face. "And you all know that it is most impolite to keep a sorcerer – waiting!"

At once, the boorleez leapt to their knuckles and arm-swung over to the tool chest. After retrieving some sledges and picks, they hurried back to the wall and began bashing away at the cracks.

Large chunks of granite were gradually loosened by the tools, before being removed by hand. It was slow and exhausting work, which required much puffing and sweating.

The obedient boorleez simply wiped their wet palms upon their loincloths and kept on with their task. Relentless. Determined. Eager to please the sorcerer and avoid a scolding. *Or worse...?*

Until eventually, just when Xebec considered granting them a brief rest to replenish their energy, it happened. One of the picks pierced a tiny peephole through the granite. A blazing beam of bright light shot out from behind the slab.

Xebec tried to peek into the chamber, but the bright light denied his eye. "Work!" he shrilled. "Swing harder! Swing faster! Make that hole bigger! Work! Work! Work!"

Now every swing seemed to break free a chunk, with each blow widening the gap until it was just large enough for a thick serpent to squeeze through. *And perhaps a skinny sorcerer?*

"Enough!" Xebec commanded, waving all of the boorleez aside. "Push me through the opening. Do it now."

Yet try as they might, the boorleez simply could not force the impatient sorcerer through the hole. They stared with befuddled minds as his feet and legs flailed wildly in the air.

"Me knows!" one excited boorleez suddenly piped up, looking very smug. "Me bashes Ruler Xebec through hole with me thick skull!"

All the other boorleez cheered the brilliant idea as one of their number lined up the sorcerer's squirming buttocks, and then lowered his thick skull like a battering ram and arm-swung full speed into his target.

"Eeeyyeeow!!"

Xebec fell hard into the chamber, bruising his ribs on the solid floor. He grabbed his cramping buttocks with one hand and tried to shield his face with the other. The searing heat scratched at his flesh. His throat became parched, and his breathers puffed and pained. Sweat dripped from his brow and stung into his eyes. His tongue licked salty drops from his lips.

"HOORRAY!!" cheered the boorleez as the hole became unplugged. They all became so engrossed in granting each other the required amount of *grats* noogies that at first they neglected to take note of the loud screaming and cussing pouring forth from inside the chamber.

Until one boorlee finally noticed the crude speech. "Not *plite* sez bad words, Ruler Xebec."

"!!#?@**??//!!?@*!!!!"

After muttering plenty additional and highly creative cuss words, the determined sorcerer was finally able to stand up. Shielding his eyes and stumbling across the chamber with one outstretched hand, he moved towards the heart of the heat. The floor was cluttered with hard objects that rolled beneath his feet, and he knew at once that they were bones.

"M-Must hurry," he panted.

His nostrils noted the stench of his own singed whiskers. *'Must find staff. Mustn't meet Morgue...'*

He could feel his skin burning towards pain. In sheer desperation, he began groping wildly about the chamber.

"Yeeoww!" he screamed as he scorched his fingers on the cavern wall. The soles of his hide slippers were beginning to smolder.

"Where!?" he shrieked in near panic. "Where are you!?"

He was rewarded as his fingers finally found the staff. Smooth. Hard. Warm. The bright light dimmed into a mellow glow and the surrounding heat ceased to rage.

"Yes!" he shouted, opening his eyes and brandishing the gold staff in triumph. "At long last, I have my prize! And...it...is...all...MINE!!"

An uneasy silence followed Xebec's shouts of triumph. Not just from within the cavern itself, but also from far and beyond the mountain's belly. All across the Isle of Countless Caverns, every breathing being could sense that something was suddenly very wrong. Back at Xebec's castle, boorleez shivered as if from a chill. In the boorleez city of Ezu, sheeleez stopped drawing water from a well and scanned up above for the source of the breathless feeling that now sank through their insides. All along The Sweet River, entire villages of cyclops farmers ceased their toil to ponder the unseen warning that rode past with the wind. On the shore of the Sweet Sea, frightened humanfolk dropped their nets and huddled together for comfort. In the Swallow Mountains, an anxious ladfolk with a long braid of black hair gazed upwards at the sky and thought, *'Something dire has just been unleashed...'*

Even as far away as The Continent, lizarme and humanfolk soldiers stopped in mid-clash to query the ill omen that suddenly swept across the battlefield. Despite the war, every combatant could sense the fangs of a much bigger foe gnawing at the pit of their soul. Yet they knew not who or why?

Firmly gripping the staff with both hands, Xebec pointed the tip at the cracked granite slab. Then, while donning an exaggerated smirk of satisfaction, he commanded his new prize, "Staff, do your bearer's bidding!"

Instantly, a thin beam of hot light shot forth and struck the slab, torching through the granite like a hot iron into hide.

Xebec skillfully guided the beam, tracing out an oval pattern just large enough for him to step through. He next tapped the staff inside the pattern and the granite crumbled into a small pile of smoldering rubble.

Bones crunched beneath his feet as Xebec stepped through the opening, barking orders at the boorleez; completely unaware that the terrified bunch had already scattered and hid, refusing to heed his calls.

The elated sorcerer was indifferent to their plite. At last, he had his prize! He somehow sensed that the staff itself would lead him safely out of the mountain's rumbling belly.

Xebec made haste across the silica floor, passing through tunnels and caverns. He then strided with a swiftness of purpose atop the meaty matting, winding his way between fibre pillars and spit-pools of saliva.

Somehow he sensed his route out of the mountain; and somehow he also sensed that something was watching his every move. *'There is an unseen presence lurking nearby. And it is stalking me as prey!'*

Xebec was well aware of his stalker's intentions. Tightening his grip about the shaft, he gleefully muttered an inaudible challenge, daring danger to expose itself. In fact, he welcomed the challenge. That is, until it actually happened.

"EEEEEEEE!!" wailed a cry of attack.

Saliva splashed across Xebec's garments as a hoofed monster emerged from the depths of a spit-pool and pounced upon the meaty matting. Foam frothed from the monster's mouth and its powerful tails whipsnapped the air. It's yellow, predatory eyes were void of mercy.

Xebec narrowly averted being struck by one of his attacker's lethal tails. He stumbled backwards and fell upon his back. *'Kymeera are for real after all,'* he thought.

"EEEEEEEE!!" wailed the monster, once again whipsnapping its tails and nearly dispatching its prey to meet Morgue.

With trembling hands, Xebec anxiously pointed the staff. "Staff, slay this beast!"

Instantly, a beam of hot light blazed forth from the tip and, in the bat of a blink, the Kymeera was burned into a swirling vortex of dust. Then the dust scattered, taking with it any trace that the departed beast had ever been.

Although somewhat shaken, Xebec still managed a slight grin. *'It seems that my new prize is most precious indeed.'*

After pressing to his feet, Xebec dusted himself off and made for the tunnel's inner mouth. Newfound strength gushed through his aging limbs and he effortlessly climbed the rope ladder. Then he hopped onto the mountain's slimy tongue. His footing was as sure as a young ladfolk's, but his senses told him that he must flee even faster.

Upon entering the sweltering tunnel, he could again feel its walls squeezing in about him; trying to crush him, constricting ever tighter and tighter. *'This mountain erupts simply to deny me my prize. I must hurry.'*

However, Scald Summit would not surrender her staff quite so easily. It had been her treasure for far too long and no mere mortal was going to snatch it from her belly without a fight. "NEVER!!"

Even before the enraged mountain tremored, Xebec braced for the jolt. Battering blasts of wet and wind slammed him repeatedly against the crystalized walls. Even the ceiling was pressing down to crush him now; for mountains exist without pity.

"NEVER!!" howled each blast of the mountain's breath. "NEVER!! NEVER!! NEVER!!"

"Staff, fare us both well!" Xebec shrieked, as Scald Summit's hot breath pinned him as her prisoner.

The staff vibrated violently before unleashing a shield of solid light. Even more newfound strength poured into Xebec's limbs. The staff had been his obsession for far too long, and no mere mountain was going to snatch it from his grasp without a fight.

"Never! Never! Never!" Xebec screamed in defiance.

"NEVER!! NEVER!! NEVER!!" howled each blast of the mountain's breath. Molten rock burned bright and orange and started to gush through Scald Summit's veins.

"Staff!" Xebec shrilled, as the lava swept and splashed its way around a distant curve, and sizzling cinders smacked off of the protective shield. "Staff, free me from this mountain!"

The staff jerked and twisted about with such a force that much effort was required for Xebec to keep it from being ripped from his grip. It quickly blew an orb of solid light around both the panicky sorcerer and itself, completely encasing them both inside.

Xebec pumped his thighs forward with a vigor far beyond any mortal's limit. Ever so slowly, the orb began rolling forward and upward against the flow of the lava, which splashed about it with a searing vengeance in its efforts to burn through the armor of light.

Famished flames continued to lap at the orb, while Scald's hot breath hurled debris at it. Ugly, black smoke sought to choke it. The constricting tunnel tried ever harder to squeeze it and pop it open.

Onward and upward the orb rolled. Faster and faster it went, spinning upwards across the surface of the raging river of molten rock it went, bouncing off the boiling walls of the chute that sought to crush both it and its raving occupant within.

Yet the orb held fast, protecting both the staff and its bearer. It easily spun its way straight through any boulders which fell into its path to prevent escape.

In desperation, Scald Summit tried every possible means to stop the spinning orb from escaping its belly. She shook! She smoked! She squeezed, split, spat and spewed! Magma! Lava! Boulders! The raging mountain spared no wrath. She even awakened her sister, Slumber Summit, from her many ages of sleep.

Together, their combined smoke spoiled the sky; like black breath blocking out blue. The entire Isle trembled beneath them. Geysers of gas and steam burst through their crust. Boulders bounded down their sides as they spilled their peaks and flexed their combined muscles of magma. Lesser summits slid into the boiling sea, which eagerly swallowed them whole until the sisters were all that remained of the Isle of Countless Caverns.

However, having been created by Seed herself, the staff possessed much more power than any mere mountain ever could, and Scald Summit's belly was not to become Xebec's tomb. The orb simply cut its own swath straight through Scald's rocky core, rotating increasingly faster and faster until, like a spinning star, it broke free of her shell and bounced down her slope to her base.

The dizzy sorcerer struggled to re-focus both his thoughts and his sights. Everything swirled around him as he tumbled heels over hearers within the protective orb, tightly clenching his prize.

Xebec's mind and vision gradually cleared and he became able to sight through the orb. And that's when he gasped. A tide of molten wrath was flowing down Scald's slope to swallow them whole!

"Staff, into the sea!"

Without hesitation, the orb rolled its way across Scald Summit's base and spun itself over a high cliff.

Xebec could feel his innards sink as they plummeted ever downward towards the steaming surf far below. Down…down…down…down…down…

"SPLASH!!"

The orb plunged deep beneath the wetrollers, down to where bubbles seldom go, before it shot back up to break atop the choppy surface. Still dry and aglow, it bobbed amongst the wetrollers of the Saline Sea, while hot pumice pelted down around it.

With his mind still spinning, Xebec hugged the staff firm against his torso. He felt ill and confused. Already, the orb was fast waning and losing its protective powers. If the Saline Sea's salty water should make wet the staff, then his prize would be lost forever. What to do?

Then the silver claws of a saber-tooth plucked the bobbing orb from the wetrollers, and a beast with golden wings and the head of an eagle whisked Xebec and his new prize off to safety.

Taleteller

"Wow! Whew! Wow! Whew! Wow! Wow! Whew! Whew! Top that for a tummy twisting escape! Whoooaa! I'm dizzy from just telling you about it!

"And check out the power of that staff! Aw-Aw-Awesome! Can you imagine taking that to class for show and tell? Straight A's from then on. And no issues with bullies. Ha!

"But there is a most serious side to these events. Oh yes. For the staff is now in the wrong hands. Very wrong hands. In fact, the very wrongest of hands. Now all plants and creatures have suddenly found themselves in a right fine mess indeed. For certain. For sure.

"Xebec never even bothered to return to his castle for more than two full cycles. Uh-uh. Noper. After all, he had matters of conquest to attend to.

"Instead of flying home, the dim sorcerer had his loyal griffin swoop south over The Baobabs and on across the channel to Ezu, City of the Boorleez and Sheeleez. The burly inhabitants were already so frightened of him that there was really no reason to remind them of who was boss, yet Xebec torched the city's entire core anyway. Just for laughs!

"Xebec began flying about Ranidae, exerting his authority over a great many creatures, both great and small.

"The staff itself was simply more powerful than all of the armies in all of the kingdoms in all of the all. Was so. Was too. For certain. For sure. And the normally passive inhabitants of Ranidae needed few demonstrations of its awesome power to assure almost their full surrender; as some brave beings chose to flee into the forests and mountains rather than succumb to the sorcerer's will.

"Cycity fell next when Xebec melted its defensive wall. Upon witnessing the staff's awesome power, the Cyclops Queen sued for peace and thus spared her beloved city from complete ruin. She reluctantly ordered her own subjects to henceforth obey all of the new rules, especially the decree demanding absolute obedience to Ruler Xebec.

Even so, some very brave cyclops disobeyed their own Queen and sneaked out of the city under cover of darkness, fully determined to maintain their freedom. Others abandoned their farms. Did too. Did so. Thus, the furious sorcerer responded in a tantrum by declaring all of them fugitives, as he continued to do with any others who fled his rule. And he decreed that they all were to be strictly shunned, even by their own loved ones.

"From Cycity, Xebec next flew upriver to Folkton, where the humanfolk dwell. Of course, he made certain to wreak havoc in each and every hamlet along the way. Just for laughs!

"Once again, terrified inhabitants surrendered their city without a fight; although some humanfolk fled into the foothills, where they joined up with other runaways in a united struggle to remain free.

"Finally, and only after nearly two long cycles of relentless seeking, Xebec at last discovered the secret whereabouts of The Hidden City.

"The Hidden City. Home to the mighty Mugwumps. Shaggy, blue beasts with big yellow feet and a most nasty nature. A most mysterious species, which greatly prizes their privacy.

"Unlike most victims of Xebec's Rule, and save for a few roving bands of rogue profiteers, virtually all of the remaining mugwumps simply refused to become his servants. Under cover of darkness, they sneaked away from their ancient city and stole north and west. Did so. Did too.

"In orderly file, they stomped all the way to the right bank of the Deep River, where the fiendish finners lurk: the fiendish finners being malicious little biters that in great numbers can swiftly strip a beast to bone in bits! Chomp. Chomp. Chomp. Gulp. Burp...

"After felling floatwood trees to bridge the banks, the mugwump column cautiously filed across the river under cover of darkness and vanished into the depths of the Dismal Jungle. Where it is said that they still dwell to this very time, greatly prizing their privacy.

"Xebec was beyond furious! He had wanted to use their might and nasty nature to help him keep all of his other subjects in line. Plus he'd also wanted them to hunt down all of the fugitives who had fled into the forests and foothills, as mugwumps are known to be expert trackers. In fact, he would have even granted the shaggy beasts some degree of self rule in exchange for such loyalty.

"In retribution for mugwump defiance, the entire Hidden City was razed by fire. In fact, virtually everything in it was so thoroughly scorched that the former inhabitants could not return home even if they had wanted to; for as of yet not a single thing can grow there, not even the toughest of weeds.

"Finally, while stuck in one of his snarky snits, Xebec returned to his castle to oversee the new order of things in Ranidae. His order, of course. And that's when he began to chuckle and mumble in the mindset of one first mating with madness.

"So-so-so, then. Of what more can I tell? Please don't close the book on me just yet, You. For there remains much more to be told. Much, much, much more...

"We shall now pick up our tale in a distant land named The Continent, which lies far north from Ranidae and across The Saline Sea. More specifically, our tale continues in the tall graingrass that grows in golden abundance all along the inland fringe of the Fluorescent Forest, which itself lies as far east and south as one can travel on The Continent.

"There a young galfolk named Shoenia is being pursued by a lizarme military unit, against whom her own humanfolk and their ape allies are engaged in open conflict..."

2

Shoenia

The young galfolk's tanned face blended in well with the tall graingrass growing all about her. Long, white hair draped about her neck and shoulders. Her alert, emerald eyes scanned between the stalks in search of any hint of movement, and her ears sought to snag any suspect sounds.

No stranger to combat, her face and body bore the scars of many clashes. She had strong limbs and possessed a tight grip; both the result of much combat training. And she had a keen mind to match. It was this combination of wit and health, matched with skill and daring, that had kept her from meeting Morgue throughout the conflict that was currently raging between humanfolk and lizarme. That and whatever good fortune Destiny had seen fit to gift her. Perhaps mostly the latter?

She was clad in a cloth tunic with a pouched skirt. Hide boots covered her swift and nimble feet. A pointy throwing blade was sheathed to one of her calves. In her hands she clenched the shaft of a sinkwood scrapstick. One well-placed whack from such a weapon could easily crack bone.

Bellybees buzzed inside her knotted-up guts as she crouched low to avoid detection. Her breathe was bated and she could almost hear her pounding heart. Painful cramps burned in her thighs, while pesky bugs bit into her flesh. She dared not move a muscle.

Her thoughts reflected back on the last battle, which had proved costly for both sides; but especially for her own. She wondered if any other humanfolk had managed to escape through the lizarme lines? Or, had they all met Morgue?

Three dawns past, her unit had been ambushed by a much larger enemy unit, which was accompanied by a pack of the vicious tracking lizards known as rexids. Just thinking of them needled her nerves.

She had somehow managed to slip through enemy lines and flee into the tall graingrass, taking care to avoid leaving a telltale swath through the fields. Keeping herself downwind of the rexids, she had prayed for Destiny to keep her concealed from the winged dacts and their mounted lizarme riders that were so often circling above.

That is where Destiny's gift of good fortune may have come into play? Thus far, Destiny had responded favourably to her prayers, and the young galfolk's position had not been betrayed. She had seen dacts flapping in flight far off in the distance, yet they had not spotted her.

For two more dusks and dawns, she had stolen due east in a vain search for more humanfolk; until her trek brought her to the fringe of The Fluorescent Forest; a mythical and mysterious place located on the southeastern shore of The Continent. A place, it is said, where none who enter will ever return. For just that reason, she had straddled the forest fringe, hoping to encounter more humanfolk; yet always mindful of not straying too close to the dancing blue curtain of light that shields the inner forest from view.

Destiny's gifts are at times meant to be spent, however, and the galfolk's keen instincts had suddenly felt the anxious tremors of trouble drawing near. Yes, something was definitely seeking her. Something threatening. Something lethal...

Then she had heard it. Faintly at first, but unmistakably the sound of blades hacking down graingrass and the crunch of many feet stomping it flat. Next came the sound of voices. Gruff voices. Foreign voices. Speaking unknown words. At once, she knew who the voices belonged to. Lizarme! A great many lizarme! And they were stomping straight towards her…

That is how she had come to find herself crouched low amongst tall stalks of graingrass; with buzzing bellybees and a pounding heart. Tormented by biting bugs. Sweat sticking her bangs to her brow.

She breathed deeply with the purpose of stilling her fear. Her habitually keen mind was racing for an out; for the lizarme had her encircled on three sides, with the Fluorescent Forest at her back.

"Destiny…" she whispered, "Guide my thoughts, for they are muddled."

The gruff voices were getting closer now, growing ever louder and more raucous. The breeze shifted and suddenly the voices were joined by the chilling squeal of a rexid as it snorted a new scent. A humanfolk scent. Her scent!

Shouting and squealing erupted from all directions as more of the tracking lizards began picking up her scent.

There was no time left for thought. With luck and her weapons, she could slay one of the beasts. Multiple rexids would tear her to pieces. "Destiny, keep beside me," she pleaded, realizing what she must do.

Spinning about, she sprang afoot and sprinted towards the blue curtain of light, fully intent on charging through it. To her surprise, the curtain parted to grant her entry to the forest and she tripped and fell upon her knees. As the curtain closed tight behind her, she became aware that the shouting and squealing had ceased. There was no longer any hint of a breeze.

Shoenia stood and struggled to absorb the strange spectacle going on all about her. It seemed as if virtually everything glowed. Vivid colours were everywhere. She surveyed her surroundings with wided eyes. Her racing mind was already cleared of all thoughts of lizarme or rexids or dacts or battle...

It was readily apparent that she had sprinted headlong into a place where the bizarre mated with the surreal? Only weirder?

Strange, fleshy flowers grew all about her. Their flushy petals circled around yellow buttons with sealed eyelids and long lashes.

Curiosity conquered caution and Shoenia reached out to touch one of the flowers, but it bent away from her. The flower's lid opened to reveal an angry eye.

"Don't touch me!" a squeaky voice exclaimed.

"Wh-Who are you," Shoenia asked, trying her best not to appear scared. "Flowers can't talk?"

"Flowers can't talk," mimicked the saucy plant.

Shoenia felt alarmed and took a step backward. "B-But they can't? I mean…"

"Go on! Beat it! Scram!" The rude blossom tilted backwards. A blinding light shone from its eye and stung into Shoenia's eyes.

"I'm really very sorry," Shoenia apologized, shielding her face from the light. Giggles became audible all around her. She pondered her own sense? Had she gone completely *'round-the-twist'?*

All of the trees were equally strange? Their woody skin glowed in such a manner that Shoenia's fingers appeared to bend upon touching it. It felt both smooth and bumpy to the touch, not unlike thinly glazed clay. And the larger trees bore a pair of thick, reaching limbs; each of which was jointed and bent at mid-length, and tipped with twigs that wiggled like fingers.

Plus there were boastful bushes. Each was supported by a pair of jointed stalks with knobby knots, and they were clothed in glowing leaves that faded and shone as if to show off.

The forest gleamed and glowed and sparkled and shone, from the soil up to the domed canopy above; which alternately sagged and inflated in breath not unlike a ginormous lung. Not even external birds were welcome to enter the Fluorescent Forest. It truly was a haven unto itself. Or a hazard?

Shoenia thought she caught a whiff of the unwelcome scent of a whitestripe, but she couldn't be certain? She wondered, *'Of all the critters from beyond the curtain, whyever would the forest allow them in? Phew.'*

The wary galfolk trekked deeper into the forest. Jitters helped hone her senses. Sight. Sound. Scent. Thought. She used them all, for it felt as though her every movement was being watched. Was she being stalked?

A skilled warrior and well tested in battle, Shoenia tightened her grip on the scrapstick. Something just didn't feel right? She wondered if she should have avoided the forest and chanced evading the lizarme instead? No, the rexids for certain would have found her. They had already locked onto her scent and no humanfolk could ever outrun any rexid. Not even one as swift on the sprint as herself. As she trekked cautiously onward, she became ever more intrigued by her surroundings.

Trees with long faces bore limbs with groping twigs that wiggled, which were adorned root to tip by blushing blossoms that giggled. Waltzing shrubs twirled about to a symphony of reeds. Some bloated beets kept good cadence by tapping their roots, while a clique of posh prissywillows strutted about in nut boots.

Then things went weird. Like a nutty dream dipped in chaos and sprinkled with crazy...?????

A slinky snapdragon coiled its thorny stem and snapped its fanged flower at a buzzing winged snack, while nasty slashthorns swiped to slice up any who passed by so that they wouldn't come back. And bug-eyed buffoons with bark boots and red noses tried to amuse one another with the zaniest of poses.

Stepping-stones stomped by and trampled flat fleshy flowers, who sprang right back up rustling their peeved petals in ire; while helmeted toadstools did drill in neat ranks, under orders of one who was really a crank. Diving dazzledills did somersaults into glistening pools, while very annoyed floatlillies tried to ignore the rude fools. Twinkling vines with orange thistles festooned from bough to terra sheen, which was matted in sections by wriggling blades of yellow and green; and a gang of tough pithpunks acted surly and mean, all to warn off some scruffy ragweeds who were in need of a preen. Grinning silkspinners bearing big beaconing butts gawked hungrily at the galfolk from within nooks, crannies and ruts.

Shoenia shuddered at the mere thought of being devoured by such grotesque looking bugs. She sensed that the entire forest was now focused mostly on her. Bellybees once again buzzed about inside of her.

"Destiny, guide me to safety," she pleaded as she veered around an enormous titan tree. She thought, *'It's amazing how open minded we are to Destiny whenever we are frightened or in need.'*

A very brief but most welcome reprieve finally came when a giant dippy dorkasaurus romped across her path. In fact, Shoenia even managed a little giggle at the spectacle of the happy beast's goofy grin and at its pink hair tied about a bone. *'So, there is some joy to be had in this strange place after all...'* she noted.

Her pleasant reprieve was cut short as the dippy dorkasaurus crashed off into the forest, amidst much cussing and rude gesturing from enraged plants and critters.

'...albeit apparently not much.' She conceded.

On the few occasions when she paused to ponder her plight, she noted that the foliage would part for her in some places, but crowd to block her path in others. *'Am I being deliberately steered through a maze? And if so, am I being steered towards safety or danger? And why does the aura about me always feel like I'm being watched?'* Her skin tingled at the thought of a presence that her mind could sense and feel, but that she could neither see nor hear. Very strange?

Shoenia continued to walk about the forest, feeling both fearful and enchanted at the same time. New genera of vegetation gradually began to encircle her. Her buzzing bellybees now had the company of knotting-up guts and she began to feel unsafe. *'Who, or what, is after me?'*

The new genus of trees were tall as towers, and quite slender of stem. Long silvery vines festooned down from their limbs, sweeping the forest floor. Their fleshy leaves lapped at the air. Despite the absence of breeze, these trees mysteriously swayed in time to a silent melody.

Shoenia almost tread on a hidden bed of flowers because their stems were reclined amongst some weeds and their petals were wrapped tightly into buds. As she passed near to them, the stems suddenly raised themselves upright and their blossoms bloomed like an awakening. The orange petals glowed like hot embers. Alert seers were unblinking as they traced the strange galfolk's movements with utmost suspicion.

In time, Shoenia chanced upon a babbling brook. Its gooey liquid flowed slowly like muck. Surface bubbles puffed up, and then popped with much splatter.

The weary galfolk opted to rest a short spell, lounging on some spongy moss in a small clearing alongside the brook. Cautiously, she looked about for any signs of danger. She noted nothing alarming, but her sharp senses warned her to keep wary despite her mounting fatigue.

Naked trees with coiled trunks and groping limbs ringed the clearing. Their twiggy claws raked at the air.

Peeking out from behind the coil trees were some flirty flowers. They giggled and blushed and batted their luscious petals. There were also smoochy blooms with transparent stems. Each bloom had two juicy red petals, and red pistons that wagged between them like lickers between lips.

Shoenia's eyelids began to fall heavy on the nod, and her head teetered and tottered in its battle with fatigue. "Need to nap," she murmured, yielding to a yaaawwnn… And then… sleep… zzzzzz...

Suddenly something pricked her leg. Then it pricked her again. And again.

With some effort, she opened her eyes and struggled to focus. Then she snapped awake with a start.

"Ouch!" she yelped, drawing herself up into a sit. "Ouch! Ow! Ouch!"

Unbelievable! Brazen blades of grass were actually attacking her and jousting her legs with their pointy tips!

"Ouch!" she yelped again. "Stop it! Ow! Stop it right now or I'll stand up and stomp you flat! Ouch! I mean…"

"BOOM!! BOOM!! BOOM!! BOOM!!"

The forest floor rolled beneath Shoenia, tripping up her efforts to stand. She watched wide-eyed and with mouth agape as the coil trees spring-pounced across the clearing; charging straight towards her!

"STOMP!! STOMP!! STOMP!!" the coil trees bellowed.

"BOOM!! BOOM!! BOOM!!' echoed the forest floor as the coil trees spring-pounced ever closer. "BOOM!! BOOM!! BOOM!! BOOM!!"

In sheer desperation, the frightened galfolk somehow struggled to her feet. Both legs shook like quakes in their effort to maintain her balance. With great difficulty, she stumbled to escape the towering titans that sought to trample her.

"CLACKITY-CLACK-CLACK!! CLACKITY-CLACK-CLACK!!"

Shoenia froze. Almost the entire forest was attacking her now, led by a hopping batch of beastly bushes with hairy stems and pincered petals. "CLACKITY-CLACK-CLACK-CLACK!!"

"Ouch!" she yelped, somewhat regaining her senses. She swatted at some grass that jousted her ankles. "Ow! Shoo! Go away! Ouch!"

"STOMP!! STOMP!! STOMP!!" bellowed the coil trees as they spring-pounced ever closer.

"BOOM!! BOOM!! BOOM!!" echoed the forest floor as it bounced Shoenia about.

"CLACKITY-CLACK-CLACK!!" resounded the pincer petals.

"Staaawwpp!" whined some wussy wimpweeds who had been moping together alongside the brook. "Staaawwpp making such a racket!"

And the brazen blades of grass relentlessly wriggled after her, squeakchanting, "Jab-jab-jab-jab…"

Instinctively tightening her grip on her scrapstick, the frantic galfolk stumbled for the brook.

"Staaawwpp with all that noise!" whined the wimpweeds.

"AW, SHADDUP!!" the entire forest retorted together; including Shoenia.

Suddenly some toughie thorn-thistles arrived and took to tumbling down the brookbank to block off Shoenia's best route of escape. Brandishing their curved sickles, they dared her to challenge them. Even double dog dared!

However, the galfolk's keen thinking and agility foiled their ploy. When next the forest floor heaved to bounce her, she tactfully seized upon the rhythm of its roll and added its energy to her own. She skillfully used her scrapstick to help her vault over the thistles, and then again over the brook; thereby narrowly averting disaster before fleeing down a winding path.

Nevertheless, her escape was brief.

"Ow!" she yelled, as a sneaky root snagged her ankle and she face-planted into the dirt. Grit and soil crunched between her teeth.

"STOMP!! STOMP!! STOMP!! STOMP!!"

"BOOM!! BOOM!! BOOM!! BOOM!!"

"CLACKITY-CLACK-CLACK-CLACK!!"

"Jab-jab-jab-jab-jab-jab..."

Shoenia struggled in vain to escape from the root, but she knew it was all over. The root bound her legs together, keeping her as prey for its forest cousins to prick, pinch and stomp her. As strong as she was, she could no more escape its binding grip than she could flap her arms and fly away. Not a chance.

The spent galfolk sighed and closed her eyes to bravely accept her fate. A lone tear blazed a trail down her dirty cheek and onto her lips. She could taste the salt. Silently, she prayed that Morgue would spare her his maze and let Seed reshape her spirit for another turn at life. *'But am I worthy?'*

"BOOM!! BOOM!! BOOM!! BOOM!!"

The rising tremors rattled Shoenia's bones.

"CLACKITY-CLACK-CLACK-CLACK!!"

Shoenia knew that the weight and wrath of the forest would soon land on her. She thanked Seed for the precious time that she'd been given. And again, she asked Morgue to gift her spirit back to Seed and spare her the maze. She begged Destiny to care for all the other humanfolk back home, and even for their enemy, the lizarme. "Please, Destiny, just bring peace back to The Continent. And let none seek vengeance, for such always lends to future conflicts."

"STOMP!! STOMP!! STOMP!! STOMP!!" bellowed the coil trees.

"BOOM!! BOOM!! BOOM!! BOOM!!" echoed the forest floor.

"CLACKITY-CLACK-CLACK-CLACK!!" clamoured the pincer petals.

"Jab-jab-jab-jab-jab-jab-jab…" squeakchanted the brazen blades of grass.

Having accepted her fate, the resigned galfolk closed her eyes, trying in vain to think past the climbing crescendo; which now surpassed the wrath of even the angriest of skybangers during even the most violent of storms. *'Destiny, please let it all end in a blink...'*

"STOMP!! STOMP!! STOMP!! STOMP!!"

"BOOM!! BOOM!! BOOM!! BOOM!!"

"CLACKITY-CLACK-CLACK-CLACK!!"

"Jab-jab-jab-jab-jab-jab-jab…"

Her attackers were nearly upon her now. Shoenia winced and braced for the final act…

"STOMP!! STOMP!! STOMP!!"

"BOOM!! BOOM!! BOOM!!"

"CLACKITY-CLACK-CLACK!!"

"Jab-jab-jab…"

……….and then… silence…

Beautiful…peaceful…silence…….

'Is it done?' Shoenia wondered, not daring to look. Her mind groped for clarity of thought. *'No, I still feel the root binding my legs.'*

Suddenly the forest erupted again.

"STOMP!! STOMP! Stomp…"

"BOOM!! BOOM! Boom…"

"CLACKITY-CLACK-clack…"

"Jab-jab-jab…"

'Wait?' Shoenia thought. *'They're all going away?'*

It was true! As the racket faded off into the distance, the forest floor ceased to roll beneath her and gradually it settled still.

Yet the root still bound her legs.

While cautiously lifting her eyelids, Shoenia pulled herself up into a sit and sighted in her surroundings. She was puzzled? All of her tormentors had vanished, save for the pesky root.

"Let go!" she commanded, twisting her feet about and beating the root with her scrapstick. She glared daggers at her captor. "I said let go! Release me this very instant! I mean it, you nasty tuber! Do so right now or I swear by Seed that I'll bash you so hard!"

The stubborn root held fast its grip. No matter how badly its captive cussed, threatened or beat on it, the tough tuber was undaunted.

Shoenia opted for pleading. "Oh please, Mr. Root. Please let me go. Please…"

No response…

The frustrated galfolk next opted for flattery. "My, you certainly are a fine-looking root. Quite a grand specimen, really. Won't you please release a galfolk in distress? I'll be your friend."

Still no response.

So, back to threats and insults and glaring daggers at her captor. "I'm quite partial to boiled root stew, you nasty tuber! And I have a blade! I'll chop you up for dinner! I will! I swear it!"

Still no response.

The frustrated galfolk continued to beg, bribe, beat and berate. She did not, however, resort to hacking away with her blade as she new the root could easily snap her legs were it really intent on harming her. Why then would it not simply let her go? Was it holding her captive for somebody? *Or something?*

Then she heard it. A voice! A very angry voice. But a voice nonetheless. A loud, gruff, obnoxious – beautiful voice! And it was coming from nearby in the forest.

"Dearest Destiny! What in Morgue's Maze has been going on in my forest! Just look at this mess. Nothing is in its proper place. Not one single thing is where it should be. Just look at this disaster!

"And just who has to clean all this mess up? Me, that's who. Yeah, me. Just let ole Snarly Grouchwhiner put everything back in order. So, what else is new? Snarly mend this. Snarly fix that.

My boughs are all broken, Snarly. Well, boo hoo. My dry roots itch, Snarly. Tough tuber toots! A dippy dorkasaurus stepped on me, Snarly. Well then, keep out of its way! It's not like ya can't hear it coming. They're ginormous. Does your mama keep your brain baked in a basket? Sheesh."

Shoenia thought, *'Snarly Grouchwhiner? Wow...'*

"Our seedlings lack water, Snarly. My leaves need a pruning, Snarly. The smoochy blooms need a kiss from you, Snarly. Yeah, right. Like that's ever going to happen! The pithpunks are teasing us, Snarly. Oh, weep me a dew puddle. My twigs ache, Snarly. Oh, wahh. Snarly this. Snarly that. Snarly, Snarly, Snarly, Snarly...

"Hey, move aside coil trees. You too, whitestripe. Spray me and you're mittens. Outta my way, all of you. Now! I said move!

"A bug-eyed buffoon has a toothache, Snarly. A slinky snapdragon has gone and tied itself in a knot again, Snarly. A weeping willow is sad, Snarly. What? It's sad? Ya don't say? Of course, it's sad. It's called a weeping flippant willow!

"Ya think it's easy being a healer, a grower and even a plant shrink? Well, do ya? As well as a seer and master magician to boot? Not to mention the full-time Keeper of this Fluorescent Forest, tasked with caring for you high-maintenance lot! And at my tender age too."

Shoenia thought, '*Well, he certainly seems stressed?*' She honestly didn't know whether she should laugh or tremble? Was Destiny playing a cruel joke on her? *'I mean, Snarly Grouchwhiner? C'mon. Seriously?'*

Yet Shoenia was undeniably in a bind. Surely the angry being behind the beautifully obnoxious voice could help her? But would he?

The exhausted galfolk briefly pondered her plight before choosing to risk calling out for help. "Uh, hello!? Mister Grouchwhiner, Sir!?" Shoenia barely buried a rising belly laugh. She had to remind herself that she really was in a serious fix. "Help! Mr. Grouchwhiner!? I'm snared by a nasty root over here! Please help me, Mr. Grouchwhiner! I'm strictly in a bind! Please help, Sir! Help! Help me! Help! Help!"

Shoenia's cries for help were met with a stony silence.

'Oh no,' Shoenia thought. *'Should I risk calling out again? This Snarly character certainly seems to be in a mood. Unless he's always this way? What if my being in his forest makes him even madder? But then again, rescuing a galfolk in distress might actually sweeten his sour spirits?'*

"As if," she muttered out loud. *'But seriously, should I call out again?'*

Destiny decided for her, as the being behind the angry voice slowly emerged from the forest and stared straight at her. *'Yikes! Too late. No going back now.'*

Shoenia was awed mute as she watched the ancient creature watching her watch him. Neither spoke a word.

The creature bore hard, silvery skin not unlike fossilized wood. A thinning patch of grey grass grew atop his head. Two hollow burls served as ears of sort, each of which had become deformed by decay. Bluish mould grew upon his nose, which had two unusually wide nostrils.

One very curious tree-toad peeked out from its cozy nook within one of Snarly's nostrils. Briefly, it and Snarly exchanged puzzled glances. Both shrugged and looked back at Shoenia.

Aged amber eyes were set deep within Snarly's puffy sockets, above which grew strips of bushy, white moss. A thin *mosstache* topped a toothless mouth, out of which wagged a reedy red licker.

Being stooped in his middle, Snarly shuffled forth on two bent trunks with knotty kneecaps. Two crooked limbs reached out from his torso, and were tipped with twiggy digits. In one shaky hand he clenched a sturdy rush; which proved most necessary to help maintain his balance as his gnarled, mossy feet were deformed from both wear and rot.

The creature stared at Shoenia with a mix of awe and ire. Thus, Shoenia nervously sucked in a deep breath as the creature approached. And her bellybees returned by the swarm.

"Uh, M-Mr. Grouchwhiner," Shoenia stammered. "H-Hello, Sir. I-I'm..."

"...in my forest!" Snarly snapped, thereby forcing his own words into Shoenia's mouth. "That's exactly where you are, Galfolk. You are in MY forest! Where you have no business being, I might add. No business whatsoever. Which begs the most obvious question – just why are you in my forest? Which begs the second most obvious question – just who are you anyway? See, that's two obvious questions for you to answer. And truthfully, too. I tend to dislike fibbers even more than I tend to dislike – well, pretty much everybody else."

Shoenia was at a loss for words.

"Speak up, Galfolk. Is your licker locked? It certainly worked well while you were doing all that hollering, disrupting the peace and tranquility of my forest. Why are you causing me so much grief?"

"Um, well, I-I am very sorry, Mr. Grouch..."

"Saying sorry won't fix my forest," Snarly interrupted. "Just look at this mess."

"Again, I-I am truly sorry, Mr. Grouchwhiner. I didn't mean to..."

"Mean to what!?" Snarly spat out. "Mean to create chaos from calm? Disorder from order? Panic from peace? Mental mayhem from mindful serenity? Because if that's what you meant to do, Galfolk, you have certainly won top prize. Would you just look at this mess. What do you have to say for yourself? Hmmm...?"

Shoenia scanned the forest. Everything seemed quite tranquil and orderly to her? She tactfully decided to swallow her pride and placate Snarly. Still bound tight by the root, she did not want to make matters even worse, and she most certainly did not wish to make an enemy of the creature who had most likely just saved her from a sure meeting with Morgue. Despite Snarly's gruff demeanor, she reasoned that enduring a sharp rebuke seemed such a small price to pay to possibly have a potential guide who actually seemed to understand the strange place in which she now found herself. In short, she needed him. And she knew it. Therefore, her current circumstance called for both tact and humility.

"Please, Mr. Grouchwhiner, if you would just allow me to speak..."

"Oh, you wish to speak, do you? Very well then, just what do you have to say for yourself? Hmmm...?" Snarly leaned forward, bracing his weight on the rush while teetering to keep his balance.

Shoenia paused, fully expecting to be interrupted again; plus she was a tad concerned that the rush might snap and then Snarly might tip over onto her.

"I'm waiting, Galfolk..."

"Mr. Grouchwhiner, I am truly very sorry for the mess I've made of your fabulous forest and..."

First Snarly snorted in derision. Then he hinted at an almost smile. "My forest truly is fabulous though, isn't it? Go on."

"It is, Sir. And I promise to do whatever you ask of me to make things right. I'll work as hard as is needed to restore order to..."

"Hah! Sure you will."

Shoenia began suspecting that Snarly Grouchwhiner may not be at all the threat she had at first assumed him to be. "No, I really will..."

"And what would a young galfolk from Ga know about keeping an orderly forest? I believe Ga is a fishing village, is it not?"

Shoenia was muted by Snarly's words. She wondered, *'How does he know where I hail from? I didn't tell him. Or did I? Am I still of sound mind?'*

"Well?"

Mustering up her courage, Shoenia braved a question: "Uh, how do you know I hail from Ga?"

Now it was Snarly's turn to stumble for words. "Well – uh, I mean, like – um, I just guessed that you – that you look like you could possibly be from Ga? That's all I'm saying, Shoen... er, I mean, Galfolk..."

Suspicion started to settle into Shoenia's mind.

"… Let's free you from this pesky root, shall we," Snarly continued, quickly changing the subject. "Root, release this galfolk."

The stubborn root held fast.

The visibly embarrassed creature stepped up to the defiant root and tapped it with his rush. "Now tuber!" he commanded. "Or should I transplant you right next to a patch of whiny wimpweeds? Hmmm…?"

This time the root obeyed at once. It released its hold on Shoenia's legs and quickly sank back beneath the soil. Gone…

"Works every time," Snarly boasted.

Having been freed from the root, Shoenia pondered the power of Snarly's rush. Plus she was in no way buying his claim that he had simply *guessed* that she hailed from the small fishing village of Ga. Yet she somehow felt quite safe with him now, even despite his dour disposition. Her stomach had finally unknotted and the bellybees were asleep. *'Still,'* she thought, *'Something very strange is going on here?'*

"That naughty root likes to be difficult," Snarly explained. "I'm just grateful that this withered and decaying old sapkeeper still holds some sway around here. Or, at least my rush does." Snarly paused and sighed, "These younger plants just don't respect order like older plants do. Always testing me, they are. Like I don't have enough problems. Sheesh."

"You're called a sapkeeper?" Shoenia asked, obviously intrigued.

"Isn't that what I just said?" Snarly sniped, somewhat rudely. "Yes, I am a sapkeeper. Somebody has to see to it that the unique plants and trees in each and every Fluorescent Forest get the exact right nutrients and minerals so that they can stay healthy. That's why everything needs to stay organized. Get it, Galfolk? Organized. Sorted. In balance. I am Seed's chosen sapkeeper for this Fluorescent Forest. Plus I'm also a seer, as well as a highly skilled master magician. I'm really very busy, you see. Fortunately, I'm also very talented when it comes to multitasking. Not to mention that I'm quite wise as well."

"And apparently quite humble too," Shoenia muttered sarcastically beneath her breath.

"What?" Snarly asked. "Speak up, Galfolk."

"Uh, you said, this Fluorescent Forest," Shoenia noted, neatly changing the flow of the conversation. "You mean there are more?"

"Dearest Destiny, Galfolk. Of course there are more. They are scattered on a grandzillion different globes that are spinning around all of Night's skytwinklers. Every single universe is teeming with life. But only I dwell here. Just one sapkeeper per Fluorescent Forest. And just one Fluorescent Forest per globe. That, my young galfolk, is the law."

"Who's law?" Shoenia asked.

"Seed's law, of course. Sheesh. Please tell me that you do know of Seed?"

"Oh yes," Shoenia eagerly replied. "Seed is the bearer of breath. Without her, there could be no life."

"Correct!" Snarly exclaimed with noted approval. "You know, Galfolk, in time I may grow to dislike you a tad less than I dislike almost everybody else."

A much-needed smile spread across Shoenia's face. She sensed that such compliments must be quite rare coming from Snarly Grouchwhiner.

"So, Galfolk, perhaps at some point during this eon you shall share with us your proper name? Hmmmm?"

"Us?" Shoenia asked, glancing about.

"Yes, I said us. Are your ears waxed? I always travel with some of my smuzzles for company."

"Smuzzles? I've never heard of smuzzles?"

Snarly pointed a twiggy digit at Shoenia's feet.

"Oooooo," she cooed in pleasant surprise.

A pair of cuddly furballs blinked up at her. Their bodies were plump at the bellies, and their stubby tails bore rings of blue. They had four short legs with wee paws. Colourful whiskers twitched atip their short snouts. One smuzzle bore blue, mask-like facial markings, while the second had a single blue patch about one of its eyes. Both sniffed at Shoenia's scent and wiggled their tufted ears.

After deciding that the strange visitor posed no threat, both smuzzles nuzzled Shoenia's legs. They chattered to each other as they playfully patted her skin.

Shoenia reached down to pet one, and it fondly licked her fingers.

But when its jealous mate nose-nudged its way up under Shoenia's fingers, a most heated spat erupted; followed at once by a tight tumble-tussle across the forest floor.

"Why, they're simply adorable!" Shoenia exclaimed, giggling with glee.

"Don't go getting them all riled up," Snarly scolded.

"I'm sorry, Mr. Grouchwhiner."

"And stop saying sorry all the time. Must you always be so polished and polite, Galfolk? Dearest Destiny, it's annoying."

"I'm sorry – er, I mean, okay. I'll try not..."

"Good. And your name might prove kinda helpful, don't ya think? Sheesh."

"Oh yes, I forgot. I'm sor... uh, my name is Shoenia..."

"Now was that so dung difficult?"

"There is never good cause for cussing, Mr. Grouchwhiner," Shoenia said crossly. "Cussing is for those who lack an intelligent vocabulary, and I will not stand for it in my presence. Kapeesh?"

Snarly appeared to be completely taken aback by Shoenia's reaction to his cuss. He looked quizzically to the smuzzles, both of whom wagged their scolding digits at him.

"It was just one minor cuss word," Snarly mumbled rather meekly.

Noting that she had the flustered sapkeeper firmly on the defensive, Shoenia adamantly pressed her point. "Which is one cuss word too many, Mr. Grouchwhiner. And cussing is cussing, there is nothing minor to it. I am indeed most grateful that you rescued me. I truly am. And I can even tolerate your dour disposition, as nobody is perfect. Not even a being with your many – uh, titles. All that said, what I will not tolerate is a cussy mouth, especially from an educated being of your age; who, I might add, should surely know better. I'd sooner take my chances alone with this forest. Kapeesh?"

Snarly looked to the smuzzles, both of whom grimaced. *'Hey Boss, don't mess with her on this one.'*

"Uh, might I inquire as to what kapeesh means?" Snarly asked with novel courtesy. "It is a word that I am unfamiliar with."

"Kapeesh, Mr. Grouchwhiner, simply means, Do You Understand? Well, do you? Hmmm...?"

For a brief bit, the entire forest joined Snarly in awkward silence.

"She's really gonna get it now, a tall tattler tree whispered to a troop of bug-eyed buffoons.

Keeping bated breath, the buffoons all nodded to agree.

"Well?" Shoenia pressed, sternly placing her fists on her hips. "Do you or do you not understand my position on cussing? Yes, or no?"

Gasps filled the entire forest.

"Uh-oh," whispered the tattler tree.

"Shush," scolded one of the bug-eyed buffoons.

"I – um, sure – I suppose I could make better word choices," Snarly offered, somewhat apologetically.

A collective sigh of relief swept through the forest.

"Very well then, Mr. Grouchwhiner. But you know, an occasional hint of humility on your end might prove kinda helpful, don't ya think? Just saying."

Gasps once again filled the forest.

"That galfolk sure has spunk," whispered a beastly bush.

"Quiet," chided a coil tree. "Do you want her to come down on us?"

Silence.........

More silence... ... ...

Finally, it was Snarly who broke the tension. "Uh, perhaps we should be on our way now, Shoenia. I'm quite certain you must be hungry and weary."

'To where?' Shoenia wondered. However, she was in fact much too hungry and weary to even care.

"Come Sneek and Peek," Snarly said, beckoning the smuzzles to follow.

As Snarly Grouchwhiner shuffled off into the forest, Shoenia and the smuzzles followed close behind. The weary galfolk never noticed the aging sapkeeper's subtle grin of satisfaction. Nor did she know that she had just passed both her *Courage* and her *Character* tests.

No sooner had they set off when Snarly turned to face Shoenia and pointed with his rush. "Do beware that slinky snapdragon. They are most cunning and forever causing me grief. Always stalking and eating my smuzzles."

"I'll keep keen to it, Mr. Grouchwhiner," Shoenia assured him, brandishing her scrapstick with one hand, while pointing to her throwing blade with the other.

"And I much prefer to be called, Snarly. Mr. Grouchwhiner makes me sound so – well, ancient. Come along now, it is quite a trek to my roost."

Shoenia thought, *'But you are ancient.'* She also wondered about his 'roost?'

Shoenia kept a watchful eye on the peculiar plantlike serpent that was slithering alongside them. A solitary fanged flower grew atop its thorny stem. It smacked its fat and juicy lips as it scented in the furry snacks.

"Try it and I'll bash you senseless," Shoenia warned with feigned courage, instinctively drawing nearer to Snarly.

Sneek and Peek now clung tightly to Snarly's back, from where they proceeded to jeer their stemmed stalker by mouthing razzberries. "Pppttthhh…"

"Don't go taunting trouble!" Snarly snapped at the smuzzles. "One should always lose any fight one picks. Besides, can't you two see that I have enough problems dealing with this headstrong galfolk? Like I really needed any more burdens. Gee, thanks a lot, Destiny. Thank you so very much indeed. Sheesh…"

'Now I'm a burden,' Shoenia mused, still eyeing the salivating snapdragon. *'Oh well, Snarly is who Snarly be. Gruff. Rude. Crude. Whiny. Annoying. And yet somehow, adorable?'*

Eventually, the snapdragon gave up its hunt and slithered away, and Shoenia was able to relax and take in the diverse splendor of the Fluorescent Forest. She watched waltzing weeds, which whirled about to an ensemble of singing saplings. Bouncing beets belted out bass, while a choir of tenor trees kept rhythm and pace. Pitch plants provided the peaks, and flute flowers fed the flow. Even some festive fiddlesticks joined, whistling a melody while stroking stretched vines. And all to the clap of the palms.

There seemed to be no end to the forest's splendor. Diving dazzledills somersaulted into clear pools, all to the annoyance of lazing lilies. Buttercups melted into yellow puddles of pollen. Thorn trees scratched biting burrs from their bark. Sad willows wept and wimpweeds whined, while some very happy husks hopped and hooted and had a grand time.

Humble hops bowed most graciously before their sapkeeper. Stemmed seers watched and batted their petals. Helmeted toadstools did drill in neat ranks, while a column of stepping-stones stomped past in pairs.

And there were strange critters too. Shoenia saw colourful crawlers with wide, crooked grins. Plus climbers and creepers, and tree dwellers with big peepers. There were bold bugs with teeth, and bugs that just buzzed. Hairy bugs. Scaly bugs. Bugs clothed in fuzz. As well as winged bugs that sparkled as they circled above. Some critters hopped, others just crept, some were quite lively, yet others just slept. And the pools were all packed with smiling finners that glowed.

In due course, they came upon a sizable grove of titan trees, which were all lined up locked limb in limb. The trees all bowed in unison to honour their sapkeeper.

'Such power Snarly wields,' Shoenia thought.

The titan trees were also home to a host of furry tenants. An odd assortment of curious smuzzles blinked down from their stick and bark boughcanies.

"Not far now," Snarly gruffed. "We'll pass through the root canals."

"Titan tree roots actually grow big enough for us to trek through?" Shoenia asked.

"Better than that, Shoenia. They actually grow big enough for us to float through," Snarly explained in a calm tone of voice.

'Snarly must be too tired to rant?' Shoenia mused. *'Of course, there is always later.'*

Snarly continued. "We'll pass through the roots on my raft. The smuzzles built it for me. They are really quite skilled when it comes to building water craft. But docks and ramps – ah, not so much. Anyway, it's not far now. Soon, you will be able to rest and take nourishment, my young friend."

'Friend?' Shoenia mused. *'Wow, a promotion.'*

"Shoenia, you will find that titanroot sap is thick with refreshing nutrients. Tastes not so bad either. A little sweet, actually. It alone has sustained many plants and creatures from Seed unto Morgue. In fact, I drink much of it myself, and see for yourself the results." Snarly slowly spun about and parted wide his limbs. "Ta-Da!"

Shoenia smiled at Snarly's out-of-character gesture. "But I am not made like you," she reasoned.

Snarly sighed. "All living things are alike in three ways, Shoenia. Seed created us. Destiny binds us. And Morgue shall claim us. In order for anything to live, something else must perish. Otherwise, the cycle of nature will be broken. Thus, while no life form can last forever, life energy is boundless and ever-changing. It evolves into new life forms, and they exist everywhere and in every universe. Even when we cannot see life, it is still there. Do you – uh, I mean, kapeesh?"

Shoenia broadened her smile. "I think I do?"

"See, I learned a handy new word from you."

"Yes, you did," Shoenia confirmed.

"And it saves me from wasting two extra words."

"Yes, it does."

Snarly hinted at an almost smile before going on. "Anyway, it is what we do between Seed and Morgue that truly defines us, Shoenia. The time spent during our journey with Destiny is what matters most. For a wasted life is the saddest sorrow of all, and far too many choose to trudge that path."

"How does one avoid a wasted life?" Shoenia asked. She was clearly intrigued.

"Love and Courage, Shoenia. Love and Courage light the path to a life well lived. Although it can be soul cleansing to get angry at times, it is soul crushing to dwell there. Anger is the greatest thief of joy – for anger was meant as a release, not as a destination. Always remember, Shoenia, that hate and love cannot both rule over the exact same heart at the exact same time. Such is the true way of things."

Snarly paused and actually stretched a lopsided smile. "And please don't follow my example on the anger part. I kinda have some issues there. Kapeesh?"

'Gee, I never noticed,' Shoenia thought, but she opted to be gracious. "It's okay, Snarly. Nobody's perfect."

"Ya got that right."

Snarly and the eager smuzzles led Shoenia to an archway that had been purposefully hewed into the base of an enormous titan tree stump. Noting the young galfolk's hesitation to step through into the darkness, the ancient sapkeeper spoke to reassure her. "Not to fret, Shoenia. Shinebulbs have been planted and strung all throughout the canals. They shall respond to our presence. Come."

True to Snarly's words, no sooner had the four passed through the archway than a pale light began to shine. It reflected gently off of the smooth surface of a sap-pool down below. A rickety ramp spiraled down and around the inner wall of the titantrunk, connecting with a crude, floatwood dock.

As the group carefully descended the ramp, more shinebulbs were awakened to their presence. Their light revealed a reed raft, which was tethered by vines to the dock. Two long punting poles lay upon its deck.

The vines instinctively released the raft as the group stepped aboard. Then the eager smuzzles grabbed the punting poles and shoved off.

"Sneek and Peek like to propel this raft for me," Snarly explained. "Although I can order it to propel itself, smuzzles are by their very nature always eager to help out. It's annoying."

The aura within the root canals was tranquil and cool, yet not uncomfortably so. Countless shinebulbs now grew in abundance along the walls and dangled down from the ceiling, adding some heat as well as light.

"Mmmmmm," Shoenia remarked, licking thick titanroot sap from her fingers. "This is deliciously sweet."

"That it is," Snarly agreed. "And it's most nourishing too. Full of nutrients. Indulge yourself as you will."

"I certainly shall. Mmmmmm..."

Shoenia had not the slightest idea of how long they spent floating through the root canals. Each canal appeared much the same as all the others; although she and Snarly were sometimes forced to duck in order to avoid a skull bonk, and, on occasion, the canals would merge with others to form large ponds within the massive titantrunk caverns. Yet the capable smuzzles always knew exactly which new canals to navigate.

Finally, they drifted into an exceptional titantrunk. Being far more massive than any of the others, it spanned a good stroll in breadth. A crude dock connected with a rickety ramp that spiralled up and around the inner wall of the titantrunk. Intricate wall carvings depicted scenes from lost legends.

"Welcome to my humble roost," Snarly stated as the smuzzles skillfully guided the raft alongside the dock. He then swept his rush in a gesture for Shoenia to disembark.

"After you."

"Why thank you, Snarly," Shoenia remarked, stepping onto the dock. She extended a helping hand to her aged host.

Well that she did too, for the struggling sapkeeper teetered for a moment and seemed to draw no breath.

"Are you ill?" Shoenia inquired with noted concern.

"I'm fine. I'm fine. Don't fuss," Snarly snapped with a mix of annoyance and embarrassment.

"Are you certain?" Shoenia pressed, disregarding Snarly's cranky retort. For some reason his moody moments no longer fazed her. His grouchy manner was becoming like water over an eel's gills. Just something natural and expected.

"I said I'm fine, did I not. Dearest Destiny, galfolk, are you certain that your hearers aren't waxed?"

Still indifferent to Snarly's ill humor, Shoenia kept on. "My ears hear well enough to take note of laboured breath. Are you sure you don't want to rest a spell?"

"Are you sure you don't want to be a spell," Snarly sniped, raising his rush. "No, I do not wish to rest a spell. Kapeesh?"

The smuzzles rolled their eyes to show empathy with Shoenia.

Shoenia smiled and thought, *'Snarly sure does like his new word.'*

"C'mon, galfolk. If I'm the problem, then why am I ahead of you? Hmmm... Sheesh..."

Both smuzzles slapped paws to brows and shook their heads.

"We're right behind you," Shoenia replied, while stifling a giggle.

"Yeah, behind me is right! This ole sapkeeper isn't fully fossilized yet! Try to keep up, will ya!"

The smuzzles covered their ears and shook their heads, while Shoenia stifled another giggle.

During their climb, the intrigued galfolk asked the puffing sapkeeper to pause and explain to her the intricate wall carvings. She also wanted him to stop and rest out of concern that his aged ticker might tock. Still, she felt quite special that Snarly proved most eager to teach her the legends behind each carving. Even his dour disposition slightly improved into something almost related to patience.

At last they reached the top of the spiraled ramp, which led them to an arched doorway. Snarly spun the latch about, while the helpful smuzzles pushed open the door. Then Snarly somewhat politely gestured for Shoenia to enter first. Well, sort of somewhat politely anyway...

Shoenia smiled a thank you and stepped inside, where she stopped abruptly and stood muted by marvel.

Snarly's roost was truly a spectacle to behold! A carpet of red thatch unrolled itself to greet them. Wall carvings literally shouted out their welcome. Smaller bells jingled and larger bells bonged. A tiered chandelier of shinebulbs spun and beaconed.

There were benches that bowed, and a crooning couch that curtsied. Four helmeted toadstools supported a breathing bedboard, upon which lazed a striped mattress of brightly coloured moss. In a cozy nook, mist wisped upward from an ornate clay cauldron that depicted etchings of alert eyes that really kept watch!

Three aproned moths wearing pointy boots and brimmed hats fluttered about the roost; a dustin' and a sweepin' and a shooin' dirt out; while a hunched butler-bug in a winged tailcoat took charge of Snarly's rush.

"Thank you, Mr. Midge," Snarly said with rare regard. "This is our guest, Shoenia."

The aloof butler-bug simply bowed to welcome Snarly's strange guest, and then turned about and scurried away down a crooked corridor.

"Wow!" Shoenia blurted out, suddenly unable to contain her voice. Snarly's roost was almost beyond belief. And yet, it was all very real.

Shoenia waltzed about the roost, meeting many new and intriguing characters. Even though they spoke in many different tongues than her own, Shoenia somehow understood every single word and responded in kind. "Hi. Adieu. How are you? Chao. Hello. Namaste. Greetings. Konnichiwa...

"I'm so very pleased to make your acquaintance, Miss Portrait. Nice to meet you, Mr. Mosaic. Oops. So sorry for bumping into you, Mr. Table..."

"No probs..."

A most fantabulous mosaic snagged Shoenia's sights. Bright beads and shinestones had been magically patterned into one entire wall. The exquisite artwork depicted a pair of wicked demons doing battle against a staff-wielding apparition.

"Snarly, what legend is this?" Shoenia inquired.

"Ah!" Snarly responded with noted passion. "That is by far my most favorite. It is The Legend of The Demon Chaser."

"Why is this legend your favorite?" Shoenia asked.

"Because, my perpetually trying galfolk, unlike most others, this legend is entirely true."

"Oh, do teach me this legend," Shoenia pleaded.

Snarly sighed. "You must nap first, Shoenia. There will be plenty of chance for you to make a nuisance of yourself tomorrow – as you no doubt will."

"I can nap after. Please teach me this legend? Please, Snarly? Please?" Shoenia planted a peck on her host's hard cheek.

"Don't!" Snarly shouted, backing away with a start and wiping his cheek.

Undaunted, Shoenia stepped forward and kissed him again. "Teach me."

"I said stop doing that – thing!"

"This thing?" Shoenia asked, kissing his cheek again. "Like this? Or like this? Or maybe like this?"

"Ooooooooo," teased the entire roost.

"Stop! No! Hey! Don't!"

"Then teach me this legend. Or shall I kiss you some more?"

"Ooooooooo..."

Hey! Stop that! Stop torturing me! I said... Oh, Dearest Destiny. Okay! Okay! I surrender! I'll teach you the legend! Just don't ever do that – that yucky lips thing anymore. Kapeesh?"

"It's called kissing, Snarly."

Snarly grabbed one unfortunate and furious frond and started wiping his face with it. "I don't care what it's called. Just don't ever do it again. Not ever. It's gross. Ick-ick-ick and quadruple disgusting ick. Throw in a few gooey yucks too. And what are the rest of you all smirking about? Get back to work! Or whatever it is you lazy lot do around here? And don't get any smoochy-woochy ideas of your own. My rush is never far from my reach. Kapeesh!"

Instantly, the entire roost went – well, sort of quiet; save for the squeals of poorly gagged guffaws, and the wheezing whine of suppressed giggles stretching near to burst.

Snarly's cheeks blushed purple. "Okay. Okay. I'll share with you the legend out on the boughcany, where at least we will have some – privacy!!"

"Oooooooooo…"

"Knock it off!"

This time Shoenia was unable to gag her giggles.

"Very funny, Galfolk. Haw. Haw. Just don't go doing that lips thing again. Ever. I'd sooner be debranched and rolled into a smelly swamp crawling with slimy wigglers."

"I won't," Shoenia said, while thinking to herself, *'Eww… are my kisses really that bad?'*

Snarly eyed her skeptically. "Promise?"

"I promise," Shoenia assured him, slyly crossing her fingers behind her back.

After some hesitation, Snarly relaxed his guard. "Well, okay then. Just don't let it happen again. Ick. Yuck. Gross."

"I've already promised you I won't. I get it, Snarly. Ick. Yuck. Gross."

"That's right. Ick. Yuck. Gross."

Shoenia secretly kept her fingers crossed, although she was inclined to quietly concede to herself that being kissed by somebody against your will was indeed gross. She vowed to herself only to do it again if the situation ever proved proper. *'After all, even gruff ole Mr. Grouchwhiner has a right to his own space.'*

"Very well then. I'll have Mr. Midge prepare us some crunchcones and cream."

Once they had received their delicious treats, Snarly began teaching his eager guest, 'The Legend of The Demon Chaser'.

Shoenia politely listened and licked her crunchcone as Snarly began tutoring her of events from countless eons past. He told her of a time when a pair of wicked demons roamed unchecked about Night's skytwinklers, seeking to destroy all of the beauty that Seed had created over all of eternity. Shoenia stared with wided eyes as Snarly described the chaos and havoc that the demons wreaked by combining their evil powers to bend gravity and divert comets from their proper paths; sending them crashing into newly thriving globes, and thereby causing widespread devastation and extinguishing many of Seed's finest creations. Even entire atmospheres were stripped away. They schemed to destroy all that was good in this universe; to be followed, no doubt, by the destruction of other universes.

Snarly told her of Seed's fury, and of how the enraged deity had created a Demon Chaser to seek out and dispatch the wicked pair to Morgue's Maze; where they would wander lost and powerless for an eternity of forevers, never to do evil again. He spoke of how the Demon Chaser was granted a staff of white gold so pure that it can actually melt even the hardest of stone; which is quite necessary in order to slay demons. The staff, he explained, also grants its bearer the power of a sixth sense; which is also quite necessary in order to prevent demons from sneaking up from behind, as the vile beings are quite apt to do.

Lastly, Snarly added that the staff can only be unpowered in the salty waters of the Saline Sea. "Seed forged it so because the sly demons were known to lurk deep beneath the wetrollers. Thus, should they somehow defeat the Demon Chaser in combat and seize the staff, eventually the pair would unwittingly unpower the awesome weapon themselves."

The crunchcones were long gone by the time Snarly taught Shoenia of the trio's epic battle, which took place high above the Isle of Countless Caverns and raged for almost three full eras. In conclusion, her aged host revealed to her how the Demon Chaser eventually prevailed and dispatched the wicked pair to forever wander Morgue's Maze. However, the price paid proved to be the Demon Chaser's own being. Morgually wounded, it plummeted downward and landed hard on the Isle's jagged rocks. *And rock beats bone every single time.*

The determined Demon Chaser, although soon to meet Morgue itself and too damaged to crawl its way to the Saline Sea, still managed to drag its own broken form deep into one of the Isle's countless caverns. There it sealed the cavern entrance with granite, lest the powerful weapon should ever fall into the wrong hands. For its possession by any mere mortal shall quickly lead its bearer into madness...

"...and then all creatures will surely find ourselves in a right fine mess indeed." Snarly nodded to indicate that the tale was complete.

A reflective silence passed before Shoenia finally spoke. "Who would want to possess such a staff if it leads its bearer into madness?"

Snarly sighed, his tone sinking melancholy. "Perhaps someone who is already there?"

"Snarly, must all who meet Morgue go down into the maze? I mean, can some return back to this time in different forms?"

"I have long pondered such, Shoenia. Truth be told, I do not know? No breathing being knows, and we will not know until our time of breath is done."

Another prolonged silence passed before the sapkeeper spoke again. This time in a surprisingly caring tone. "Anyhow, Shoenia, your heavy eyelids shout of your need to nap. As do my own. I'm afraid that the energy I once enjoyed in my youth has long since waned. Come, Mr. Midge has fixed you up with a comfy cot. He has also warned the mattress not to tickle you, so you should sleep well."

Shoenia gulped, then nervously followed Snarly as he shuffled in from the boughcany. She conceded that her host was exact, for she was spent in both mind and body. After all, she had missed several sleeps in a row, and it had been a very long and eventful trek since the battle.

Snarly guided Shoenia over to a mossy mattress, which had been placed beside the mosaic depicting The Legend of The Demon Chaser. "If I should be out and about when you awaken, Mr. Midge shall tend to your every need. Nap well, Shoenia."

"Snarly?" Shoenia said as the aged sapkeeper laboured towards his own mattress.

"What now, Shoenia? I too am weary."

"I'm happy we met."

"Yeah. Yeah. Whatever…?"

Shoenia simply smiled and flopped down upon the mattress, where she quickly entered the realm of deepest dreams. There she saw diving dazzledills and stepping-stones and crawlers with grins and wall carvings that shone and…

….zzzzzzzzzzzzzzzzzzzz….

…gradually the groggy galfolk became aware of voices drifting in from the boughcany. They seemed to be arguing. Wiping napsand from her bleary eyes, she drew her torso up into a sit.

Only Snarly's gruff voice was familiar to her. The stranger's voice was flat and unfeeling, and Shoenia found it unsettling.

"Fine morning to you," greeted a voice out of the wall mosaic.

Shoenia was startled. "Oh, fine morning to you too," she replied, exchanging pleasantries with the Demon's Chaser's image while ignoring those of its two evil foes.

"Destiny has urgent need of you, Shoenia of Ga," stated the Demon Chaser.

"Huh? H-How do you know my name?"

"Pay no mind to that one," growled one demon.

"Take heed of us!" demanded the other.

"To Morgue's Maze with you both!" shouted the Demon Chaser, brandishing his staff. And with that, the three eternal enemies clashed into combat.

Uncertain of what to do, Shoenia leapt off the mattress and sped barefoot for the boughcany. "Snarly! Snarly!"

"What is it, Shoenia?" Snarly asked, meeting her at the boughcany entrance. His tone bore some concern, yet he seemed not overly alarmed.

"Snarly…" she gasped… "Th-The mosaic is doing battle. The demons…"

"Shoenia. Shoenia!" Snarly interrupted, "It is that mosaic's very purpose to portray such a battle."

"But they spoke to me, Snarly. All three of them…"

Snarly sighed and gently gestured for the excited galfolk to calm down. "Wind down your worries, Shoenia, no harm shall come to you here. My mosaics often perform dramas for my guests. I fashioned them to do so. Tell me, what words did the players speak?"

Despite being wound up, Shoenia took note that Snarly didn't seem quite his usual cranky self. She wondered, *why?*

"Well?" Snarly pressed. He waited impatiently while Shoenia drew in a deep breath, before exhaling slowly to still her nerves.

Once her nerves were somewhat settled, Shoenia attempted to explain what had happened. "The Demon Chaser said that Destiny has urgent need of me. But the demons said that I should listen to them. Then they started fighting…"

Snarly raised a palm to shush her. "Never, ever listen to demons, Shoenia. They are not created by Seed and they do not exist to tell truths. Kapeesh?"

"But if Seed did not create…"

"Shoenia, chill. It's all good. See, the play is over now. See how the mosaic has reverted back to its still image."

Shoenia stared back at the mosaic, which had indeed reverted back to its original scene. Even though she could almost swear that the Demon Chaser blinked?

Snarly beckoned for her to follow him the rest of the way out onto the boughcany. "Shoenia, I want you to meet an old acquaintance. He was by far my most capable apprentice."

An exceptionally tall and lanky grandfolk offered Shoenia a curt nod. His pale flesh was well wrinkled with age. He had thinning white hair and a bleached beard. Bushy white brows topped his empty eyes: rare in that one eye was coloured green and the other blue. Both eyes stared straight through her. His stony scowl was so deeply set that Shoenia suspected a smile might crack his face.

His attire attested that he was a magician of sorts? He donned a pointy red hat with blue streamers dangling freely from its peak. His blue robe was patterned with red crescent moons. Well worn sandals padded the cracked soles of his much-travelled feet. His crooked fingers clenched a wand of pink crystal.

Shoenia mutely returned the nod. Something about this magician knotted her guts? Something unseen, but fully felt. Something sinister? As if an angry aura surrounded his gaunt frame. Not lighthearted anger like Snarly's. No, not at all. This anger went much deeper and was far more dangerous. *'Scoundrel?'*

An awkward silence temporarily settled over the boughcany.

Noting that his two guests had clearly taken an instant dislike of each other, Snarly tactfully moved to soften the atmosphere. "Shoenia, do you recall the last legend that I taught you?"

The moody magician moved to interject, but Snarly motioned for him to hush.

"You mean the legend from the mosaic that just spoke to me?"

"Yes, that's it. The Legend of The Demon Chaser."

"Yes, I remember. Seed had created the Demon Chaser and forged for it a powerful staff of white gold so pure that it could melt stone and slay demons. But the Demon Chaser itself also met Morgue."

"You remember details quite well, Shoenia," Snarly noted, nodding approval to the scowling grandfolk.

"Why do you ask?" Shoenia inquired. "Is it ..."

The moody magician cut her short. His ill-mannered tone and words went well beyond rude. "My mystic mist has revealed to me a most disturbing illusion. I have come to confer privately with my Mentor, and to seek his wisdom. I did not come to listen to the pointless prattle of some silly galfolk."

Shoenia glared daggers at the offensive grandfolk. Bullying had long been her prize peeve, even more so than cussing. She never backed down in such circumstances, for backing down to bullies always invites more abuse.

"Perhaps Snarly should have mentored his most capable apprentice better?" Shoenia sniped back. "One would think that by now a learned grandfolk should have at least learned some basic manners."

Her pointed rebuke caught the moody magician completely unawares. In confused and steaming silence, he looked to Snarly for support.

Snarly merely shrugged him off. "I did warn you, Zebu. This spirited young galfolk is not shy on spunk. Pick a fight with her and you shall get one."

'So, this miserable magician's name is Zebu,' Shoenia discerned.

Zebu's tone was respectful, yet firm; albeit tinged with more than a trace of resentment. "Mentor, I have great need of your wisdom and your magic, not the ignorant designs of some simple-minded..."

"You know, Zebu, the first step in climbing out of a hole is you have to stop digging," Snarly scolded. He was clearly losing patience and growing cross with his former apprentice. "Perhaps you need to drop your shovel? Just drop it. How is that for wisdom?"

Zebu's face burned with embarrassment.

Shoenia fought back a gloat.

"Besides, I cannot leave this Fluorescent Forest. Zebu, you know full well of my responsibilities here. Snarly do this. Snarly do that. Sow this seed, Snarly. Trim that bud, Snarly. This nectar isn't sweet enough, Snarly. It just never ends. Snarly-Snarly-Snarly-Snarly-Snarly…Blah-Blah-Blah-Blah-Blah..."

Shoenia took comfort in the rant. *'Yes! The real Snarly is back!'*

"Mentor, she wields no magic? She cannot even…" Zebu complained.

"Zebu, how much magic did you wield before I mentored you?" Snarly asked with noted annoyance. "Well, apprentice? Tell me. How much?"

"Well, none. But she…"

"And have you not since mastered magic?" Snarly pressed.

"Yes, I have. But Mentor…."

"And yet you mock my wisdom? The very same wisdom that mentored you. The very same wisdom you claim to seek?"

Shoenia silently savoured the one-sided exchange, while struggling with limited success to contain a gloating grin. She did not like this Zebu character; not one tiny bit.

"No, Mentor. I would never…"

"Splendid!" Snarly cut him short. "Then there is no cause for wasteful debate. Shoenia shall become your apprentice and aid you in your purpose. Together, you both shall voyage south and east to Xebec's Island and…"

"Whoa!" Shoenia cut in, every trace of the grin instantly gone from her face. "Snarly, what are you going on about? Apprentice? Purpose? Voyage? Island? Uh, together? Like, with him? I don't think so."

Now Snarly and Zebu both seemed at a loss for words.

"Well?" Shoenia pressed, folding her arms across her chest. "Hmmm?"

Snarly sighed. His tone sank somber. "Shoenia, come sit with us on the toadstools."

Once all three were seated, Snarly carried on. "Shoenia, we have need of your help." The sapkeeper paused to shoot the stewing magician a warning look. "We are faced with a looming crisis – and by we, I mean most living things. Perhaps even the gravest crisis since that posed by the very demons themselves?"

Shoenia could not help but glance her ill will at Zebu.

Zebu responded in kind.

Snarly ignored the glaring tension between his guests. "Shoenia, Zebu's *seers cauldron* recently boiled over, which of itself is never a good sign, and the mystic mist revealed some disturbing illusions."

"What sort of illusions?" Shoenia asked.

"Perhaps it is best that your new mentor explain," Snarly said. "He nodded to Zebu.

Zebu eyed Snarly with nil gratitude. "Perhaps it is," he grumbled.

"Explain what?" Shoenia asked, clearly irked that Zebu would try to tell her anything.

"Patience, Shoenia. Go on, Zebu."

The tepid magician made a face. "Oh, very well then. As the mystic mist cooled it revealed to me the whereabouts of the Demon Chaser's long-lost staff. No longer safely entombed inside a cavern, it has indeed fallen into the wrongest of hands...

"Whose hands?" Shoenia cut in.

"Patience, Shoenia. Allow Zebu to speak his words."

Zebu stretched his scowl, yet kept on. "The staff is now the prize possession of that loony sorcerer, Xebec of Ranidae. Xebec was once an ethical magician such as us…" Zebu paused to indicate both Snarly and himself. "… as he had once been apprenticed to the master magician, Spidey Smells..."

"Spidey Smells? Seriously? That's his real name? Ha! That is funny."

"This is no joke or game, Shoenia," Snarly scolded. "Do keep focus and knot your loose tongue."

"I'm sorry," Shoenia mumbled, accepting that she had rudely crossed a line.

This time it was Zebu who barely contained a gloating grin. "Although a capable magician of the highest order, Spidey Smells is also a very poor judge of character. After all, it is he who trained Xebec in the fine art of magic. And it is he who failed to note that his sly apprentice schemed behind the dutiful words that he spoke.

"Xebec patiently bided his time waiting for the perfect chance to act. While Spidey dangled in trance, he skulked into Spidey's lair and stole off with his webscroll."

"His web what?" Shoenia asked.

"His webscroll," Snarly put in. "Spidey spun his most secret of spells and chants into a webscroll so that he could always keep them with him."

"As with the staff, the webscroll too can also be quite dangerous in the wrong hands," Zebu added, before continuing with his tale. "Anyway, when Spidey finally untranced and realized that he had been duped by his most capable apprentice, he promptly tasked his other apprentices to chase down the thief and retrieve his precious webscroll. But Xebec…"

"Zebu, can you imagine how such a betrayal by an apprentice must feel to the mentor?" Snarly asked. "It must slice deep?"

Zebu was puzzled by Snarly's interruption. "Uh, yes. I do suppose it would, Mentor. Anyway, getting back to my story. Xebec was by far the most skilled apprentice of the lot, and, having acquired new knowledge from Spidey's webscroll, he easily dissolved all of his pursuers into smelly moo-pies. You see, galfolk, Sorcerer Xebec does have a rather twisted sense of humor."

'At least he has one,' Shoenia thought.

"Xebec then escaped to the island that now bears his name," Snarly added. "Which is why we need your help."

"Why didn't this Spidey Smells give chase himself? After all, is he not also a master magician?"

Zebu toned sarcastic. "Because, my dear apprentice, being mortal ourselves, even we master magicians have our limitations. And one of Spidey's limitations is that he is a blanched arachnid."

"A blanched arachnid?"

"Which means that he is in a very rare breed of silkspinner who must avoid the direct rays of the sun at all cost," Snarly explained. "Lest his skin should frizzle from his frame. This is why Spidey dwells only in his subsurface lair. Up top means Morgue to him."

"Which explains why this sorcerer, Xebec, fled to a faraway island," Shoenia concluded.

"Exactly!" Snarly exclaimed.

"What of this purpose then?" Shoenia asked.

"Xebec is not worthy to wield even a pebble of power, hence he must be relieved of the staff," Zebu stated quite matter-of-factly.

"Not simply relieved of it, Zebu," Snarly responded in the strictest of tones. "The staff must straightaway be flung into the Saline Sea. It was never meant to be seen by mere mortals, and none of breath are worthy to wield it. Do you hear me, Zebu? None."

"Of course, Mentor," Zebu said, bowing his head in mock respect.

Snarly turned to Shoenia. His tone was pleading. "Will you not help us, Shoenia? Zebu shall mentor you in magic. You will learn much."

Shoenia's racing mind cramped at the mere thought of voyaging anywhere with Zebu, or of having him teach her anything. Besides, what of her friends and allies who were still engaged in conflict against the Lizarme? Surely she should return home and fight alongside them?

Despite all of that, Shoenia knew deep down that the staff must be unpowered in the salty waters of the Saline Sea; or else all will be lost anyway. Snarly had almost certainly spared her an early meeting with Morgue. How could she refuse to help him now? Had she no honour?

Shoenia thought, *'Destiny, guide my thoughts to make the right choice?'*

Both master magicians sat still and mute as Shoenia further pondered her dilemma. One hoping that she would voyage to Ranidae. The other hoping that she would not.

Finally, she made her choice. "Snarly, I owe you a debt that I can never fully repay. I shall do as you ask."

The sapkeeper shook his head. "No, Shoenia. You owe me nothing. This choice could cost you your very life, as you shall surely be assailed by evil on many fronts. Therefore, I cannot play any role in your choice, nor can I condemn you for it. You alone must choose. Kapeesh?" Snarly stretched a soft smile of compassion. It was clear that he understood the depth of the dilemma with which Shoenia now grappled.

Shoenia responded by nodding and matching Snarly's smile with one of her own. "Kapeesh."

Aged amber eyes locked with youthful emerald eyes. They exchanged an unspoken bond of mutual respect and affection.

Shoenia carefully rethought her position. Oh, how she ached for her family. Her friends. Her village. They were never far from her thoughts. And what if the lizarme should actually win the conflict? It was in fact a possibility. Just the idea of such sank in her stomach. How could she simply abandon her own in their time of need?

'But all other creatures are in peril as well. We humanfolk do not own this globe. All that breathe have value; even the rotten, for Seed does not create useless fruit. In this role called life, we all play our part. For better or for worse. And the staff in the wrong hands will surely destroy all that is good and beautiful. How can I ever face Morgue if I allow that to happen? Much worse, how will I ever face myself?'

The torn galfolk finally resolved her dilemma. She would forgo sentiment for logic. "Snarly, I will voyage to Ranidae to seek out the staff and unpower it in the Saline Sea. Or else I will breathe my last trying to do so."

Zebu was vigilant to mask his thoughts.

"Splendid!" Snarly exclaimed.

'Yeah, splendid,' Zebu thought. *'Simply splendid. Yay.'*

"Well then," Snarly continued, "There is nary a moment to waste. I've already told my smuzzles to gather up their tools. They really are highly skilled boat builders, you know. Thus, we shall set out for the southern coast at once, where the smuzzles shall construct for you a pliable yet sturdy boat from a boulder-pea pod. Plans have already been drawn up. They shall use a dandytall stem for the mast, and stitch together palm leaves for the sails. The boat will be steered by a fanlilly rudder with a wooden tiller. And it shall be both swift and seaworthy!"

"A boulder-pea pod?" Shoenia stated, rather skeptically. "Seriously?"

"Seriously," Snarly assured her. "Boulder peas are so named because they are – well, big as boulders. And some pods can float over a hundred of them."

Snarly then pointed a twiggy digit to the above. "Skytwinklers and the sun shall take turns guiding you, and Destiny shall protect you. Come, let us be off at once!"

And so it was that all three ventured forth for the southern coast, along with an eager crew of tool-toting smuzzles.

In the Fluorescent Forest, one can never be fully certain of just how many dusks and dawns have passed because most regions of the forest were forever vibrant and bright. At such times it was often uncertain as to whether Day or Night ruled beyond the breathing canopy above. As a result, sleep patterns were quite disrupted, which added greatly to fatigue. Yet the determined group pressed on and on…

They carefully threaded their way through thickets of slashthorns, and about brush budded with bows. Plus they passed by silly shrubs with crossed seers, and proud plants with schnobb noses. In fact, they even encountered a spinney of shy saplings who crept away on root digits.

All the while, Snarly kept ranting and whining and brandishing his rush. "Get outta our way! I said move aside, floppy ferns! Ya'd think with ears that big you lot would have heard me the first time. Now scram! Hey, you there. That's right, I'm talking to you, proud plant. How would you like my rush shoved up that schnozz? Hey, slashthorns. Yeah, you four. Wanna become kindling? Dearest Destiny, why was I stuck with this loopy lot? Why me, Seed? Why ole Snarly? Wad I do? Wad I do?"

At one point during a brief break, they were entertained by a trio of tapsticks who just loved to show off; alongside cacti with shiny needles, who trumpeted tunes through conch horns. For you see, in the Fluorescent Forest, not one thing fits in with the norm.

Careless stepping-stones stomped flat hapless flowers, who sprang back up burning with anger; leading Shoenia to ponder, do the plants here expire?

"Hey, you stones over there. Why don't ya watch where you're stomping? Kapeesh! Or do ya wanna become magma!?"

Silkspinners dangled down from their glistening webs, while passion fruit made smacking sounds whenever they kissed. In fact, it seemed like the whole forest was just teeming with pests.

On and on the group trekked, along trails and through thatch, topping up their bellies from each chow-veggie patch; although eating only those eggplants that Snarly said could not hatch. They nibbled on fiddle heads from feed ferns, and downed berries by the batch. Plus they gulped down the sweet cream of milkweeds, and slurped root sap by the pail; in fact, once all was considered, they faired really quite well.

At long last they passed through a parting curtain of blue light and stepped out from under the shelter of the breathing canopy. They had finally broken free of the Fluorescent Forest and had arrived at the coast.

Monster wetrollers swept in from the deep, and then curled over to splash the beach. Surf spat foam at the wind, and the retreating tides sucked silt back out into the depths. Yet a patch of boulder-pea pods held fast, being well anchored by long stems and deep roots. They bobbed about in the surf with nary a care, knowing that only the severest of storms packed the power to uproot them.

Bended palms swayed in the refreshing seaside breeze. Hairy bonker beans littered the beach. Shore squawkers flapped their wings and voiced their annoyance at the new arrivals. Although it was still light out, a full moon was already chasing the sun back beyond the western horizon.

It would soon be dusk, and time for a much-needed sleep. Which is exactly what the weary group elected to do…

….zzzzzzzzzzzzzzzzzzzz….

…even before the sun peaked atop the eastern horizon, the skilled smuzzles were already up and hard at work on the construction of a sturdy boat. They laboured hard in their race against time. Snarly wanted the craft completed before the moon's return, and the ensuing assault of the tides.

They cut the craft's hull from an enormous boulder-pea pod, and fitted it with a flexible dandytall stem as its mast:

meant to bend but not snap during rogue swells and severe storms, both of which they were most certain to encounter. Special palm leaves were chosen and stitched together to make sails; chosen because their tough fibres were difficult to tear. A thick fanlilly was found and fashioned into a rudder. It would be steered by a floatwood tiller. A hole was painstakingly bored through a stone, which would suffice as an anchor.

The retreating sun still ruled the sky when the boat was deemed to be seaworthy and made ready to sail. The smuzzles were kept busy loading rations and supplies right up until the moon's tidal scouts started creeping ashore. Soon, Day would surrender its blue sky to Night, and to its army of skytwinklers.

While Zebu personally oversaw the final packing of provisions, Snarly quietly took Shoenia aside to chat free from unwanted ears.

Shoenia could sense Snarly's desire for discretion.

"Speak softly, Shoenia. And do not waste words. Kapeesh?"

The cautious galfolk nodded that she understood.

"I have some items to aid you in your purpose, Shoenia," Snarly whispered, slinging a full stalkhollow over her shoulder. "Remember, besides refreshing your energy, this specially brewed titanroot sap will also help hasten the healing of wounds. Apply it sparingly as it is quite potent. Don't fret, it is still quite safe to drink."

Next, the anxious sapkeeper tied a dormant shinebulb to Shoenia's scrapstick. "Just tap it gently to make it glow and unglow."

Shoenia nodded discretely.

Snarly glanced cautiously about before secretly pressing some hard objects into her palm. "Hide these three items in your pouch, and reveal them to absolutely no one. I mean it, Shoenia. Until the staff has been unpowered, you are to trust nobody. And I do mean nobody."

"I trust you, Snarly." Shoenia opened her hand, exposing a stone flint and striker. The third item was a tiny glass vial, which seemed to be empty even though it was plugged with a cork. She was puzzled. "Why are these items so secret," she asked, dropping all three objects into her pouch.

Snarly's tone was warning. "Because, Shoenia, I too can read mystic mist."

Noting that his tone had further alarmed the already wary galfolk, the sapkeeper gently held her shoulders and softened his words to calm her. "My final gifts have neither shape nor weight, yet their value goes well beyond the others. Shoenia, I give you my trust, plus the gift of true friendship."

Shoenia had never known 'true' friendship before. Few ever do. Emotion welled up in her throat, making speech difficult, and she grew misty-eyed from her fondness for the cranky sapkeeper with the dour disposition who was now placing so much of his trust in her. "Isn't it sad, Snarly?"

"Isn't what sad, Shoenia?"

A lone tear trickled a crooked trail down Shoenia's cheek. "That we should meet as we did. I mean, I was forced into your forest haven only because the land beyond is currently embroiled in its Second Continental Conflict. Isn't it sad how we mere mortals are so lacking in sense that we need to number our wars? One should think we would have learned our lesson after the first one? You are old and wise, Snarly. Tell me, what is wrong with us? Why can't we all learn to get along?"

Snarly solemnly shook his head. "I cannot answer those questions, Shoenia. Even after such a long life, hate still remains a sealed riddle to me? I suspect hate is fueled by either fear or greed? Perhaps it is even a toxic blend of both, but with a twist of wilful ignorance mixed in just to sweeten the taste? It likewise baffles me how Hate or Love can so often and so readily outwit reason – and how such fiery opposites as they can both burn inside the same soul? It all makes no sense?

"At least we did meet, my young friend. Regrettably, we shall not meet again. At least not in this age, anyway. Even as we speak a new sapkeeper is sprouting to take my place in the Fluorescent Forest. Such is the will of Destiny."

"Where are you going?" Shoenia asked, visibly concerned.

Snarly gently squeezed her hand. Sticky sap seeped from his puffy sockets. He shrugged. "Back from whence I came, I suppose?"

As Shoenia took in the meaning of her friend's words, she felt a sinking in her stomach. More tears trickled down her cheeks. Trying to keep it together, she swallowed hard. She barely choked forth her wish. "Snarly, I so hope we meet up again in the beyond."

Snarly smiled as only true friends can. "Perhaps we shall? Or, perhaps our spirits will return to repeat this strange journey we call life? Only Destiny knows?"

Deciding that the situation now proved proper, Shoenia wiped sap from Snarly's rough cheek and gently kissed him. "I had my fingers crossed," she confessed.

"I knew that," Snarly replied. He awkwardly kissed her brow, noting that it felt just as warm being the kisser as it did being the kissee. He added, "I do wish that I had learned of this peculiar humanfolk custom much sooner."

Shoenia smiled through wetted cheeks. "At least you did learn of it."

"I did at that. But now it is almost time for you to set sail. Shoenia, listen to me. I know you are prone to speak what you think, but from now on you must think what you speak. And especially think of to whom you do speak it. Words have power, Shoenia. And consequences. Which is why a wise grown-up never wastes words."

Snarly paused a moment to let his advice settle before he continued. "I knew that you would come to meet me a long time ago, Shoenia. Keep keen of wit and speech. And always beware *the dumps of alone.* Many of life's poorest choices are born out of loneliness.

"And always remember this about fear. You cannot wish away fear. You cannot hide from fear. You cannot go around fear. You cannot climb over fear. You cannot tunnel under fear. Shoenia, you can only go through fear. And at some point in life your mortal courage will fail you. Of that you can be certain. It is at that point that you must trust in Destiny to guide you and give you your courage. *Then, when you find yourself in the proper place and at the proper time, you shall know to do the proper thing*. Kapeesh?"

"I understand, Snarly."

"Good." Snarly kissed Shoenia's brow a second time. And with that the ancient sapkeeper turned and shuffled away.

Tears flowed freely down Shoenia's face as her competing emotions messed with her mind. "Snarly!" she called out after him. "I think you're adorable!"

"Ah, whatever?"

"And you really suck at being mean!"

The sapkeeper simply raised his rush to acknowledge her, but neglected to look back.

Suddenly Zebu barked that it was time to cast off.

Thus, Shoenia set sail for the Land of Ranidae with only the moody magician's empty eyes and stony scowl for company. She silently wished that some others had come along. Anyone. Sorrow and guilt were her only companions now, as she had just abandoned her own in their time of conflict. Plus she had left Snarly to meet Morgue alone. She had even forgotten to seek out Sneek and Peek and hug them goodbye. So selfish... *'And what of Snarly's claim that he had already known that I would come to meet him a long time ago? Very strange...?'*

Shoenia could not know that the ancient sapkeeper shared in both her sorrow and her guilt from his final perch high atop a rocky crag. Sticky sap seeped freely from his puffy sockets as he watched the tiny boat bobbing atop the distant wetrollers, taking his three friends ever closer to danger. He kept watch in somber silence as the craft became but a speck, before vanishing altogether beyond the southern horizon.

"Destiny, I have done all that you have willed of me," Snarly prayed, still watching the empty horizon. "Do not let my actions be for naught."

With that final thought, the ancient sapkeeper bowed his head and fossilized to meet Morgue.

3
Tiptin

Snow devils spun and danced their way across the mountains' naked slopes, while biting gusts of wind blew about the needle trees that carpeted the deep valleys of Ranidae's Swallow Mountains. Lesser branches cracked, or even snapped from the weight of the icicles that hung down from them like spikes.

"Dung," the ladfolk cursed, his frosty breath tumbling forth from between his chattering teeth. He wrapped his thick woolen cloak tightly about his shivering frame, trying to trap in body heat. His sopping wet trousers were tucked deep into his highboots, where his frozen toes refused to wiggle. Blowing breath to thaw his numbing fingers, he whispered, "Destiny, shall I ever know warmth again?"

The ladfolk blew breath across his fingers several more times before reaching inside the cloak and dipping them into the pocket of his hide vest. He smiled as his fingers felt two hard and familiar objects amongst a handful of dry straw. He would soon need them, lest he should meet Morgue from the cold.

His alert, brown eyes darted back and forth, seeking the right spot for a much-needed rest. A long braid of black hair dangled down his back. Although tall and thin, the ladfolk's frame was not lacking in strength. Wiry muscles ached beneath his dark skin. Thighs and calves burned with each crunching step. Yet onward he trudged.

For more than a cycle he had hidden out in the forest, only sneaking into hamlets that were known to him, and only on rare occasions. And always under the protection of darkness, lest he be captured by Xebec's suck-ups and shackled as a fugitive. He had no intention of ever obeying any ruler's decrees. To him, freedom was well worth such hardships. He would rather test Morgue than become any sorcerer's subject.

He had always kept close to home before, relying only on trusted friends or family for supplies. That is, until his narrow escape from a patrol of Xebec's suck-ups forced him deeper into the forest, putting him further away from both home and help.

The humanfolk patrol had pursued him for nearly three phases, forcing him to flee north and east into the Swallow Mountains. Twice the ladfolk had barely dodged arrows. And one time he had even hidden and shivered inside a tree hollow while a gang of mugwump river pirates made camp nearby; for the shaggy beasts would have happily bartered him over to the suck-ups for a small bounty. Or tormented him just for fun.

However, Destiny smiled on him twice; first when the mugwumps broke camp during Night's rule and cast off in their riverboats, and then again when the suck-ups departed promptly at the crack of dawn, having decided that they had wasted enough time chasing after just one fugitive. This left the exhausted ladfolk still shivering in his hollow; all alone and hopelessly lost. Yet still free!

He had next waited out a severe ice storm by taking shelter inside of a small cave, hoping that others would not smell the smoke from his small fire. And there he had eaten the last of his smoked meat and hardtack. Hence, he now found himself both hungry and cold, while trudging about a mountain slope that was covered knee deep in wet packing snow. His eyes were desperately seeking shelter from the mountain's frigid breath, for he was tired, lost and all alone. At least until…

"Keeps still, Bam!"

"Snff. Lets Biff pull, Bam! Snff."

"Ahhh… Schtops pulls. Dooz hurts. Ahhh…"

"Duhh – ?????"

"Bam's tongue dooz be stuck."

"Snff. Me knows, Mr. Stinks Gross. Duzz??"

"Me not stinks gross!"

"Ye dooz too stinks gross. Snff."

"Dooz not!"

"Snff. Dooz too."

"Ahhhhh… Schtops pulls."

"Duhh – ?????"

The ladfolk didn't know whether to howl or weep. Four burly boorleez with bald heads, skinny legs, hairy torsos, and thick arms reaching down to touch the ground were gathered in a nearby clearing. Each was clad in naught but a loincloth. One boorlee had his tongue stuck to a frosted chopping axe? A second boorlee had a firm grip on the axe handle. The third had a drippy schnozz. While the fourth boorlee simply looked lost?????

"Not nice ye sez me stinks gross!" screamed the biggest boorlee, releasing his grip on the axe handle and brandishing his knuckles high atop his thick skull. "Dooz pologize, or ye gets hard hurts noogies!"

"Me not pologize. Snff. Ye gets nasty knocks noogies," countered the boorlee with the drippy schnozz, likewise brandishing his knuckles high atop his thick skull. "Snff. Bam too sez ye smells stinky gross like yucky finners. Guffaw!"

"Ahhh… Uh-uh, me notth sezth," denied the boorlee with his tongue stuck to the axe.

"Sees! Me not smells stinky gross like yucky finners!" the biggest boorlee belted out with a smirk. "Bam not sez!"

"Bam dooz be big fibber. Snff."

"Be nodth."

"Be too. Snff."

"Nodth!"

"Snff. Too."

"Bam not fibs!"

"Snff. Uh-huh. Bam dooz too fibs," the boorlee with the drippy schnozz smugly insisted. Quite clearly, he rather enjoyed taunting the two bigger boorleez.

"Not! Not! Not!"

"Too. Too. Too. Snff."

The intrigued ladfolk stared almost in disbelief as the biggest boorlee and the one with the drippy schnozz started circling about with knuckles raised high. Noogie combat seemed certain.

"Boog, ye dooz pologize cuzz ye sez Bam be fibber!"

"Snff. Me not pologize! Bam dooz be fibber. Ye dooz stinks gross! Guffaw! Guffaw! Snff."

"Me stinks nice!"

"Gross. Snff."

"Nice!"

"Gross. Snff."

"Nice! Nice! Nice!"

"Snff. Gross. Gross. Gro…huh?"

"What ye sees…huh?"

Having now spotted the staring ladfolk, three of the boorleez scrambled to hide behind each other. While the fourth boorlee simply looked lost?????

"Don't be scared," Tiptin assured the boorleez as the frightened trio kept backing away across the clearing in a frantic effort to hide behind one another. He stepped out from amongst the needle trees and began trudging through the deep drifts towards them.

"Stops!" shouted the biggest boorlee, brandishing his knuckles. "Ye not *catches* me *brudz*! Ye gets nasty knocks noogies! Gets hard hurts noogies too!"

"Snff. Dooz ye be *suck-up*?" inquired the boorlee with the drippy schnozz. "Dooz ye be *meeny*?"

"No, I am not a suck-up or a meany. Nor do I wish to catch or harm anybody," Tiptin calmly assured them. He knew from past encounters with boorleez that brudz was boorleez speak for both brother and brothers, and that family bonds were extremely strong amongst them. However, brudz was not to be confused with *budz*, which simply put meant friend; and that friendship to boorleez meant sharing and caring about each other, despite their penchant for quarreling about, well, pretty much anything and everything. He also knew that, despite their size and strength, they were a very gentle sort who would never hurt anyone or anything unless they themselves felt threatened.

"I am just a simple ladfolk. My name is Tiptin of Folkton and I..."

"We likes simple! Snff."

Tiptin thought, *'Gee, I never would have guessed.'*

"Dooz come ye be here in woods?" inquired the biggest boorlee, still notably suspicious. He leered askance at the little stranger. "Dooz come ye not be in Folkton with humanfolks, huh?"

Tiptin granted the wary boorlee a warm smile. His tone rang soft and disarming. "Well, actually, I am lost and..."

"We be lost!" the biggest boorlee interrupted, splashing a great big smile clear across his face.

"Duhh – ????? – desserts?" asked the lost-looking boorlee, while rubbing his belly.

The ladfolk was caught somewhat unawares by the boorleez' sudden swing in mood. "Sorry, but I don't have any food at all. As I was saying, my name is Tiptin and I..."

"Greets! Me be Biff!" announced the biggest boorlee, slapping a palm to his own skull. He proudly pointed to the others. "And them dooz be me brudz!"

The others boorleez suddenly felt the need to compete. The boorlee with the drippy schnozz arm-swung directly up to the startled ladfolk. "Greets! Snff! Me be Boog! Snff."

"Uh, greets, Boog."

Biff also arm-swung up to Tiptin. "Bam dooz licks cold axe."

"Gotsth schtuck," the unfortunate boorlee confirmed, pointing to the axe as it dangled freely from his tongue. "Hurtsth."

"Oh, I bet it does hurt," Tiptin acknowledged.

Next, the lost-looking boorlee arm-swung over to Tiptin and extended a wet and hairy foot in greeting.

Tiptin hesitated, and then tapped feet with the boorlee as it only seemed *illogical?* "Uh, and what is your name?" he asked of the lost-looking boorlee.

"Duhh – ????? – ?????"

"Branehurts not sez much," Biff explained.

"Snff. Too muches nasty knocks noogies," Boog added, rapping his knuckles loudly upon his own skull. "Branehurts dooz be boink. Snff."

"Oh, I see," Tiptin said. "Still, I must be getting on…"

"Me sees too!" Biff cut in, using his fingers to widen his own eyes. "Sees, me gots eyes?"

"Snff. Him sees ye gots eyes, Mr. Stinks Gross! Duzz??" Boog stated sarcastically, offering up an eye roll.

"Me stinks nice!"

"Not nice. Snff. Ye stinks gross."

"Me stinks nice!"

"Uh-uh. Snff. Ye stinks smelly gross like yucky finners."

"Dooz not!"

"Snff. Dooz."

"Not! Not! Not!"

"Dooz. Dooz. Dooz. Snff…"

"Hey!" Tiptin hollered, stepping directly between the circling combatants. He pointed at Bam, causing the unfortunate boorlee to flinch. "Instead of fighting, why don't we try and get that axe off of your brudz' tongue?"

"Axe be schtuck," Bam added with a sulk.

Tiptin drew a deep breath before he resumed speaking. "If we start a fire and slowly warm up the axe, then it should peel off without tearing away the skin. It really is quite simple."

"Snff. We likes simple."

Tiptin rolled his eyes. "I'm most certain you do, Boog."

"Dooz ye sez? Snff."

"I said I'm most happy to help you."

"Tiptin dooz be boorleez' budz?" Biff inquired.

"Yeah, sure. I'll be your buddy. Now, let's gather…"

"HOORRAY!!" shouted the four boorleez, suddenly grabbing the startled ladfolk and rubbing their knuckles briskly across his skull. "NOOGIE!! NOOGIE!! NOOGIE!! NOOGIE!!"

"Stop it! Hey! Cut it out! I mean it! Hey! Dung!"

Suddenly the brudz stopped giving Tiptin noogies.

Biff donned a serious look. "Not plite sez bad words, Tiptin."

The other boorleez all nodded with wided eyes.

Tiptin rubbed his aching crown and met Biff's serious stare with one of his own. It was readily apparent that the boorleez were beginning to rattle his reason.

"Not plite sez bad words," Biff repeated.

"Okay. Okay," the fuming ladfolk conceded with a sigh. "I do apologize. It's just that we humanfolk don't much care for knuckle noogies."

The boorleez were visibly stunned. Each dropped his lower jaw and looked to the others in utter disbelief.

"Ye not likes nice *no-hurts* noogies even?" Biff asked.

"Ye not likes plays noogies ever? Snff." Boog pressed.

"Bam was equally perplexed. "Ye be schik, Thipthen? Ahhh..."

"Duhh – ?????" Branehurts began, but lost his kernel of thought.

Tiptin tried to explain. "No, Bam, I am not sick. You see, my skull is not nearly so thick as yours and..."

"Waits!" Biff suddenly exclaimed. "Me gets it! Tiptin likes dooz plays zings!"

"HOORRAY!!" the others cheered, before chanting, "ZINGS IN SKY!! ZINGS IN SKY!! ZINGS IN SKY!! ZINGS IN..."

"Hey!" the startled ladfolk screamed to no avail, suddenly finding himself being tossed heels over hearers high up into the air. "Whooaaa..." Over after over he flipped in mid air; falling back down only to be caught by huge, hairy arms and promptly *zingsed* back up into the air. He quickly grew dizzy. Plus very, very angry.

Tiptin's cheeks flushed red with rage as he frantically flailed about in mid toss, grasping at the breeze. "Hey! Stop it! I said stop! Whooaaa..."

"ZINGS!! ZINGS!! ZINGS!!"

"Guffaw! Snff. Tiptin zings high up to trees! Guffaw! Guffaw!"

"Hey, I'm not kidding! Whooaaa... Stop it! Put me down! Now! Whooaaa..." Tiptin's stomach spun to spew.

"Tiptin's face dooz turns green. Sees."
"Snff. Brudz dooz too high zings, Tiptin?"
"Ye wanth brudz schtopth playth zingth, Thipthen?"
"Whoooaaaa..."
"SPLUNCH."
All the brudz gawked down at the ladfolk's legs, which were now kicking furiously up out of the snow.
"Ooops. Dooz pologize, Tiptin. Boog spozed dooz catches."
"Not me. Snff. Ye spozed dooz catches, Biff."
"Uh-uh."
"Uh-huh."
"Uh-uh."
"Uh-huh."
"Mmmmm!? #*!?"
"Dooz Tiptin sez?"
"Mmmmmm!! #*!??!!*#!??#*!!!"
"Snff. Tiptin sez plays noogies now maybe?" Boog suggested with a shrug of his broad shoulders.
"Him nodth sez plays noogeeth," Bam noted. "Him sez beeth schtuck in snow!"
"Ooops," Biff offered up with a shrug.
Of course, the customary round of post zings *joy* noogies was required before Biff and Boog finally yanked the livid ladfolk free from his frigid fix and laid him down gently atop the snow. There Tiptin lay panting and shivering and scolding Seed for the very being of boorleez, and begging forgiveness from Destiny for whatever it was he had said or done to deserve the four brudz.
"Destiny, grant me patience," Tiptin pleaded, staring up at the swirling sky while holding on tight to the spinning ground.
"Dooz Tiptin sez?"
The other boorleez simply shrugged.
After his spins had somewhat settled and he had shaken much of the mush from his mind, Tiptin slowly wobbled to his feet; only to encounter three approaching boorleez bearing full armloads of broken branches. Brainhurts lagged behind, dragging along a massive log.

"We gots wood for fire," Biff proudly noted.

"But nodth gotsth flintsth?" Bam pointed out, with the axe now dangling freely from his swollen tongue.

Tiptin sighed and stuck his fingers into his vest pocket. "It's okay, I have flints and dry straw for starting a fire."

"HOORRAY!!" the brudz shouted, each throwing their arms up in the air.

Tiptin dove for cover as branches landed all around him. Once he felt it safe to do so, the livid ladfolk yet again pulled his face from the cold snow. Obscure yet pointed words mumbled through his gnashed teeth.

"Dooz ye sez, Tiptin?" Biff inquired.

"Just dig a fire pit!" Tiptin snapped. "And somebody drag more logs over here for us to sit on!"

"Tiptin dooz be mad at boorleez, huh?"

"Yes!" Tiptin railed, brandishing a forefinger. "Now, you brudz listen to…"

Tiptin ceased in mid-shout as all four boorleez had started to shake.

"*Pleeze* not scolds brudz, Tiptin. Pleeze."

"Snff. Brudz dooz pologize cuzz we be dense boobs."

All four boorleez nodded in agreement.

The ladfolk lowered his forefinger and tamed his harsh tone. "Very well, then. I not scolds – I mean, I won't scold you."

"HOORRAY!!"

"Hey! No! Ow! Ouch! Aaahh! Stop it!"

"Ooops. We dooz forgets, Tiptin not likes noogies."

"Dooz pologize. Snff."

"That is right. I not likes……Dung! Sure as Seed, now I'm even starting to speak like them!"

"Not plite sez bad words."

Tiptin bowed his head in prayer. "Destiny, can you please put a rush on that patience?"

"Snff. Dooz Tiptin sez?" Boog asked of his brudz.

"Seth him not liketh noogies?" Bam offered.

"Snff. Plays zings again?" Biff suggested.

"No!" Tiptin screamed out in frustration. "I do not want to play zings again! I prefer to keep my belly inside my skin. Nor do I wish to play noogies either. My skull feels just fine without the lumps. In fact, I don't want to play any games. Can we just keep things simple and focus on getting a fire started? Please."

"We likes simple."

Despite their apparent lack of wit, the boorleez actually proved to be most capable workers. Digging like canines, their large hands quickly scooped away a sizeable patch of snow right down to the bare ground. Of course, they displaced much of the snow and sod onto one very annoyed ladfolk.

"Snff. Where be Tiptin too?"

"Guffaw! There him be! Tiptin dooz be snowfolk. Guffaw!"

"Duhh – ?????"

"Wants zings snowballs, Tiptin?"

"No!" Tiptin snapped, shaking and slapping the snow and dirt from his cloak and trousers. "I do not want to zings snowballs…"

"WHAP!"

"Grrrrr!" was all that Tiptin could manage after a giant snowball to the face knocked him flat on his butt.

"Branehurtsth zingth," Bam tattled, pointing at his lost brud.

"Cuzz ye sez him to zings!" Biff railed in Branehurts' defense.

"So, Branehurtsth shtill…"

"Enough!" Tiptin shrilled, standing and wiping slush from his face. "I don't give a flying flick who threw it. One more snowball to my face and I'll leave you here to start your own fire. Got it."

Tiptin glared daggers at the muted boorleez. "Good. Now, dig that fire pit."

At once the boorleez took to fist pounding the frozen ground and breaking it up into large chunks, which they carelessly zingsed aside without caution.

"Branehurtsth still dooz zingth snowball."

"Cuzz ye sez him to, Bam."

"Deeper," Tiptin cut in, barely dodging an errant chunk of dirt.

"Ooops. Dooz pologize."

"We dig ye nice pit, Tiptin."

"Hey!" Biff suddenly exclaimed, tearing a large chunk of root from the fire pit. "Me finds tuber! We gots food!"

"HOORRAY!!"

"NOOGIE!! NOOGIE!! NOOGIE!! NOOGIE!!"

Tiptin could merely roll his eyes as Biff was well rewarded with a rousing round of grats noogies.

"Ye wants dooz plays noogies, Tiptin?"

"No!"

While Branehurts and Boog fetched more logs, Biff and Bam kept on scooping out soil; until they had dug a deep pit.

Upon noticing that Branehurts was wandering back into the woods all by himself, Tiptin huffed, "Now, where is he off to?"

"Branehurts dooz gots piddle," Biff explained, busily washing his hands with snow.

It intrigued the ladfolk to discover that Boog and Bam were likewise washing their hands.

Noting Tiptin's puzzled expression, Biff explained, "We gots tuber, so we gots wash hands cuzz we eats.

Bam and Boog nodded to concur, while Branehurts swift-swung back from the woods. Then he too joined in the hand washing ritual.

"Dooz make fire now, Tiptin? Pleeze?" Biff pleaded.

"Pleeezth. Axe beeth schtuck," Bam whined.

Tiptin took the flints and some dry straw from his pouch, and hopped down into the pit. "It is time we got warm."

Soon, the entire group were all warm and cozy, seated on dry logs about a raging fire, while famished flames feasted on the crackling branches in the pit.

"Ahhh-ahhh-ahhh..." Bam moaned as Tiptin gently tugged on the axe.

"It shouldn't be long now," Tiptin assured the sulking boorlee. "Just don't lean too close to the fire. We don't want the metal to get too hot and burn your tongue."

"Uh-uh," Bam agreed, shaking his head and causing the axe-handle to swing. "Ahhh!"

"Ye wants eat tuber?" Biff asked, offering Tiptin a charred chunk of root.

The famished ladfolk eagerly snatched it from the boorlee's outstretched palm. "Thank you," he said, before chomping off a chunk and greedily gulping it down into his gut.

"Tuber be yummy, huh?" Biff inquired. "Be juicy too, huh?"

"Oh yes," Tiptin replied, biting off another chunk and thinking, *'Food always tastes so much better when you're hungry.'*

"Snff. Tuber not tastes beddar dooz yummy desserts," Boog noted. All of the brudz nodded to agree.

"No, I don't suppose it is beddar – uh, I mean, I don't suppose that it tastes better than desserts. Still, given our current circumstances, it is rather delicious. And much more nutritious too, no doubt."

"Dooz ye sez, Tiptin?"

"Oh, I said tuber is good for us."

"Tuber makes us be beddar strong, huh?"

"Yes, eating tuber will make us all stronger, Biff."

"Snff. Me dooz be strong."

"Not so strong dooz be me."

"Dooz be too. Snff."

"Dooz be not."

"Snff. Be too."

"Uh-uh. Be not."

"Uh-huh. Be too."

"Not."

"Too..."

"Duhh – ????? – desserts!?"

All stopped to stare at Branehurts, who calmly went about biting off another chunk of tuber. Clearly, his mind was happily at play in some faraway place?

"Hey, brudz! Axe dooz be off! Sees!"

It was true. Bam was standing and proudly displaying the tool high atop his thick skull. He began wagging one very swollen, purple tongue.

"Tiptin thinks muches smart. Snff. Him dooz gets axe off Bam's tongue!"

"HOORRAY!!"

"Tiptin gets grats noogies!"

"NOOGIE!! NOOGIE!! NOOGIE!! NOOGIE…!!"

"Hey! No! Stop!" Tiptin protested, albeit to no avail. Still, he got off rather easy this time by only being grats noogied about twenty times.

After the clamour had finally dwindled to a calm, Tiptin asked, "I hope you all thought to save Bam some tuber?"

The confused boorleez exchanged quizzical glances.

"Boorleez dooz always share, Tiptin," Biff finally stated, holding up a large piece of root and passing it to Bam.

"Bam spread his arms to the max. "Be lotsth of tubers cuzz we be in woods. Just gotsth digs."

"Yes, Bam, I suppose that there is ample food about. But only if one knows where to look. Just don't you go eating anything hot. Your tongue needs time to mend."

"Ampeel food? Snff. Ampeel be like apples, huh?"

"No, Boog. Ample means lots. We have lots of food."

"HOORRAY!!"

"Hey. Ouch. Stop. No. Don't. Ow. Stop it!"

"Ooops. Brudz dooz pologize, Tiptin. We forgots ye not likes noogies. Plays zings?"

"No!"

Having finally filled their bloated bellies near to burst, the group then fed more logs onto the flames. Next, after Tiptin had checked Bam's tongue to make certain that the swelling was going down, they all sat down around the fire pit for a chat.

The boorleez eagerly told Tiptin all about how they had *sneeked* away from Ezu because the sorcerer *dooz be big meeny and sez not nice things.*

"Ruler Xebec bosses nasty to boorleez," Biff explained.

"Him scolds boorleez muches lots," Bam added.

"Snff. Him not likes boorleez," Boog put in.

"Duhh – ????? – ????? – desserts!"

The brudz also spoke of how much they missed netting finners and playing *swims-in-sea*, and even more so of how much they missed the sheeleez.

"Cuzz me likes hot noogies," Biff explained, wriggling his brows.

"Ooooooo….," the others teased, smudging their blushing brudz with a vigorous volley of *razz* noogies.

Tiptin thought, *'At least Bam's tongue is healing rather quickly. Perhaps a little too quickly? Hopefully these four brothers have all learned a good lesson about licking frosted metal? Yeah right. As if...'*

The boorleez yacked well into Night's rule. They talked about Ezu and sheeleez, and, of course, about knuckle noogies. They marveled at the moon and the skytwinklers; for the clear sky was filled with them. And they quarreled. Incessantly. Over everything from who was the strongest to who was the smartest. To whose feet *stinked* the worst; with Bam being branded *Mr. Stinks Feets.*

"Me feets not dooz stinks like yucky finners!"

"Uh-huh," his three brudz disagreed, while taunting him with plugged noses.

Tiptin felt his eyelids shutting against his will. He struggled to stay with the chat, yet he could not. Losing his battle with fatigue, he closed his eyes and slowly slumped to one side. Then, just as he entered the realm of dreams, he became vaguely aware of strong arms scooping him up and gently snuggling him against something warm and soft and hairy. There his dreams danced to the beat of Biff's big heart…

….*zzzzzzzzzzzzzzzzzzz*….

"…not so hard skull squeezes, Branehurts. Snff. Cuzz ye skull dooz caves in!"

"…see, Branehurts' tongue dooz flaps out. Guffaw! Guffaw!"

Tiptin awakened to find himself still lying atop Biff's belly. The other boorleez were already up and about. Day had long forced Night from the sky, triumphant once again in their never-ending battle to rule the skies. Warm embers still hissed and crackled within the fire pit.

"Wakes, Tiptin," Biff said with a welcoming smile. "Sees. Branehurts squeezes hims skull so hims tongue flaps out. Guffaw!"

Tiptin stretched the knots from his frame and palmed his cheeks to awaken his face. He then rolled off of Biff's warm belly.

Branehurts was now stretching his yap wide apart and wagging his tongue at Bam and Boog, both of whom were holding their bellies and rolling about in the snow.

"Dearest Destiny, whatever did I do?" Tiptin muttered, looking above the trees. The sun was high and warm, and the icicles were dripping in melt. "Whatever it was, I'm sorry."

"Dooz ye sez, Tiptin?" Biff asked, knuckling himself up off the ground.

"Oh nothing. Just muttering is all."

"Huh?"

"I mean, I was just talking to myself."

"Tiptin, dooz ye be boink?" Biff asked.

"No, I'm not boink, Biff. My thinking is just fine," Tiptin assured the concerned boorlee. He wrapped his cloak tightly about his frame to help trap in body heat. "I really must be getting on now. It certainly was nice meeting you and your brudz. I do wish all four of you well."

Biff's eyes wided with shock. "Tiptin not stays with brudz?"

The other boorleez instantly ceased their antics and swift-swung over to join Biff. Bam and Boog shared in Biff's look of shock. While Branehurts, of course, simply looked lost?????

"Snff. Why Tiptin not dooz stays?" Boog asked.

Bam added, "Cuzz boorleez be so dense, huh?"

"No. No. That's not it. I really do like you brudz. It's just that…"

"HOORRAY!! ZINGS IN SKY!! ZINGS IN SKY!! ZINGS IN..."

"No. Wait. Hey! Stop! Put me down! Now!"

"Ooops. Dooz pologize," Bam offered.

"Brudz forgots ye not likes plays zings. Snff."

"Why cuzz Tiptin not stays with brudz?" Biff asked. He was visibly hurt and confused. "We dooz be ye budz."

Looking at the brooding brothers, Tiptin realized that there was probably little chance of his simply saying good-bye to them and being on his way. With their superior speed and stamina, they'd surely follow and catch up to him in no time. Only to noogie him nutty. He knew he would need a distraction. But what?

Not that the ladfolk disliked the burly bunch. In fact, he had grown somewhat fond of them. But their ceaseless antics were starting to prick under his skin. Plus his skull was already plenty sore enough. Thus, he knew that he needed to somehow fool all four brothers and give them the slip at the same time. But the question remained: how to do it?

Still, he felt more than just a tad guilty for leaving them all alone and lost deep in the woods. Except that they weren't really all alone, he reasoned. *'After all, they do have each other, do they not? In due course, are they not likely to find their own way home to Ezu? Or to wherever Destiny intends for them to be? Are they not then much more Destiny's problem than mine? Just suppose we had never met. How then would things be any different than if I leave them behind now? No difference at all as far as I can tell?*

'Oh well, I'm certain they'll forget all about me soon enough. Probably won't even remember my name come dusk. Or I theirs for that matter. What do I owe them anyway? Or anybody else for that matter? That's right – nothing.

'Is it my fault Xebec found that stupid staff? No. Did I seed his lust for power? No. Am I responsible for choices made by others? No. One is only responsible for ones own self, right?

Besides, these boorleez must learn to solve their own problems. Their current plight is not my prob...'

"Tiptin not go," Bam pleaded. "Pleeze."

"Brudz dooz be lost," Biff pointed out. "Ye dooz be lost too."

"Snff. We be beddar budz. Not zings ye no more. Snff. Pledges."

"Pledges!" promised the others. "We clunk skulls to seals it!"

Tiptin felt his heart tugging at his chest as the four brudz all clunked their thick skulls together to seal their promise.

"Dooz pologize cuzz me sez for Branehurts dooz zings snowball," Bam said.

"Ye not go, Tiptin. Snff. Branehurts just dooz mistake."

"Duhh – ????? – desserts!"

All glanced briefly at Branehurts, who was clearly somewhere else.

"Hey, I have an idea!" Tiptin suddenly exclaimed, stretching a fake smile. "Why don't I stay here and we'll play a fun game?"

"HOORRAY!!"

"Hey! Ow! Stop it!"

"Ooops. We dooz forgots."

"Snff. We dooz pologize."

"Plays game?" Biff asked skeptically.

"Yes, Biff," Tiptin said, stretching his smile. "It is a totfolk game called hide and seek."

"Hides and sees?" Boog asked, clearly confused. "Snff."

"Me dooz sees?" Biff noted, pointing to his eyes.

"No," Tiptin explained, "Not hide and see. Hide and seek."

"Hides and seeks? Seeks be finds, huh?" Bam inquired.

"Yes, Bam. Seek means to try and find something. It's really quite simple to play."

"Duhh – ????? – hides!"

Tiptin began turning the burly bunch about so that they were all facing the same direction. "Here, I'll show you how to play," he explained. "First you must all look this way..."

"Dooz for?" Biff asked with some suspicion.

"Cuzz Tiptin sez, Dungskull. Duzz??"

"Me not be dungskull! Ye be…"

"Whoa!" Tiptin intervened, just as Biff and Bam began raising their knuckles to engage in open noogie combat.

"Bam sez me dooz be, Dungskull," Biff pleaded in his own defence.

"Cuzz ye dooz be Dungskull," Bam stated to justify his part in the spat.

"So. Ye dooz gots stinky feets like yucky finners," Biff countered.

"Me feets stinks nice!"

"Uh-uh. Ye feets stinks muches gross like..."

"Enough!" Tiptin cut in. "Dearest Destiny. The reason you must all look this same way is so that you won't see where I hide while you brudz are counting."

"Counts?" Bam said with marked concern.

"Yes. First you all count to twenty…"

"Huh?"

Tiptin paused, then rephrased. "Let's make it to ten then. You can count to ten, can't you?"

The boorleez hesitated, and then nodded with zero confidence that they could.

Slighting his mounting guilt, Tiptin kept on. "Very well, then. While you brudz are counting, I'll go hide. But you can't turn around and look until you've counted to ten, and you must cover your eyes with both hands like this." Tiptin pressed both palms over his own eyes to demonstrate.

"Hides dooz seeks be fun?"

"Oh yes, Bam, hide and seek is quite fun. But you must cover your eyes while you count."

"Duhh – ????? – seeks!'

All four brudz pressed their palms to their eyes, although Branehurts needed several attempts to get it right. Each burly beast teetered from side to side as their thin legs buckled beneath their bulk.

"Brudz lean on brudz so stops us tips."

Following Bam's suggestion, the boorleez did in fact start leaning on each other for support and began teetering to-and-fro as a group.

"Okay, then. Start counting," Tiptin said as he started sneaking away. "And no peeking."

"Brudz not peeks," Biff assured him.

Tiptin felt the gnaw of guilt as he trudged in amongst the needle trees and started his climb up the mountain's slope, reasoning that it would be fully to his advantage if he were to gain the higher ground. There may be some tight caves or chasms that the much bigger boorleez could not follow him into?

"One – three – six – uh – five – uh...?"

"Snff. Me thinks dooz be four?"

"Uh-uh. Dooz be nine."

"Uh-uh. We spozed sez six again."

"Dooz not."

"Dooz too."

"Not!"

"Too!"

"Duhh – ????? – simple!"

Tiptin pumped his legs hard to make haste. He had no idea how much time would pass before any one of the brudz suddenly said the number ten. After that, the counting sequence would matter for naught. Without looking back, he continued winding his way in and out of the trees while climbing ever higher.

Soon, the slope steepened and the temperature dipped towards freezing. Dropping down to all fours, the ladfolk scrambled up a narrow ravine; twice sliding back down over rock and ice and slush.

His fingers numbed and ached as he clawed his way back up towards the treeline. Flesh was stripped from his palms, and bruises throbbed about his battered knees and shins. Each of his weary thighs and calves cramped in revolt. His parched throat pleaded for a cool drink. Frosty breath tumbled forth from his lips. As the air waned thin, he grew giddy of sense. Yet onward and upward he climbed.

At last Tiptin broke free from the trees; however, with nothing to block its wind, the mountain's frigid breath blasted down from its peak, berating the puny pest for intruding upon its face and fiercely whipping Tiptin's cloak about his shoulders and head.

Tiptin turned his back to the biting wind and wrestled with the unruly cloak. He pondered his dilemma while watching snow devils spin and dance their way across the mountainside.

The determined ladfolk was also aware that Night would soon charge back atop the eastern horizon, bringing with it a severe plunge in temperature. He also sensed that, should he climb any higher, he may not be able to descend back down from whence he'd came; as it is often easier to climb up a mountain's face than it is to climb back down. Yet to remain exposed above the treeline could well mean a frigid meeting with Morgue. Perhaps he should have thought things through a bit more?

"Must stay of sense," he muttered. "Mustn't lose control…"

"Tiptin! Here we dooz be! Sees!"

"Sees, Tiptin! Dooz be us brudz!"

Tiptin felt his stomach sink. All four boorleez were swift-swinging clear of the treeline.

"Stops plays seeks game, Tiptin! Mountain not dooz be safe!" Biff shouted. The big boorlee stopped and began frantically waving his arms about. "Stops, Tiptin! Game not dooz be fun!"

"Stops, Tiptin! Snff."

"Pleeze, Tiptin!" Bam pleaded. "Stops plays game!"

"Game dooz be dense! Snff. Stops!"

"PLEEZE!!"

"Dung!" Tiptin cussed in sheer frustration, charging back down the slope and in amongst the needle trees. "Am I to be bound to this burly bunch for all of my being?"

"Stops, Tiptin! Snff."

"Ye wins game, Tiptin! Gets grats noogies!"

"Duhh – ????? – Morgue!"

Tiptin could tell by their mounting voices that the much swifter boorleez were quickly gaining on him. Regardless, the determined ladfolk wasn't ready to surrender the chase just yet. He thought, *'Destiny, help me to lose these…'*

"Whoops….whoaaa..." Tiptin failed to negotiate the thin crevice in time and he tumbled heels over hearers down into a narrow ravine. "Ouch! Ow-ow-ow-ow! Ouch! Yeow! Dung!"

An exposed slab finally brought Tiptin's acrobatics to a jarring halt. He winced as he struggled to regain his footing on its icy surface. Pain shot through his ankle. A badly bruised elbow caused him to wince. He gasped to suck in a breath.

Despite being dizzy and disoriented, and while cupping his injured elbow, the determined ladfolk somehow managed to find his footing and he began limping his way through slush and snow. Twice he stumbled over rocky rubble, but both times he managed to retain his balance without face-planting onto the frozen ground.

Upon reaching the base of the ravine, Tiptin was surprised to discover a complete absence of snow. In fact, here the mountain's aura was inexplicably warm. He wondered, *'Am I still of sense?'*

Veering clear of a gooey puddle of gob, he hobbled in amongst a patch of coarse bristles; where his injured ankle failed him and fell to the ground.

For several painful moments Tiptin lay still, wincing in pain and holding his ankle. All too familiar voices shouted out to him from somewhere well above. Only now he no longer cared if the boorleez found him.

"Tiptin, dooz be us! Dooz be brudz!"

Tiptin felt like giving up. And he would have. Except that just then he spied a tight cleft in the rock face, which had been obscured by the coarse bristles growing about its stony lips. *'I must reach that cleft…'*

Tiptin wriggled into the cleft, wedging himself between two stony lips. Hot breath blew forth from the blackness. He noted that the surface inside the cleft felt soft and – fleshy?

"What the...?"

"Aaaaayy!" Tiptin shrieked as the stony lips smacked shut and something fleshy curled about him. Then the mountain gulped him down into a dark abyss.

"Whooaaa...!" Down, down, down, he plummeted. No sounds. No sights. No shapes. Only blackness and his own sinking stomach.

High above him, the stony lips parted and belched, before stretching into a satisfied smile.

Down, down, down, down, down.......... "Sploop!"

He plunged deep into – *slop?* A sense of motion indicated that he was caught up in some sort of a goopy swirlpool...

'Gotta reach the surface,' he thought. *'Before my breathers burst...'*

The frightened ladfolk fought for his very being, thrashing his limbs wildly to reach the surface and fill his breathers. All to no avail. It was like swimming in swirling sinksand. His limbs hung heavy as strength was sapped from his body. He felt himself slipping away into the realm of oblivion.

Suddenly something nudged his legs? Something lurking in the slop! Then it nudged him again. And again. And again.

'No,' Tiptin realized, *'I'm still of breath. This something below me is real!'*

Panic seized his mind as the *something* shoved him from below and surged upward to break the surface. It flung him off into the blackness.

Tiptin's frame slapped against a spongy surface, where he slid down to sit in soggy – *stuff?* He choked for breath and strained his eyes to sight in shapes. His nostrils burned as he inhaled the stench of ammonia. Evidence of blackwings?

However, nothing stirred inside of the Mountain's belly. Nary a draft nor a flutter. All was silent, save for the occasional gurgle and pop of bubbles bursting. And the sound of Tiptin's own heart pounding to burst open his chest.

"Tiptin discarded his sopping-wet cloak and poured slop from his boots. After easing his swollen ankle back into his boot, he stood and patted about in the blackness until his palms found the spongy surface. While tracing his fingers along its squishy plane for balance, he began slowly hobbling his way through the soggy stuff; completely unaware that high above, two stony lips parted to giggle.

"Schmuck-schmack-schmuck-schmack..."

After a few painful steps, Tiptin paused to rest his ankle.

"Schmuck – schmack – schmuck – schmack..."

The second sound seemed to come from behind him. *'A delayed echo? No, I hadn't been limping along that slowly. Can it be the 'something' from the slop stalking me?'*

Tiptin took two cautious steps, then stopped to hone his hearing.

...silence...

Two more steps before he stopped abruptly. While holding his breath and carefully twisting about, he cupped his ear to listen.

...silence...

Next, he tried stepping in place. "Schmuck-schmack-schmuck-schmack..."

...silence...

"Is somebody there?" Tiptin asked.

...silence...

"I mean nobody any harm. I'm just lost, is all." Tiptin thought of the Grinning Reaper. Legend stated that he dwelled in The Swallow Mountains, and that he was so named because he took immense pleasure in escorting beings who had passed beyond breath down into Morgue's Maze. Could it be him? Tiptin had always thought that the Grinning Reaper was only a myth. But was he?

Once again, Tiptin tried stepping in place. "Schmuck-schmack-schmuck-schmack..."

...silence...

A few paces forward... and stop.

...silence...

It seemed that he really was all alone after all. Perhaps angst and fatigue were teasing his mind? "Yes, that must be it," he muttered, shrugging and starting on his way.

"Schmuckschmackschmuckschmackschmuckschmackschmuckschmack..."

That was definitely not his imagination! He hobbled as quickly as he could through the soggy stuff, tracing the spongy surface with his fingers. His mind was now racing through a range of possibilities? Not a one of them good.

'What is chasing me? Where is it coming from? Where am I going? Will I bang into an object? Or fall into a pit? Or meet up with a beast? Or beasts? And what of the Grinning Reaper? Will I be condemned to wander Morgue's Maze? I must escape? I must! But how? Is there even a way out of this mountain?'

"Schmuckschmackschmuckschmackschmuckschmackschmuckschmack..."

'There it is again! Gaining on me! Is the 'something' alone...? Or are there many 'somethings' chasing after me...? Trying to trap me? Flee! Faster! Don't think! Mind your mind, Tiptin! Do think! There must be an out! Ignore the pain! Wait? What is that? Light? Can it be? Yes, it can!'

Tiptin's mind was not playing tricks on him. There really was a dim glow up ahead.

Driven by a fresh burst of hope, the ladfolk hobbled in haste towards the light. He ignored the pain in his screaming ankle. He ignored the 'something' or 'somethings'. He ignored the Grinning Reaper. All that mattered was reaching the light.

'There it is! It shines through a narrow split in the spongy surface. Can I squeeze through? Probably. But what lies beyond?'

"SCHMUCKSCHMACKSCHMUCKSCHMACKSCHMUCK...!!!!"

'Who cares!' Tiptin lunged for the narrow split and barely wriggled through to the other side. His foot caught a snag and sent him sprawling onto rock. Hard and rough and cool. Yes, it was all real. He was lying face down on unyielding, beautiful rock!"

Tiptin sat and propped his back against a wall, panting with purpose as he took in his new surroundings. He was now inside an immense cavern, which sprawled out about him for as far as his eyes could see.

Its walls and ceiling were clothed in clear, sparkling crystals. Scarlet fibres spiraled from the floor to the ceiling, throbbing forth both heat and light. Flexible tentacle trees wiggled their feelers and bent towards the intruder.

Silkspinners webs were festooned between the scarlet fibres and sculpted pillars of stone. Yet there were no silkspinners about?

"Dearest Destiny," Tiptin whispered, forgetting all about the something beyond the split.

He stood and took to hobbling about the cavern, weaving in and out of the fibres while keeping well out of reach of the tentacle trees. Eventually, he grew weary and felt the need for a nap, but the vacant silkspinner's webs kept him alert. He sensed that he wasn't alone, so he picked up a rock. Just in case.

Creepy shadows teased with his mind. Some stretched and shrank as the fibres throbbed forth their heat and light. Others simply loomed over him.

Suddenly his ears snagged a sound. It was faint and distant at first, but unmistakably the sound of claws clicking upon rock. And they were coming closer!

Tiptin began to panic. He scanned the vicinity for a better weapon and a hiding place, almost wishing that he had just stayed with the brudz.

He wondered, *'Should I flee? But to where? No, sound will only give me away. And what of my scent? I can't just stay...'*

"Ouch!" he exclaimed as his arm brushed up against a hot fibre.

Suddenly the clicking ceased.

"Dung," Tiptin cussed beneath his breath.

He slowly began backing away from the area. Cautiously. Upon tippytoes and with darting eyes. His shaky hands were ready with the rock. His chest was pounding near to burst. The very thought of becoming a silkspinner's snack moved him to gulp.

"Come to me," he muttered, trying to find his courage. "I'll bash you."

Backwards he crept. Each step placed with care to nix noise. Softly. Stealthily. Back… Back… Back… However, Tiptin was fully unaware of the huge form now looming over him, silently mimicking each of his steps.

"Ah," Tiptin blurted out as he bumped up against – flesh! He spun about with the rock held high.

"AAARG!!" roared the one-eyed giant, brandishing a log-sized club. "AAAAARRRGGG!!"

"Aiyeee!" Tiptin wailed as he dropped the rock upon his own toes. In raging agony, he commenced to hop, scream and cuss. "Yeow! Ouch! Ouch! Dung! Ow! Ow! Ow! Dearest Destiny, it hurts! Dung, it smarts! Ahhhh…."

"HARR!! HARR!! HARR!!" roared the giant. "HARR!! HARR!! HARR!! HARR!!"

Tiptin fumed as he took in the jovial joker, who was clearly much amused by the success of his prank in spite of Tiptin's ensuing pain.

Even as he was stooped over in hysterics, the giant still looked straight down at the much smaller and quite irate ladfolk. Tall, even for his kind, his brawny body would surely tip the scale at well over one hundred stone. Easy.

His blotchy skin bore a greenish tinge. Frizzes of coarse, orange hair covered much of his broad back, chest and shoulders. Ditto his thick and meaty forearms.

Pointy ears sided his smooth, shiny dome. One bushy brow bridged a solitary eye. A large, hooked schnozz topped two fat lips.

His broad shoulders were so muscular that he seemingly lacked a neck. Both of his fists were as big as boulders. Muscles ripped within thighs thick as sinkwoods, threatening to rip apart his ratty shorts. Each oversized foot was complimented by a trio of clawed toes. His enormous belly bounced in raucous laughter.

"HARR!! HARR!! HARR!! HARR!! Wow, were you scared or what! HARR!! HARR!! HARR!! You shoulda seen your face! Oooweeee! Too much, I tell ya! Simply toooooo much! HARR!! HARR!! HARR!! HARR!!"

Tiptin finally ceased hopping about and addressed the jovial joker. "Y-You're a cyclops?"

"Wow, you are quick! HARR!! HARR!! HARR!! No shortage of smarts in your mind. Too much. Simply toooooo much. HARR!! HARR!! HARR!!" The giant lowered his club and grabbed his bouncing belly. He slapped Tiptin's back, nearly stopping the startled ladfolk's heart. "Dribble my drawers, this is just too funny. HARR!! HARR!! HARR!! HARR!! Tooooo much, I tell ya! I can barely stand it! This puny guy is simply toooooo.... EEEEYYYOOOWWWWWWW!!!!"

While the now *not-so-jovial* joker hopped about clenching one foot, Tiptin gloated and patted the rock.

"OUCH! OUCH! OUCH! OW! OW! Mighty Morgue, it smarts. Ah. Ow. Eee. Oh, my aching tootsies..."

"Well, it serves you right," Tiptin scolded, "Sneaking up behind strangers and terrifying them like that. Not to mention stalking them through dark tunnels."

"Ah. Ow. Eee – huh? Dark tunnels? What dark tunnels? Oh, it smarts. Ohhhhh..."

Tiptin gulped, and then warily scanned the vicinity. He could almost feel somebody watching them. Or something?

The moaning giant plopped down onto the cavern floor and stuck a swelling toe between his lips. "Mmmmm..."

"Well then," Tiptin continued after a bit, "Might I ask just what in Morgue's maze is a cyclops doing sneaking about a mountain's innards?"

"Ohhhhh..." The giant stopped sucking his toe and took to rubbing it. "Ahhhhh..."

"Well?" Tiptin pressed.

The giant's face was flush with pain. "I – I was fleeing a group of boorleez brudz I had met at the base of this mountain. They were seriously needling my nerves. Had I stayed with them any longer, I most surely would have gone completely round-the-twist. So, I gave them the slip."

Tiptin smiled knowingly.

Using his club as a makeshift crutch, the cyclops stood and stepped closer to the ladfolk. He returned the smile and extended a huge hand in greeting.

Tiptin was skeptical and hesitant to shake.

Noting such, the cyclops withdrew the gesture; all the while keeping his smile. "Anyway, I spied the mouth of a large cave and figured I'd give them the slip. I crawled into the cave and soon I could no longer hear them calling after me. All seemed to be going well until I accidentally brushed up against the side of the cave wall and it – well, it…"

"Smacked shut and swallowed you whole," Tiptin stated from experience.

"Uh, yeah."

"And then you landed in some mucky slop, right?"

"Uh, no. I landed in a silkspinner's web. And a right sticky one at that. Took me forever to gnash free." The cyclops chomped his teeth together for effect. "Sadly, the web held no insects for me to snack on. I so enjoy the crunch of fresh bugs between my biters. Yummy for the tummy. Mmmmm..."

Tiptin soured face in disgust. "I am Tiptin, Stonemason from Folkton. What is your name and title?"

"What is my title?" The giant smirked silly, then snapped straight his spine and palmed his chest. "I am Thwack, Fleshfeed for a Mountain's Innards. HARR!! HARR!! HARR!! HARR!! Oh, Dearest Destiny. Too much, I tell ya. This puny guy is simply tooooo much. What is my title? Seriously? HARR!! Like it almost matters down here. HARR!! HARR!! HA…. EEEEYYYOOOWWWWWWW!!!!"

"Harr, harr, harr," Tiptin mocked with noted sarcasm. "How about Thwack, Smarty Cyclops with Twin Throbbing Tootsies."

Thwack soon ceased with his hopping and howling. Once again, he plopped down and stuck a swelling toe between his lips and started moaning. He viewed Tiptin with hurt pride, his silly smirk seemingly silenced for good.

"Well, nobody likes to be poked fun at," Tiptin rebuked, sitting down to rub his own throbbing toes.

"Most certainly not," a dignified voice concurred from above. "Nor does one usually favour having their digits bashed with rocks."

Thwack and Tiptin exchanged panicky looks before scrambling to their feet.

Dangling from the ceiling was the strangest silkspinner that either of them had ever imagined. Its plump body was covered with white hair. All of it's flesh bore a pinkish tinge. Eight skinny arms led to withered hands with long, hooked fingers. Two stubby legs joined with a pair of flat feet with hooked toes.

Its scalp was ringed to the temples by a wreath of white hair, and its face was wrinkled with knowledge. Bulging pink peepers nearly popped from their sockets. A long nose bent to one side of its face. A round mouth separated its white beard from a thick moustache.

The muted pair continued gawking as the silkspinner reeled out thread and dropped down towards them. Thwack tightened his grip on his club, while Tiptin clenched the rock with both hands. Both were intrigued, yet uncertain? Silkspinners knew naught of speech? Or so they had always believed.

"W-Who are you?" Tiptin asked as the silkspinner touched solid. Words tripped over his tongue. "I-I..."

"Nap your nerves, Tiptin. I have no desire to harm either yourself or Thwack."

"How is it you know our names?" Thwack asked in a tone of suspicion.

The silkspinner chortled. "How? Hee, hee. You two were raising enough racket to awaken the very stones themselves, let alone a napping arachnid."

"Arachnid?"

"Yes, my dear clops, I am an arachnid. Or silkspinner. Or even spider if you so prefer. Take your pick of names."

"Who are you?" Tiptin asked again.

"Oh dear. It does seem that I have neglected to formally introduce myself. Tsk. Tsk. How improper of me. I do offer you both a humble apology. Really. Just haven't been quite myself of late. But no excuses! This boorish behavior simply will not do. Most unseemly of me. In fact, it's downright rude."

Thwack and Tiptin shared relaxed looks.

"Ahem. I am Spidey Smells, Master Magician and Metal Forger, and your humble host." Placing its four right arms behind its back and simultaneously sweeping the four left arms majestically across its plump body, the strange silkspinner executed a gracious bow. "At your service."

"Spidey Smells?" Thwack bit his lip, lest he launch into laughter. Despite a stretching smirk, he somehow managed to bottle up a brewing belly burst. Only a saucy squeak slipped between his sealed lips.

"Correct. Although some call me Mr. Smells, and others just call me Spidey. I so prefer the latter."

"And your title is Master Magician and Metal Forger?" Tiptin asked, uncomfortably conscience of the cyclops cooking up some sort of quip about Spidey's name.

"It is. I am a stable student of both ancient arts. One can never know everything about anything. We are all always learning. Or at least we should be."

Thwack spouted another saucy squeak, which surely would have boiled over into a bouncing belly burst were it not for a heel crunching down onto the tip of his already aching toe.

"Ahh-ahhh…"

"Pardon me, Thwack?" Spidey asked.

"Ahhh..."

"He's awed speechless by the presence of a real master magician," Tiptin explained, shooting a warning glance at the wincing cyclops and grinding his heel down even harder. "Isn't that right, Thwack?"

"Ahh – yaahhh!"

Tiptin grinned with palms up. "See?"

"Hmmmmm?" Spidey stroked his beard as he examined Thwack's face. "Interesting. I've never seen a green face flush purple before.

"Anyway, I'm still not behaving like a proper host. Tsk. Tsk. Come. My lair is quite comfy. Tiptin can clean up from his dip in the swirlpit. Then we shall break bugs together. I do hope you've both brought along ample appetites. Hmmmm?"

Tiptin's stomach wrenched. "Break bugs?"

Spidey smiled knowingly. "Or we can eat maize bread and fruit instead, if you so prefer. I can never keep it straight which species consumes which grub? Anyway, my apprentices often go up top and bring me back food delicacies that are not growable down here."

"Can I still put bugs on my bread?" Thwack asked with deep concern.

"Certainly, my dear clops. You know, I have been told that I prepare the best pestzels anywhere. Hee, hee. Hardly surprising when one considers I bake the only pestzels anywhere."

"Mmmmmm…" Thwack rubbed his belly and smacked his lips.

"Gee, I can hardly wait to taste those, Tiptin mumbled with overt sarcasm."

"Pardon me, Tiptin?"

"Uh…"

"Tiptin says he'd love to try some pestzels," Thwack said with a smirk, squeezing the back of the ladfolk's neck until his tongue gagged out. "See?"

"Marvelous. I shall bake up an extra big batch. Plus prepare a light insectasalad as well. Along with creeper cake for dessert. Come, let us feast."

Thwack released Tiptin's neck and patted the choking ladfolk's back. "Remember that you also have toes," he warned in a whisper, supplemented with a show stomp.

Tiptin was too busy sucking in breath to reply.

"Come," Spidey beckoned with sweeping arms. "Don't fret, Tiptin, for I have ample bread and berries as well. Just in case you should change your mind about the pestzels."

"Spidey, you will still bake pestzels, right?"

"Of course, my dear clops. I do aim to please. Come. Come to my lair. And do avoid being snagged by the tentacle trees. They don't get on very well with strangers, I'm afraid."

Together, they weaved in and out of the stone pillars, while the silkspinner's webs simply lifted from their path. Until at last they came to the edge of a wide pit.

"I'll spin you a strong climbing cord," Spidey explained as he commenced circling a pillar. "You need not fear falling. My silk does stretch, but it shall not snap."

"Naaaww," Thwack responded. "I'd have never guessed."

Spidey skillfully attached his climbing cord to a boulder, and then he scurried across the floor and dove brazenly into the pit. "Wheeeeeeee..."

Tiptin motioned for Thwack to descend first. Should their host be in error about the strength of the silk, he had no intention of landing beneath a hundred stone of falling cyclops.

The climb down into the pit proved to be much easier than they had imagined. Ample fissures in the stone allowed for secure footing until the vertical shaft gave way to a slight slope. Sparkling silkwebs brightened the tunnel, aided by the shine off of a spring of cool water.

Thwack and Tiptin soon caught up with their host, who was standing before silkspun curtains with shell beads woven in for décor. The plump arachnid parted the curtains, then bowed into an arm-sweep to usher his guests inside. "Welcome, my fine friends. Welcome to my lovely lair."

Tiptin and Thwack took in the awesome splendor of Spidey's lair.

A tiered chandelier swung from the glittery ceiling. Spun of sparkling silk, it brightened and warmed the entire lair as if the sun itself was shining in. The floor was set with stone tiles, and covered in areas by mats spun from fine silk. Two silkspun cots swung between carved pillars; one of which was far larger than the other and clearly meant for a giant. The furniture was of polished wood, including chairs that were padded with pillowy cushions. A table was set with goblets and plates, along with a large bowl of fruit. A second bowl was packed to the brim with nuts.

Iron pots and skillets dangled from metal hooks. A small, brick kiln squatted beneath a chimney stack. Wood shelving supported an assortment of clay jugs. Four barrels were lined up along the wall and labeled: BUGS, BIG BUGS, BIGGER BUGS and BIGGEST BUGS. Two spouted urns bore the inscriptions: WASH and THIRST. Three drying towels hung from wall pegs, marked with identifying insignias stating either SPIDEY or GUESTS. One of the guest towels was blanket-sized and clearly meant for a giant.

In a far corner, a caldron swung from an iron tripod. Beside it stood a wooden cabinet. To the other side, an iron workbench supported a small anvil. A much bigger anvil squatted on the floor. Bellows were placed to each side of a second, larger kiln.

A round seer's web covered much of an entire wall. Spun of dyed silk, it depicted a watchful eye. Beside it hung a portrait of a plantlike creature with amber eyes.

"Who is this?" Thwack inquired, pointing at the portrait.

"A very old and very dear friend," Spidey replied.

"Where does your friend dwell?" Tiptin asked.

Spidey sighed. "Not anywhere that we still of breath could grasp?"

"Oh," both guests responded in one voice. "Sorry."

Spidey smiled. "Sorry? Whatever for? All that starts must end. Whatever arrives must depart. Lest there could be no order in this universe, nor space enough for those yet to come. Besides, perhaps the beyond is just another stage of one eternal journey? Sort of like we're all climbing a stepwell through different levels of time? I often ponder such matters."

"So, what's at the top?"

"The top of what, Tiptin?"

"The top of the stepwell?"

The arachnid stroked his beard. "I honestly don't know, Tiptin. Perhaps a path back to the beginning? Only time and the deities hold the answer to that riddle."

"But is it proper that we mere mortals should even ponder such matters?" Tiptin pressed. "I mean, won't the deities be angered if we question such things? Teachers of faith tell us that such is so."

Spidey produced a lopsided grin. "The deities would probably be more amused than angered. Only mortals would be offended by such. After all, Seed did grant us minds to use. Maybe to ponder about the universe and our role in it is in fact the natural purpose of our being. I've little doubt that the deities ponder over many choices made by mortals. I know I do."

"Perhaps eating is the natural purpose of our being?" Thwack cut in. "Like, I ponder when we're gonna?"

"Hee, hee. Perhaps for some it is." Spidey patted his own plump belly and winked at Tiptin. "We can speak about such matters another time. For the moment, somebody's natural purpose growls for bugs."

Spidey retrieved a huge bowl and a wooden chow-pounder from one of the shelves and handed them over to Thwack. "While I flame the kiln, do be a dear clops and start crunching bugs into fine pellets for our pestzels. I have found that the biggest bugs bake best."

"Sure, Spidey!" Thwack exclaimed, beaming a broad smile. He merrily sped over to the appropriate barrel.

"Help yourself to fruit and drink, Tiptin. But be certain to peel the skin from the crescent pulpy. And only eat the ripe, yellow ones. The green ones are crunchy dry and bitter to the bite."

"Thank you," Tiptin said, snagging one of the drying cloths enroute to the wash urn.

Together, Spidey and Thwack prepared a fabulous feast of insectasalad, pestzels, and chocolate-covered creeper cake. Almost all of which they eagerly devoured, while Tiptin struggled not to retch in disgust.

When their bellies had been properly filled, all three settled onto the padded chairs that had been placed before the seer's web. The wary eye watched their every move.

"That was deeeelicious!" Thwack exclaimed, smacking his fat lips for effect and sinking deep into the cushion of his oversized chair.

"I'm glad my pestzels pleased your palate, Thwack." Spidey smiled at Tiptin. "I trust that the maize bread and berries were likewise satisfactory?"

"Mmmmmm..." Tiptin replied, rubbing his bloated belly. "I feel like a big ball with limbs."

Spidey chortled. "Splendid. Perhaps now we can talk free of distractions."

"Talk about what?" Tiptin inquired.

"Hmmmm..." Spidey stroked his beard and sank his thoughts deep into his pool of knowledge. After a prolonged silence, his thoughts resurfaced and he was able to share them with the others. "Well, for starters, you both might share with me news of current events up top. I seldom venture to the surface, and absolutely never during Day's rule." The arachnid paused and pointed at the vigilant seer's web. "However, my seer's web has recently revealed to me that all is not well in the Land of Ranidae. I do wish to know more."

Both guests proved most eager to chat. They routinely interrupted one another in their vivid and emotional accounts of the New Order of things.

Details of how a sorcerer, bearing a staff of white gold, had encroached upon their peaceful communities and invoked his unwanted decrees intrigued the arachnid, who listened patiently until each guest had exhausted his own version of events.

"...and now many of us are in hiding," Tiptin sighed out upon completion.

"Hmmmm..." Spidey stood and, interlocking all eight arms behind his back, commenced pacing back and forth.

Thwack and Tiptin exchanged shrugs, yet kept mute. Neither wished to divert their kind host's flow of thoughts.

At last, Spidey ceased pacing and stopped the silence. "This sorcerer you speak of, what exactly does he look like?"

"I don't know," Tiptin replied. "I have never seen him."

"Few actually have," Thwack put in. "Although, most have heard tell of him."

"Oh? And what have you heard?" Spidey pressed.

Thwack was eager to reply. "He is said to have the wackiest of grins and the most sane-wanting of stares. The buzz is he has the laugh of one whose mind has trekked too far past the point of koookoooo…" The cyclops rolled his eye as he wound a forefinger about his ear for further emphasis.

Tiptin next added his own remarks. "Talk also tells that he rides a magnificent flying beast with wings of gold and the head of an eagle. It is even said that his staff can hurl forth balls of light so hot they burst timber into flames!"

"Plus it can stream forth searing beams of light that can even melt stone," Thwack added. "It is true. I have seen such melted stone with my very own eye."

"I've heard many fugitives speak of the destructive power of the staff," Tiptin said. "Many who have witnessed it for themselves. That is why the sorcerer was able to subdue so much of Ranidae so very quickly. All because of the staff. It is said that none can defend against it."

"All fear the sorcerer and his staff," Thwack put in.

Spidey nodded his head in sympathy. "One can hardly blame them. I too am frightened of both."

"You, Spidey?" Thwack asked, somewhat surprised. "Even though you are a master magician?"

"Yes, me. I know this sorcerer well, and you cannot find grace wrapped up in madness."

"You know him?"

Spidey's tone sank solemn. "Yes, Thwack, I do. I also know of this staff of which you speak. Together they are a most dangerous and frightening mix. The sorcerer's name is Xebec, and he has found The Staff of The Demon Chaser. May Destiny help us now. My previous lack of judgment has played its own role in creating this mess in which we all now find ourselves. And a messy mess it is."

"Staff of what?" Thwack asked.

"Do you know this Xebec well?" Tiptin cut in, appearing somewhat uneasy.

Spidey sighed and bowed his head. "Clearly not as well as I should have."

Both guests blinked uncertain.

"Please permit me to explain." Spidey directed their attention to the seer's web, then commenced chanting out in cadence:

"OH MAGIC EYE WHO ALWAYS PEEKS…
SPIN FORTH TO VIEW WHAT MY MIND SEEKS…
BRING XEBEC FORTH FOR US TO SEE…
SHOW US WHERE THAT SCROLLTHIEF BE!"

Slowly, the web began to spin and the eye faded to form a floating portal. Within it a wavy shape began to take on form.

"Yikes!" Tiptin shrieked as a ferocious fangaclaw appeared and snapped its jaws at his head. Only a boulder-sized fist knocking the beast gaga spared the lucky ladfolk from a messy meeting with Morgue.

Spidey acted quickly before the dazed beast could regain its senses:

"OH SPINNING WEB, I CLAPPED IN ERROR,
NOW WISK THIS BEAST AWAY FROM HERE!"

The fangaclaw screamed as it was sucked back into the portal. Then the portal faded and the watchful eye blinked alert.

Spidey blushed with embarrassment. "Oops. Sorry about that. Tee-hee. Sort of chanted out the wrong cadence there. My bad. No messy matter, I'll just opt for a second swat at the skitter."

Both guests stepped backwards and poised to bolt.

"OH MAGIC EYE WHO ALWAYS PEEKS,
SPIN FORTH TO VIEW WHAT MY MIND SEEKS,
BRING XEBEC FORTH FOR US TO SEE,
SHOW US WHERE THAT SCROLLTHIEF BE!"

Once again, the web began to spin and the watchful eye faded to form a floating portal. Ever so gradually, a wavy shape took on form. It was of a glumdreary figure in a black cloak and matching skullcap, who was standing alone on the brattice of a pink limestone tower and clenching a staff of white gold.

"Right there!" Spidey exclaimed with unrestrained venom. "Feast your eyes upon my former apprentice! The seediest schmuck to ever skulk about civilized Ranidae! Lower than a toad's tush, he is! Recreant! Rascal! Rogue!"

As the pair listened, Spidey told them of Xebec's treachery. Their openly resentful host revealed how his former lead apprentice had sneaked into *'this very lair'* while he himself had dangled in trance, and then stole his webscroll right out from under him. Spidey also related to them how Xebec escaped by dissolving virtually all of the lesser apprentices into smelly moo-pies.

"Can you believe it? Moo-pies. Moo-pies! All before fleeing to a faraway island. Blade! Scoundrel! Coward!"

Next, Spidey related to them The Legend of The Demon Chaser. Both had heard it told as youngsters, but had long since forgotten.

"So, you see..." Spidey warned in conclusion, pointing at the sinister shape who was now smirking and pointing back at him, "...unless that moo-pie making maniac is somehow defeated and the staff tossed into The Saline Sea – well, I'm sure you both fully grasp the dire consequences to us all should you fail in your purpose."

Thwack and Tiptin exchanged puzzled looks. "Uh, purpose? Fail? Us? Huh? Say what?"

"Yes, your purpose." Spidey spread out all of his arms. "You two can't just watch from here while that cloaked cuckoo becomes madder and madder until he takes to burning down all of Ranidae just for chuckles!"

Thwack raised a forefinger. "Ah, excuse me, but I think you just implied that we two are somehow supposed to take on this loony sorcerer?"

Spidey beamed with enthusiasm. " That is correct, my dear clops! Rather challenging concept, don't you agree?"

"And what exactly is wrong with your own legs?" Tiptin asked with overt suspicion.

"Oh, nothing really. You see, it's my skin."

"Your skin?"

"Yes, my skin. Should I be exposed to Day's penetrating rays, my skin will fry to a frizzle. No, really. It will. Honest arachnid."

"Yeah, sure."

"Uh-huh."

"No, it's a fact. I wouldn't fib ya. Absolutely not. That is why I dug the tunnel. Honest. I swear to it on my mama's eggs – and if I'm fibbing, may I be stung and scarfed down by a scorp."

"Tunnel?" Tiptin raised a skeptical brow.

"Well obviously I didn't dig a tunnel all by myself. Let's be realistic here. To undertake this fantastic feat of engineering, I've enlisted an elite crew of *gravel grinders*."

"Gravel grinders?" Tiptin asked, growing ever more skeptical.

"HARR!! Sure, Spidey. And Tiptin can lift more than me."

"No, I speak the truth. Gravel grinders are plumpanormous, limbless wigglers with mushy heads and many rows of stone-crushing chompers. They chew through rock like worms through dirt. Each shift they gulp down thrice their enormous body weight in rocks and clay. Terrific workers, they are. Eat. Eat. Eat. Eat. Never stop. Never complain. How can they with their mouths always full? Hee, hee. And any chompers they break or lose are quickly replaced by simply growing new ones. Seed designed them so."

"Uh, and just where exactly does this tunnel lead?" Tiptin pressed.

"Why, straight over to Xebec's Island, of course. Where else would it lead? It was my intent to tunnel clear through to his castle and retrieve my webscroll myself. According to my calculations, it would have taken another forty cycles to complete the dig; by which time Xebec may very well have met Morgue, but at least my webscroll might still be there. As it was my burden to keep it safe, it is now my burden to fetch it back.

"But things have changed now that the staff has been found. There is no longer enough time to dig the entire length of Xebec's island. That is why you two must go now. If someone doesn't unpower the staff, then soon all shall be lost anyway. As it is, your own have already been robbed of their freedom by that ratsbutt."

Tiptin wondered, *'Just how many cutting names can just one master magician have for just one apprentice? Yikes!'*

Spidey's pink peepers pleaded with them to consider his words carefully.

Tiptin and Thwack obliged by drawing away from their host and whispering amongst themselves. No matter what excuses to refuse Spidey's request that they aspired to make valid, the arachnid's last statement always kept them invalid: *'As it is, your own have already been robbed of their freedom by that ratsbutt.'*

Finally, and despite their own misgivings, the pair agreed to go. Not out of bravery, but rather out of fond feelings for their loved ones, most of whom were still suffering under Ruler Xebec's New Order. Proving once again that love rules fear.

"We'll go, Spidey. I suppose that loving others sometimes means making tough choices."

"Loving others often means making tough choices, Tiptin. But splendid! Splendid!" Spidey clapped his eight palms together like a small audience. "Now then, there is no time to waste. We must soon be on our way! But first I have gifts for each of you. Come with me."

Thwack and Tiptin followed their host over to a shelf, where he procured a furled bundle of hide. Spidey held the hide up high, letting it unroll to reveal a big bag with drawstrings to seal the mouth. Sewn onto the bag was a long shoulder-strap befitting a giant.

Handing it to Thwack, Spidey smiled and pointed to the bug barrels. "Help yourself, my dear clops."

Thwack beamed with delight. "Wow! A big bag of bugs! Thanks, Spidey."

Spidey led Tiptin over near the larger kiln. "You shall require some mode of defense," he explained, swinging the cabinet doors open to reveal an ample array of assorted tools and weapons.

There were hammers and chisels and files and tongs, plus a wide variety of clamps of all sorts. In addition, there were jewelled daggers forged from the finest of gold, and silver throwing stars inlaid with cut diamonds. And there were maces moulded of precious metals; some of them spiked.

Tiptin watched as Spidey reached in and removed the most impressive item of all. It was a spectacular fibre sword with a shimmering blade and a woven hilt. The blade pulsed with life, radiating both heat and light.

"Ahhh," Spidey remarked with noted pride. "My fibre Masterpiece. Weightless and with its own pulse, it can almost wield itself. Here, take it."

"But I know nothing of weapons," Tiptin said.

Spidey grabbed the hesitant ladfolk's wrist. "What is there to know? You swing your weapon at your foe, they swing their weapon at you. Whoever slays the other first wins. See, simple."

Tiptin grimaced as the cynical arachnid grinned and pressed the sword's hilt into his palm. Instantly, the startled ladfolk felt the weapon's charge vibrate up his arm and spill into his body.

"Now, about that swollen ankle," Spidey remarked, stooping to get a better look. He gently lifted his young guest's knee and then moistened the dangling ankle with hot, damp breath.

His patient could actually feel the tendons tingling in repair.

Spidey lowered the foot back down. "There now. How does that feel?"

Tiptin hopped up and down on the ankle. It no longer screamed in pain. In fact, it was as though it had never been injured at all. "Wow, it's entirely healed!"

Spidey beamed. "Another triumph for the science of magic medicine. Come, let us be off. Ready, my dear clops?"

Thwack slung the big bag of bugs, which he had crammed near to burst. Ditto his bulging cheeks. "Schorr, Schpidey."

They stood before the seer's web as the arachnid commenced to clap and chant; while both of his nervous guests prepared to duck and bolt:

"OH MAGIC EYE OF SILK AND BLUE,
MY FRIENDS HAVE A DEED TO DO,
BY MY COMMAND I ORDER YOU,
TO OPEN WIDE AND SEE US THROUGH!"

Immediately, the eye snapped shut and the seer's web took to spinning. Slowly, at first, and then faster and faster and faster, until a strong syphon threatened to suck Tiptin in; but a meaty forearm held him in check.

A vacuum suctioned from behind the spinning web as a tiny hole opened up in its center. The hole expanded wider and wider until the silk had completely detached to expose the entrance to an expansive shaft. In fact, the shaft was so large that even Thwack could trek through it fully upright. Wherever one looked, bite marks scarred the rock.

Tiptin thought, *'Wow, these gravel grinders must be behemoths to behold?'*

"Come on," Spidey beckoned, stepping across the threshold and on into the shaft.

No sooner had the others entered the shaft, when the entrance spun shut behind them. Beyond it, the alert eye resumed its blinkless vigil.

The shimmering blade breathed forth ample light as the trio made their way down a steep slope. Spidey scurried along in the lead, while Tiptin followed with newfound vigor and energy. Thwack thumped along in the rear, merrily stuffing his yap with bugs.

The shaft eventually levelled off and led them into an even larger tunnel. Its walls were mostly of black onyx, occasionally broken by wavy bands of brown and yellow agate. As with the shaft, bite marks were everywhere. However, additional light was now availed to them by peculiar, glowing plants that quivered as the group trod past.

"What unusual plants," Tiptin said.

"Ah, they are that," Spidey concurred. "To exist where light does not, plants down here must produce their own. The seeds to grow these jellyglow plants were given to me by an old friend."

"Your friend in the portrait?"

"Yes, the very same. He also provided me with spores for scarlet fibres and seeds for tentacle trees. As well as other nuts and seeds to plant a variety of foodstuffs in my underground garden. Unfortunately, time prevented me from showing it to you."

"I would have very much liked to have seen it," Tiptin assured him.

"Perhaps someday you shall," Spidey stated hopefully.

"Issth thith the main tunnel to Schebecth Island?" Thwack wanted to know, while munching down yet another fistful of bugs.

"It is. And I would conserve those crunchy delicacies, my dear Clops. It is a long and arduous journey to the far end of this tunnel."

"Oh, I wouldn't fret too much over him, Spidey. None of flesh can match the stamina of a cyclops. It is myself who lacks nourishment."

"Don't fret, Tiptin. While you hold the fibre sword, you shall require little nap or feed. The blade's own energy shall enter into your body and help to sustain you. I myself designed it so."

"I have noticed that I do seem to feel much more fit and aware than ever before?"

"Oh, you are, Tiptin. You surely are."

True to Spidey's warning, the journey through the tunnel proved to be long and arduous. Even more so, it was boring. Boring! Boring! Boring! Naught about the immense tunnel ever changed. The rough walls of onyx and agate went on and on and on and on and on and..................

****

..................on and on and on.....

Until, just when Thwack wondered if they might not find themselves passing through the boring tunnel for far too long to ever achieve their purpose, his pointy ears pricked to snag sound. "Wait, I hear something?"

"Such as?" the arachnid inquired.

"It sounds like – ummmm…"

"Like deep, bass music, perhaps?"

"Yeah!"

"What is it?" Tiptin asked. "I don't hear anything?"

"You shall," Spidey assured him. "It's the grinder bosses blowing orders to the grinder workers. The bosses blow bass notes through their horny hearers. Of course, the gravel grinders all take turns at being both boss and worker. Thus, each gets their chance to feel weighty. Hee, hee. Which, as you shall soon see, they certainly are."

And they most certainly were! PLUMPANORMOUS!!

Both guests gawked in muted fascination at the limbless wigglers with horny hearers sticking out of their mushy heads. The grinders greedily devoured the onyx and agate, and literally anything else that came within biting range; their many rows of crunching chompers quickly grinding each substance into dust. Being much too busy burping and slurping and gassing, they paid the newcomers no heed.

"Gross!" Tiptin hollered, pinching tight his nostrils.

"Revolting!" Thwack concurred in disgust. *And coming from him, that was really saying something.*

"It is both of those!" Spidey readily agreed. "Terrific workers though! Always chewing! Never complain! Just keep your distance, my friends! They are blinder than blackwings, and they'll gobble up anything! And I do mean anything!"

Thwack embraced his big bag of bugs.

"This way!" Spidey beckoned. "We're almost there!"

Tiptin scrambled after the arachnid, with Thwack breathing down his back.

"Hey! Quit shoving, Bugbreath!"

"Hurry it up then, Slowpoke! It stinks worse than whitestripes down here!"

"Come!" Spidey beckoned, scurrying off into a diverging artery. "This shaft leads back up to the surface!"

They ascended up and up, and then up and up some more. The mere thought of finally exiting such a long and boring tunnel put strength in their legs and lifted their spirits.

Then, just as Thwack began to wonder if they'd ever reach the surface, his schnozz sniffed the fresh fragrance of a forest. "Thank you, Destiny," he muttered.

They climbed up out of the shaft and stepped onto soft soil; venturing into a dark and creepy place where trees grow so vast even cyclopes can abode in their trunks. A place where sunbeams seldom kiss the forest floor. A place where the only colour is shapes. A place where the blackness is blinking with peepers. A place where nerves cannot nap.

"Where are we?" Tiptin inquired, tightening his grip on the sword's hilt so as to brighten the blade.

"This place is known as The Baobabs," Spidey explained. "No need to fret, the critters hereabouts are mostly harmless."

"Gulp. Mostly?"

"Yes, Thwack. Not to worry, you two should fare rather well. After all, you both have your wits and your weapons. Even more importantly, you also have each other. Now don't forget, in order to get to Xebec's castle, you travel south by east until you reach the distant seashore. From there you simply trek northward along the coast for as far as you can go. You can't miss it. There is only one pink castle that I know of."

"But Spidey, how will we know which direction leads to the seashore? We will be trekking below this forest's canopy, where neither sun nor skytwinklers can guide us."

"Allow the sword to guide you, Tiptin. It is its own compass, and its blade always points true. Now remember, the staff can only be unpowered in The Saline Sea. One of you must cast it into the deep first chance you get, without giving it any thought. No pause to think, straight into the drink. Do not allow your minds to be seduced by ambition. The staff must be unpowered. Nothing matters more. Everything matters less.

"Also, if at all possible, do try to retrieve my webscroll for me. But only if an opportunity should present itself. The staff remains your only priority. It must be, or else all will be lost anyway. You do realize the grave future that awaits all of Ranidae should you fail?"

Tiptin and Thwack both nodded that they did.

"Very well then. Venture forth in high spirits, for your purpose is a noble one. Travel with Destiny and you shall never get lost. Go on now. Quickly. Go. Too much time has already passed us by. Go. Go."

Neither Thwack or Tiptin uttered a reply as they stepped forth to find their fate. Although shielded from the crackling flashbolts that ripped open the unseen above, both were quite aware of the angry skybangers now battling for space well atop the canopy; all announcing the arrival of some serious sky showers.

Never had the pair experienced such a torrent. Soon, raging rivers of muck flooded the forest floor. To trek further was futile. To stay put was to perish. Their only escape was up↑.

Using the blade as a lantern, they began climbing up one of the broader baobab trees. With Thwack boosting his puny pal from bough to bough, eventually they clambered atop a sturdy platform. There they slumped down to rest.

"I can't believe it!" Thwack shouted to top the storm.

"Can't believe what!?" Tiptin asked.

"I can't believe the strength of these massive boughs! Even the droopy ones barely bend beneath my bulk!"

"I hear you! The tree branches in this forest are much thicker than most trunks elsewhere! I wonder how old a tree such as this…"

"Whooooo!?"

Chills shivered up their spines as both jerked about to face the voice.

"Whooooo!? Whooooo!?"

Blinking in disbelief, Thwack dropped his precious bag of bugs and two-fisted his club.

Too startled to stand, Tiptin pushed hard with both feet to slide his body backwards until his back banged against a bough.

"Whooooo!?"

Finally, the defensive cyclops untangled his tongue. "Wh-Who are you!?"

Taleteller

"Hi! Hi! Hi! Hi, You! It's me, Me! So, so, so, so. What can one possibly say about those boorleez? Definitely not the sharpest sticks in the woods, but certainly the most honest. Perhaps being simple minded like them brings one closer to true happiness than many of us pseudo intellects shall ever be? Just saying.

"Now, where were we? Oh yes. Xebec now possesses both the staff and the webscroll. Dearest Destiny, what a scary combo.

"And what of this moody magician, Zebu? Poor Shoenia. Imagine undertaking a long sea voyage with only ole scowlface and his empty eyes for company. If I had lips I'd bobble them. I mean, it's certainly not my idea of a luxury cruise. Uh-uh. Noper! No way! Not at all!

"Lastly, we have Thwack and Tiptin trapped high up in a baobab tree and cornered by a, "Whooooo?". Which, I suppose, is still better than a, "GRRRRR!!" Or an "AAARRRGH!!" Or even a whiney, "Whaaaaat?". For certain. For sure.

"But you shall never find out more of what happened if I keep yackity-yack-yackin. Uh-uh! Noper! No way! Not a chance! Which is why I shall, as you earth types would say, stuff a sock in it! Will so! Will too! Ciao for now..."

4
Baobabs And Beakers

With its palm sails filled and its dandytall mast bended by wind, the little boulder-pea pod pitched and dipped and listed its way across the rolling, blue sea. Capable hands gripped the tiller, safely steering the sturdy vessel through the deep swells.

A tall and lanky grandfolk in a blue robe peered south from the pod's bow. Blue streamers fluttered from the peak of his pointy, red hat. His wrinkled hands clenched a wand of pink crystal.

"Uhggg," Shoenia grunted, heaving hard on the tiller. Day had battled Night many times since she and the moody magician had bid Snarly farewell and cast off from The Continent.

Shoenia had long passed the point of weary; although not of energy. Titanroot sap was quick to replenish her stamina. Rather, she had grown weary of her muted companion's constant scowl and arrogant attitude.

Zebu had barely even acknowledged her presence since the very moment that they had cast off. Not once had he even offered to spell her on steerage or assist with trimming the sails. Nor would he even respond to her questions. In fact, he mostly behaved as if she did not exist.

All the moody magician ever did was peer south from the bow and occasionally chant to his wand. Except on those rare occasions when he would point out a slight change of direction, always without so much as looking back at the labouring galfolk; which actually suited her just fine, since his empty eyes only served to sink her spirits anyway. *'Oh, how I loathe you, Zebu of Narcissily...'*

Tossing her hair back behind her shoulders, Shoenia savoured the sensation of the spray splashing across her cheeks.

Shutting her eyes, she licked salty drops from her lips, while enjoying a beautiful piece of natural music that she inwardly titled, *The Waltz of the Whirling Wind.*

Even the pod took part, rocking in sway to the tempo. It timed its climb up each wetroller so as to top the crest at high pitch, and then slooped down into the trough right on cue at each rest. It then climbed back up with the next roll of the sea's skin, only to once again crest at high pitch...

Opening her eyes, Shoenia spied a beautiful blue spouter far off in the distance. Then it was gone? And she again felt the dumps of alone.

Lashing the tiller in check, she reached for her stalkhollow and granted herself a satisfying sip of titanroot sap. Taking hold of her scrapstick, she stroked the attached shinebulb to glow; then giggled as she returned the objects to their place at her feet.

Suddenly some movement snagged her sights: neither of spouters nor of her *so-called* mentor. No, this movement was mid-pod, amongst the supplies. *'Wasn't it?'* She couldn't be sure?

Then it happened again. One of the larger acurns shifted slightly and its stemmed lid jiggled. Her mind wasn't playing tricks on her after all. Something was hiding inside the acurn!

Unsheathing her blade, Shoenia stepped softly towards the container. Upon gripping the stem in one hand, she readied her weapon with the other. She quickly lifted the lid. "Don't move or…?"

Shoenia gasped. A pair of furry faces blinked up at her. One bore mask-like facial markings, and the other bore a patch about one eye. Each chattered uncontrollably, while pointing an accusing paw at the other. Scampering free of their hiding place, both smuzzles clutched hold of the startled galfolk's tunic.

"Sneek!? Peek!?" she shouted. "What a pleasant surprise."

Shoenia scooped the furry pair up in her arms and began to giggle as both smuzzles licked her cheeks. "I don't believe you two, hiding inside an acurn all this way. Why didn't you…"

"Ew-ew-cootchy-coo, now I'm sailing with a zoo," Zebu taunted. "Just don't get too attached to them. Both of these stowaways are being marooned on Orange Island."

"Stowaways? They're not stowaways." Shoenia protested.

"Oh really," Zebu scorned. "Not stowaways? Then tell me, dear apprentice, what else are they to be? Other than fresh bait for finners, that is."

Although the magician's empty eyes stared to daunt her, Shoenia bluffed a stern rebuke. "They're – they're stowfriends. And they're not going anywhere."

Zebu actually smirked amused. "Stowfriends?"

"Yes," Shoenia said. "Stowfriends. And I'm no longer your apprentice. In fact, I don't even like you."

Zebu toned sarcastic. "Well wiggle my wand, Shoenia doesn't like me. Oh, teary-bleary-boo-hoo-hoo, but I just so love you."

That's right, I don't like you one tiny bit. And neither do my stowfriends."

Both nervous smuzzles clung tightly to Shoenia's tunic.

"Not many do like me, Galfolk. In fact, I can't think of any who do? So what? And you can call these two stowaways whatever you want, but they're still getting off at Orange Island. And I'd mind my flippant tongue if I were you…" Zebu wielded his wand in a most menacing manner. "…lest it should find itself tied tight into a knot!"

Bellybees buzzed about Shoenia's guts. She knew that the moody magician had both the mind and the means to carry out his threat. Yet with two innocents now clinging to her for protection, she dug deep within herself until she struck courage.

"Do so, Zebu, and you can just find somebody else to sail this pod!" Shoenia spat back, bluffing a brave front. "And to help you unpower that stupid staff, too!"

Zebu rolled his eyes. He knew of spells that would mute the saucy galfolk. Sadly, such spells would also numb her mind and impair her ability to sail the pod. He had always preferred that others should tend to all matters of toil, which he regarded as being too far beneath himself to pursue. Therefore, he decided to tolerate her only as far as the coast of Xebec's Island. But no further.

"Oh, very well," he grumbled. "Your stowaways can stay..."

"Stowfriends."

"Those!" Zebu snapped, pointing his wand at the trembling smuzzles. "But they had best chop the chatter and keep clear of mischief, or else into the drink they shall go! And they must work for their keep! Do you understand me, Galfolk!?"

Shoenia merely nodded her reply. This battle she had already won, but she knew that to push the enraged magician any further could mean losing the entire conflict. She recalled Snarly's warning advice: '*...but from now on you must think what you speak. And especially think of to whom you do speak it...*'

"Good! Glad we're all agreed! Now tend to your tasks! Move!"

All three obeyed at once.

It immediately became apparent to Shoenia that her furry friends were quite quick to learn. Each smuzzle grasped with just one demonstration how to tie the knots necessary to secure the sheets. With very little instruction from her, they almost instantly took to trimming the sails like seasoned seafarers. They calmly climbed aloft to untangle rigging, even in the foulest of weather.

Shoenia had crewed for several seasons before her mates permitted her to attempt such tricky tasks. Even then, she first honed her seafaring skills upon the much calmer wetrollers of The Bay before she was entrusted with such tasks out on the open sea.

Yet the nimble rodents happily scurried up the swaying stem with neither a slip nor a care. In fact, they seemed to be at play in their own element. *Almost as if they had done such many times before?*

Their voyage took them due south, through both calm seas and torrents. Whether the pod was climbing up steep wetrollers or slooping down into deep swells, they saw naught but sky, water and some blue spouters; plus one titanic tentacone with suckers covering its wiggly bouquet of arms.

That is, until, early one windless dawn, when they found themselves bobbing in calm off the coast of a lonely isle.

The isle's plants were a bright orange and a dull orange, as well as an in between orange. The shore silt was striped many hues of orange. High, stony bluffs were of a glittery orange. Even the stilted beakers wading through the surf were plumed in orange.

Yes, virtually everything about the isle was orange. Orange! Orange! Orange! Orange! Orange!

Throughout all of Day's rule, the pod bobbed at anchor just shy of the shore. Then, just as Night launched its assault upon Day, the winds awakened and the anchor was weighed. Thus, by the time Day next charged back atop the eastern horizon to reclaim the sky, the lonely isle had long departed.

During especially strong torrents, when crackling flashbolts spread their crooked claws to rake the sky, and angry skybangers deafened the very sea itself, monster wetrollers would spill their whitecaps into the pod. At such times the tough little smuzzles were forced to take the tiller on their own, while Shoenia lashed herself to the mast and used an acurn to bail. Zebu, of course, cowered and held on tight for his very being; as even his magic was no match for nature's ultimate wrath, which ebbs for no mortal.

Still, they persevered, regardless of the elements. After all, what other choice did they have? They were just four specks in a pod surrounded by sea. Captive to Morgue's mercy.

At one point during the long and treacherous voyage, they encountered a hostile spouter. Unlike the blues that they had observed from afar, this nasty nemesis was black of back and white of belly, and it had mean red eyes. It soon took to ramming and bashing the pod; once even lifting the tiny craft clear of the drink and pitching its crew haphazardly about.

As Shoenia and the smuzzles stumbled and fell and rolled about the pod, one extremely irate magician sought revenge upon their tormentor. Securing himself by grabbing hold of the mast, he pointed his wand at the water and began gyrating its tip.

Almost instantly, the choppy drink began to swirl. As Zebu chanted and increased the tip's speed, the swirlpool likewise advanced until a spinning vortex sucked wind and sea down into a void.

Zebu directed the sucking swirlpool directly into the path of the charging spouter, which wailed in terror as it struggled to swim free. But the panicky beast's slapping tail was of little match for the trap that engulfed it, and it was soon siphoned from surface to ...?

As they sailed further south into calmer waters, the climate climbed and they started crossing paths with many unique forms of sea life.

There were squadrons of gilled mantas with thin tails like whips, plus pods of striped dolphins that performed back flips and tricks. They saw shell-dwellers with fins, and squishy sacks with eight arms, plus they spied crabs by the cast amongst sea polyp farms. Even a school of flying finners skimmed past without causing them harm.

Day battled Night battled Day battled Night battled.... *yet, still no sight of land?*

That is, until, while under a setting sun, they spotted a thick mist far off in the distance; and, shortly thereafter, a smoking peak rolled atop the horizon. It was soon joined by a lesser, docile peak. To the south and east stretched a white ribbon of sandy beach. It served as a welcome mat to a much larger land mass, which sustained a forest of ginormous trees. Clearly, they had found dry land. But where were they?

"Dung!" Zebu cussed, realizing his error. "The Baobabs. We've wrongly hit the opposite coast of Xebec's Island. Stupid skytwinklers!"

'More like, stupid you,' Shoenia thought. *'I tried twice to tell you that our course was much too far to the west.'*

Upon deciding that the battered pod was no longer seaworthy enough to risk sailing it around the treacherous coast of Xebec's Island, the moody magician ordered them to put ashore. This they managed to accomplish with little difficulty, thanks to favorable gusts and the low tides that scouted along the shoreline in prep for their dusk assault higher up onto the sand.

The pod rode the rolling surf into a shallow cove, drawing alongside a partially submerged trunk of rotwood. The experienced smuzzles quickly lashed the battered craft to some exposed boughs, while Shoenia took in the mysterious forest about them.

The baobab trees grew so large that creatures could actually become lost in their trunks, their girth far surpassing even those of the Fluorescent Forest. It was readily apparent that sunshine seldom struck soil in this place.

"You three stay put in the pod!" Zebu growled, stepping atop the rotwood.

"Where are you going?" Shoenia inquired, suddenly feeling quite unsafe and wondering if perhaps she hadn't been a tad hasty in dismissing her former mentor.

Zebu neither broke stride nor looked back. "To explore. Remain in the pod until I return. The Baobabs are home to hordes of hideous horrors. All who enter unprepared shall surely perish."

Shoenia felt uneasy as the smuzzles clung to her legs, especially when Zebu paused to tap some tree vines with his wand. Even though none could see the gloating grin pasted on his face or read inside his wicked mind, each of them sensed that something was off-the-up?.

After Day had once again surrendered the skies back to Night, the three friends cuddled together in the darkness for comfort. Each tried to stave off fatigue as best they could, trying in earnest to keep their senses primed. Shoenia much wanted to conserve the titanroot sap. As well, she was hesitant to use the shinebulb, lest its glow should attract skitter bugs. Or worse, alert the hordes of hideous horrors?

As each in turn yielded to fatigue and nodded off into the realm of deepest dreams, they were entirely unaware of the vines slithering down from their boughs and skimming across the water towards them. The sleeping trio never noted the muffled plops of the stringy stalkers dropping into the pod, nor felt them winding about torsos and limbs.

Day had returned by the time Shoenia awakened. Immediately, she realized their dilemma. Sneek and Peek were tied together into one tight furball with eyes. Even their short snouts were lashed shut. While she herself was bound from shoulders to feet.

The furball looked at her, its four moist eyes blinking for help.

Shoenia fared no better than they. In fact, the harder she struggled, the tighter the vines squeezed. They would choke off her wind, thereby gagging her speech. All she could do was stare at the pathetic bundle of fur, and pray of Destiny for help before the sun's searing rays baked the flesh from her face.

Silently, she wished they'd ignored Zebu's order and taken refuge beneath the canopy. At least they'd be spared the wrath of the sun. But what other dangers lurked in the forest?

Shoenia recalled Zebu's off-the-up manner when he'd departed, and how he had tapped these very same vines with his wand. Realizing that it was he who was responsible for their plight told her that he was not coming back to save them. His treachery caused her to grow angry. She struggled to burst free of her binds, but to no avail. They simply squeezed ever tighter. Only this time there would be no Snarly coming to save her. Oh, how she wished that he could have come with them.

'Wait!' she thought, recalling the glass vial in her pouch. *'Why else would Snarly give it to me, if not for in a bind such as this? But how can I retrieve it? Or uncork it? And what is contained in its emptiness?'*

Stretching with all her strength, she attempted to scoop the object from her pouch. It was no use. The vines constricted ever tighter about her wrists, cutting off the feeling in her hands. As her fingers numbed, she ceased trying to overpower her stringy captors and paused to ponder her plight: *'Think, Shoenia. Your mind's not a melon. Make use of your wits.'*

A hopeful thought leapt into her mind. Her limbs may be bound, yet the vines were only lashed about her body. *'I may still manage to retrieve the vial!'*

Shoenia began rocking her body back and forth until she was finally able to roll over onto her belly. She took to squirming about like a wounded wriggler, until three objects finally rolled free from her pouch.

In an effort to halt her movement, the vines latched onto the mast and commenced reeling their catch across the pod; while squeezing ever tighter about her torso and limbs.

Shoenia choked and gasped for breath. She knew that she was soon to meet Morgue. She must dislodge the cork, or else…

Snagging the vial with her tongue, she tried to scoop it into her mouth. But it rolled away from her lips. Now her mind was dimming and dizzy.

'I need to simplify this. To Morgue with the cork!'

Squirming enough to bend her torso, Shoenia opted for one final try. Out of sheer desperation, and despite the certain pain to follow, she whipped her brow down hard upon the glass vial. Red shades of pain shot through her blanking mind. Defeat had all but engulfed her aching limbs as the vial rolled away almost intact, save for a slight crack.

'Oh no… It didn't shatter…'

Even so, a slight crack proved to be all that was needed. Never one to quit at anything, Shoenia fought to keep from passing out. She found new strength in the spectacle now playing out before her.

A slight wisp of smoke appeared within the vial, fed by the tiny bubble of air that was slowly seeping in. It gradually expanded into a glowing green haze and the vial itself swelled near to burst.

"Pow!" The cork popped clear of the vial, and instantly the haze spewed free of its glass prison. Within its growing mass hunched an apparition with rough, silvery skin and amber eyes set deep within puffy sockets.

The apparition wasted no time in pointing its rush at the vines. "Be gone or be mulch!"

Without a blink of delay, the vines unwound to release their captives. They slithered in haste from pod to rotwood to water to shore to forest to...?

The apparition floated over the gasping galfolk, tapping her with its rush so as to refill her breathers. "We do not have much time, Shoenia. Already, my image is fading."

"Snarly?"

The gruff voice was familiar, although its tone was haunting and distant. "Not Snarly, Shoenia of Ga. The sapkeeper you once knew has wilted. What your eyes see is his life spirit given shape by a spell."

"I do not understand?"

The apparition pressed a twiggy forefinger to Shoenia's lips. "Shush, Shoenia. We need not understand everything, for some things will never make sense. Just listen.

"Zebu knew that Snarly was fast wilting from age. He only wanted Snarly along on the voyage so that he could make use of his mentor's vast knowledge of skytwinklers. Zebu never could grasp basic astronomy. His weakness has always been a mind much too obsessed with his own ambitions.

"Zebu has no desire to unpower the staff, Shoenia. His only aim is to have it. Snarly had often pleaded with Destiny that Zebu would stray from his scheme and choose grace over greed. Yet his pleas found no favour. Zebu's passion for power won out."

"But why then did Snarly send me along with Zebu?"

The apparition was fading quickly now. "Snarly knew his time to wither was near, and he needed a noble being with enough grit and wit to defeat Zebu and unpower the staff. Somebody he could trust not to betray him."

"But how can I defeat a Master Magician like Zebu? I wield no magic?"

"No, Shoenia, you do not. Instead, you have something much more powerful than magic – *Honour*. A fine quality that seems to have dwindled greatly with the passing of time, I might add. Now, listen carefully. You must take note of each word I speak, for they are meant from Snarly to You."

Shoenia nodded that she understood.

The apparition offered up a riddle; only now the voice was undeniably Snarly's:

"WHEN NEXT YOU MEET UPON A SHORE,
HOW SHALL FLAMES LICK CLOTH NO MORE?"

"I do not understand? What does that riddle mean?"

"A life spirit's sight into future events has strict limits, Shoenia. It can aid you no further." The apparition paused briefly as if it was carefully choosing its words. "Remember this – *in the proper place and at the proper time, you shall know to do the proper thing.* And perhaps you will also learn something of Love's own magic along the way? I do trust you, Galfolk. You are so very special to me, even despite your making a complete mess of my forest. My smuzzles are most fortunate to have you."

"Did you send them along, too?"

The apparition was almost gone now. "I did. To help ease your *dumps of alone.* Kapeesh?"

As the apparition vanished, Shoenia smiled and unscrambled her thoughts to find just the right words. "Kapeesh. Snarly… I love you!"

"Ah, whatever?"

"And you still suck at being mean…"

A fading voice responded from the nothingness:

"WHEN NEXT YOU MEET UPON A SHORE,
HOW SHALL FLAMES… lick …cloth… no…more….?"

Then came silence… save for the intermittent crash of wetrollers breaking onto the shore, and the soft blow of the gentle seaside breeze. Off in the distance, a shore squawker railed at a defiant crab.

Both smuzzles whined and whimpered after the scattering wisps of haze; providing proof positive that pain over loss does indeed transcend species.

Shoenia gently stroked her little companions' fur. She quietly gathered up the flint and striker, before palming the shinebulb to glow. Her demeanor was calm, yet deliberate. She was now quite determined to settle a score. "Come on, you two. We're going to find and unpower that staff."

Together, the three friends trod warily beneath the canopy and entered the dark forest. Sneek and Peek stuck close to Shoenia, while the shinebulb dangled from the tip of her scrapstick.

Peepers blinked at them from the shadows and grunting sounds shivered their skin, but the brave trio trudged onward. Doing their best to stay brave, they passed beneath root archways draped with mangy moss, and they clambered over broken branches by the cord. Shoenia wondered just what types of hideous horrors belonged to the blinking peepers, and what manner of unseen beasts were making the grunting sounds?

After what seemed like forever, it became readily apparent that they were hopelessly lost. Both body and mind were spent. In utter frustration, Shoenia wiped her sweaty face on her sleeve and sought out a soft mat of moss at the base of an exposed root. There she and the smuzzles snuggled up for a nap.

"Destiny, watch over us," Shoenia whispered. "Mask our presence from all that would harm us."

Yet no sooner had Shoenia tapped out the shinebulb, when…

"Whooooo?" a deep voice inquired from the darkness above. "Whooooo are you?"

Shoenia snatched up the scrapstick and sprang to her feet. Palming the shinebulb to glow, she scanned the above shadows for shapes.

Sneek and Peek balled their wee paws to box.

"Whooooo?" the deep voice repeated.

Bracing her back against the tree, Shoenia prepared to swing at even the slightest hint of movement.

"Whooooo?" This time the deep voice was attended by rustling and flapping.

"Go away!" Shoenia warned. "Or I'll whack you!"

"That wouldn't be very nice," replied the deep voice. "Would it, Dearest?"

"No, Dear," concurred a mellow voice. "Not very nice at all."

"I mean it. I will whack you really hard. Now, go away!" Shoenia lowered her tone in an attempt to sound menacing. "I'm big and I'm bad."

Several tense moments passed before the deep voice broke the silence. "You don't look very big to me. Does it look big to you, Dearest?"

"No, not at all, Dear," responded the mellow voice. "Nor does it look to be bad. Does it look bad to you?"

"No, Dearest. I'd suggest it appears somewhat more frightened than bad. Wouldn't you agree?"

"Most definitely, Dear. Not that I blame the poor…"

"Well, I am bad!" Shoenia retorted over her pounding heart. "And I grow much bigger when I get angry! So you had best leave us be!"

A prolonged silence ensued before the deep voice spoke again. "It doesn't appear to be growing any bigger to me. Does it to you, Dearest?"

"No, Dear," replied the mellow voice. "Perhaps it is not really angry at all and simply fibs out of fear? Wouldn't you agree?"

"Absolutely, Dearest. But it certainly has nothing to fear from us."

"Of course, it doesn't. The poor thing is simply afraid of that which it cannot see. Perhaps it is best if we swoop down there and reveal ourselves?"

"Yes, let's do that," concurred the deep voice.

"No!" Shoenia exclaimed as unseen flapping approached. She tightened her grip on her scrapstick.

Sneek and Peek dove beneath a pile of leaves.

Still, Shoenia did not swing her weapon. Instead, she was struck still by the two figures that descended into the glow of the shinebulb.

Circling above her was a plump beaker, whose big brown eyes blinked behind his oversized spectacles. He had matted brown feathers, which were long overdue for a preening. Tufted ears and tiny horns topped his wide head. A pair of powerful flappers kept him aloft. Sharp talons dangled at the ends of his bony legs. Short arms led to pudgy hands with stout fingers.

Fluttering in place was a second, beautiful beaker with brilliant blue eyes. She had soft down and feathers; white like fluffy skysheep. Her soft stare was somehow disarming.

"No, it certainly isn't very big," observed the bespectacled beaker in his deep voice.

"Nor is it bad," noted the beautiful beaker. "I have a sense for these things."

"You most certainly do, Dearest. You know, I believe I've read of this species in the Scholarship Chronicles."

"Is it an ape?"

"No. No. I rather suspect it to be humanfolk. And given its features, I'd guess it to be a galfolk."

"Are you sure, Dear?"

"Not fully, Dearest. But it does fit the description as best I recall."

"Perhaps you should ask it? Well, go on. Ask it."

The bespectacled beaker nodded, and then looked down at Shoenia. "I say, you down there. Are you in fact a galfolk?"

Being awed speechless by the strange avian couple, Shoenia barely managed an affirmative nod. All she could think was, *'Wow...'*

"Well, go on," prodded the beautiful beaker. "Ask her name."

"Yes, Dearest. Galfolk, do you have a name?"

Shoenia managed another weak nod, simultaneously lowering the scrapstick.

Both beakers exchanged bewildered blinks.

"Well?" pressed the bespectacled beaker, touching talons to moss. "Might we hear it?"

The beautiful beaker landed beside her mate. "Can't you see she's still frightened, Dear? Perhaps we should introduce ourselves first?"

"Absolutely, Dearest." Extending a pudgy hand in greeting, the bespectacled beaker introduced himself. "Hello, Galfolk, my name is Hoot Beaker."

Shoenia still stared in silence, but she shared in the handshake.

Hoot then gestured to the beautiful beaker. "And this pretty hen is my missus, Hweet Beaker. We've hatched twenty-three chicks together."

Hweet shot her mate a stern stare. "We?"

Hoot grimaced forth an *oops*. "I mean, I helped hunt our chicks' chow."

Hweet pecked him gently on the cheek. "You did at that, Dear. That's why I love you so much."

Hoot blushed clean through his down.

Hweet stepped forward and executed a flap-sweeping bow. "Welcome, galfolk. I do hope we didn't scare you too badly. We were really quite startled ourselves. Strangers are quite rare here in the Baobabs."

"Perhaps she's gone mute?" Hoot suggested.

"Her ears seem to function just fine," Hweet pointed out.

Shoenia finally found her voice. "I – uh, we were already scared."

"It speaks again!" Hoot declared.

"I can hear her just fine, Dear."

"Sorry, Dearest. Young galfolk, do you have a name?"

"Uh, my name is Shoenia."

Hweet clapped her palms together. "Oooooo, what a nice name."

"Ahem, do those rodents have names?" Hoot asked, pointing at two trembling bumps beneath the leaf pile.

"Yes, they do. Their names are Sneek and Peek."

"They certainly look tasty," Hoot noted.

Hweet smacked her mate in the chest, then firmly pinched shut his beak. "Pay ole growlguts here no mind, Shoenia. We are not in the habit of devouring our guests."

"Guests?" Shoenia remarked with some skepticism.

"Yes, guests," Hweet confirmed, releasing Hoot's beak. "You really can't expect us to simply up and abandon three lost strangers way out here in the forest. Whatever would that say about us?"

"Especially with some serious sky showers approaching," Hoot added. "If you were in our feathers, would you abandon three strangers in need of help?"

"Uh-no," Shoenia conceded.

"It's settled then," Hweet asserted. "You and your rodent friends will wait out the flashfloods in the dry safety of our den hollow."

"Flashfloods?"

"Yes. There are no sky showers like Baobab sky showers," Hoot explained. "Where we now stand shall soon be a raging river of muck. Isn't that right, Dearest?"

"Absolutely, Dear. Spread your arms, Shoenia, so that I can fly you to the safety of our den hollow. Ole growlguts will bring along the rodents."

"They're called smuzzles," Shoenia said, nervously eyeing Hoot with evident distrust. "And I adore them."

Hweet winked knowingly at the anxious galfolk. "Perhaps it would be best if I flew your smuzzles to our den hollow. Hoot will fly you along. Won't you, Dear?"

Hoot knew that his mate wasn't really asking. "Yes, Dearest."

Shoenia smiled as she stood up. "Thank you, Misses Beaker."

"Please, Shoenia, just call me Hweet. Misses Beaker makes me feel kinda old."

"And just call me Hoot," said the bespectacled beaker. "That way I won't feel old either."

"But you are old, Dear. He really is, you know."

"Don't tease, Dearest."

Hoot and Hweet both beaked bird smiles at each other, and then at Shoenia.

Shoenia returned the smiles and clapped her hands. "Come on out from under there, you two. Sneek. Peek. C'mon. The Beakers are going to help us."

Two furry faces poked out from beneath the leaf pile, viewing both beakers with obvious skepticism.

"Come on out. It's okay. The Beakers have offered to shelter us in their den hollow. Come on."

Hoot gently clamped his strong talons gently about Shoenia's shoulders, while Hweet carefully snagged the still trembling smuzzles. They then flapped aloft, dodging and dipping about barely visible shapes.

Whenever the group passed by an obstacle, the shinebulb's glow revealed it to Shoenia and the smuzzles; while the Beakers' big blinkers enabled them to sight far past the glow. To those who dwell in the Baobabs, darkness poses no barrier. Indeed, it is a blessing that has long protected them from rare intruders; time and time again.

Shoenia rather enjoyed the refreshing gusts from Hoot's powerful flappers, which whooped quietly enough to permit conversation. "Hoot, what belongs to all of these peepers?"

"Oh, a great many creature's dwell here, Shoenia. More than we together could even begin to count during all of our being."

"Are you not afraid? I mean, this forest is so dark and spooky."

Hoot chuckled. "Maybe it seems spooky to you, Shoenia. But it's not spooky to us beakers. I once ventured above the canopy just to see the sun for myself. Now, that was spooky. My blinkers went blind and the missus had to guide me back home to our den hollow. That's how I came to need specs. Much worse, though, I was forced to listen to 'I TOLD YA SO' so many times that I nearly leapt with wings wrapped!"

"I heard that, Dear."

"Love you, Dearest." Hoot winked at Shoenia.

"Don't any of the other creatures around here pose a threat?"

"No, not really. Beakers pretty much rule this forest. There are a few howlers about, but only the *whoomees* are really dangerous. Thankfully, around here they are even rarer than strangers. Personally, I have never chanced to meet one. Nor do I know of anybody else who has met one. I have, however, read that they do come in many colours, shapes and sizes."

"Whoomees?"

"Yes, whoomees. Bogus beings who are so fond of self that they only accept others who always agree with them on everything. Also, whoomees will never take any blame for their own behaviour. Not ever. Hence their name, *Who - mees?*"

"Why would anyone end a friendship just over somebody not always agreeing with them? I mean, if two friends always agree on everything, then something just isn't right about their friendship. Somebody isn't being real."

"Because whoomees are control freaks, Shoenia. They fancy themselves as being forever flawless. Hence, only their own opinions will ever matter to them. And if you dare to disagree with even one single whoomee on even one single point, then they and other whoomees will unite to call you all sorts of names. And they'll even try to ruin you. Apparently a group of whoomees all acting out together is called a Mob, and sometimes those in power use these mobs to keep their plebes cowed and in line. Quite simply put, whoomees are rash and gullible bullies."

"Sounds like they are very vain to me. Nobody is flawless."

"No, nobody is. But whoomees are a lofty lot. Angry and glum too. Always blaming others for their own failings. No whoomee ever looks at their own faults. Quite convenient, really. If we're never at fault, then we needn't grow up. Shoenia, have you ever noticed how the more you focus on the faults of others, the blinder you become to your own?"

"Uh, I suppose. I kinda have."

"Do take care to avoid whoomees at all cost. But if you should ever chance upon one, remember this - never, ever give in to a whoomee. Do so once and a whoomee will bully you forever."

"What do they sort of look like?" Shoenia pressed.

"I have read that whoomees come in all sizes, shapes and colours. That's why you can't really spot a whoomee just by looking at it. Oh no. You spot whoomees by their know-it-all attitude and their quick reaction to criticism. In fact, I recall an old joke that went something like this: You can always tell a whoomee, but you can't tell it much. Ha!"

"Can one heed a whoomee's hateful energy? I mean, can one feel it beforehand so as to avoid them altogether? Like, does their aura vent anger?" Shoenia asked.

"I'm not sure, Shoenia? I'd have to research the Scholarship Chronicles about that. I do suppose expending all that hateful energy to bully and control others, combined with being forever offended about – well, about pretty much everything, must surely warp one's aura. I don't see how it couldn't?"

Shoenia sighed. "I hear that. There are humanfolk who behave very much like whoomees."

"Really? There are?" Hoot was clearly intrigued.

"Yep. Unfortunately, amongst we humanfolk, whoomees are not so rare."

Hoot suddenly changed the subject. "Uh-oh! Keep your paws poised to touch down hard, Shoenia. My sight and landing skills aren't quite what they used to be."

"Feet. We humanfolk have feet, not paws."

"Hmmm? Interesting? According to the Scholarship Chronicles, so do whoomees. Hang on tight!"

Hoot touched down hard onto a large boughcany, just as the first skybangers blasted their wrath from somewhere high atop the canopy. Hweet landed gently beside him, bearing two excited and chattering smuzzles.

A natural archway had been split into the baobab tree's enormous trunk. It was sealed by droopy drapes, all fashioned from flax and feathers.

"Welcome to our den hollow," Hweet stated with much pride. Drawing aside the drapes, she gestured for all to file inside.

Hoot led them down a narrow shaft, through a tight corridor, and on into a large, vaulted hollow with rough-hewn walls rising from floor to ceiling. Worn hide scrolls were rolled up and stacked neatly inside rows of cubby holes. Clearly, they were quite old and had been very well read. The uneven floor was crisscrossed with thick slats of tree bark. Two napping nests were set against one of the walls.

Vibrant vines dangled from a clay planter, providing faint yet ample lighting. A stumpwood table squatted beneath the planter, supported by its own sturdy roots. Two wooden bowls, each brimming over with nuts, were placed in the table's center; and it was ringed by six smaller stumps, which plainly served their purpose as stools.

Hweet's mellow voice put the trio completely at ease. "Relax, you three. You will be kept warm and dry and safe up here in our den hollow. Just be prepared, the skybangers may rattle things about a wee bit."

"Yes, please treat our home as your very own," Hoot encouraged. "First, we shall munch nuts dipped in bumble sweet, and then you shall share with us where it is that you hail from and what led you to the Baobabs?"

"If Shoenia so chooses," Hweet scolded. "Don't be so beaky."

"Uh, but of course, Dearest. Only if Shoenia so chooses."

Shoenia smiled and unslung the stalkhollow. "Oh, I don't mind. Perhaps I would benefit from sharing our tale. Does anyone care for a taste of titanroot sap?" she offered, smearing dabs on her bruised brow and sore wrists.

With that the three travelers settled in to wait out the sky showers in the dryness and safety of Hoot and Hweet Beakers' den hollow. Shoenia thought, '*We could not have met kinder hosts. I must remember to thank Destiny for being so good to us...*'

5
Madness

A glumdreary figure in a black cloak and matching skullcap fixed his mad stare upon the blooming bush before him. It was all that remained of the vibrant floral garden which had been planted by the boorleez, and that had once beautified the entire castle courtyard.

Pointing the staff at his latest victim, the figure grinned in anticipation of his next senseless act. It had certainly been a most splendid use of Day's time, filled to a feast with much needless carnage; and, as a result, many lovely things were no more.

Xebec smirked as he mumbled his command. Instantly, a blue beam of light blazed forth from the weapon and the pretty bush burst into flame.

With that, the spinny sorcerer launched into the cackling laughter of a loony spun completely round-the-twist. "Ha-Ha-Ha! Ho-Ho-Ho! Hee-Hee-Hee," he howled, as tears of folly squirted from his eyes. "Ha-Ha-Ha! Ho-Ho-Ho! Hee-hee..."

Quite abruptly, his laughter cut to silence and his anxious eyes darted back and forth. His muddled mind sought to seek out what his senses could already feel.

Procuring a vial from his cloak, Xebec scowled and flung it forcefully against the broken remnants of a stone sculpture, where it smashed into slivers.

A yellow fog poofed into being, and Xebec commenced to chant:

"FOG OF FOCUS, I SET YOU FREE,
TO SHOW MINE EYES WHAT THEY MUST SEE,
EXPOSE MINE EN-EM-EEZ TO ME,
UNCLOAK WHERE THEY'RE MOST APT TO BE!"

The fog curled and shifted until it revealed the distinct outlines of both Scald and Slumber Summits. A boulder-pea pod was sailing past the sisters and heading straight for the shore of Xebec's own island. Four distinct forms occupied its hull.

Xebec squinted and leaned closer to the fog. "Ohhh, and what have we here? Hmmmmm? One magician, plus one galfolk, plus two furballs? Ha! That equals four dopes for my dungeon! "Ha-Ha-Ha! Ho-Ho-Ho! Hee-Hee-Hee…huh?"

"Ohhh, and just what have we now?" Xebec bit a knuckle. "My old nemesis Spidey Smells scurries through his tunnel. Old fool. Does he really think I'm unaware? Hee, hee. But wait! Who else shares his trek? Well, I'll be a goblin's goo if ole Spidey hasn't enlisted the help of a tall ladfolk and a one-eyed giant in ratty shorts. Hmmmmm? Yes, we must expand our facilities to accommodate Mr. Hookschnozz. Anybody who dresses that shabby deserves to be punished. Oh yes, and we'll also need a much longer stretching rack for him too. Ha! To think, all that mighty Destiny can manage to gather against me is this pathetic gaggle of gaffes? Whooda thunk it? Oh, goody-goody gleeglobs."

Entirely overcome with joyful anticipation, the spinny sorcerer did *'The Lipsbobble Boogie'* clear across the courtyard and on up the long and winding corridor that ascended in stages to an oversized antechamber.

He paused to torch one of the few unscorched wall paintings, the meanings of which are known only to magicians and sorcerers. He briefly savoured the portrait's splendid squeals before silly-skipping with satisfaction on through the antechamber, fully indifferent to its charred furnishings.

After twirling merrily beneath a narrow archway, he waltzed up a spiraled stairwell, past two heavy sinkwood doors, and on into his tower chambers. Flopping down onto his floating mattress, he flailed his limbs about wildly until he giggled himself off into the twisted realm of demented dreams: *'ZZZZ?!!#@ZZZZ*?!!ZZZZ&$?!!!!....'*

Taleteller

"Wow! Wow! Wow! Wow! Wow! What a spin case! Kooooookoooooo! Time for the nice blokes in the long white coats, and the pink room with the padded walls. But that's what becomes of any who bear the staff. Is so. Is too. Uh-huh.

"Oh well. Xebec can't claim he wasn't warned by the very legend itself. Uh-uh. Noper. No way. Not a chance. The longer he possesses the staff, the madder he'll grow. For certain. For sure. Cross my beams and hope to get snuffed out by a comet.

"And what of poor Shoenia and the smuzzles? Dumped on a foreign coast by that scoundrel, Zebu. Can you just imagine if Mr. Personality ever gets his greedy hands on the staff? Eeeeeyikes! Zebu will make Xebec look like a psycho wannabe.

"Thank Destiny for Hoot and Hweet Beaker. Two fine flappers if ever there be. Not to mention Snarly Grouchwhiner's cagey foreplaning before he met Morgue. Some serious grey matter went to work there. Shrewd. Sly. Quick. Brilliant!

"Anyway, you still won't discover the final outcome of this adventure unless your humble taleteller gets on with the story. So, on with our tale. On! On! On! On! On!..."

6
East Then North

"Who are you!?" Thwack asked of the strange, bespectacled beaker, who calmly parted some feather drapes with one hand, while dangling a clay planter of vibrant vines in the other.

The beaker blinked and stepped out from the archway. Colliding skybangers high atop the canopy, coupled with the incessant swush of leaves slapping at wind and wet, forced him to shout. "Well, I'll be a howlpack's chow! If it isn't a young ladfolk! Although I'm not at all familiar with your features, my greenish friend! Might I inquire as to your species!?"

Thwack slackened his grip on the club, and exchanged a glance of bewilderment with Tiptin before responding. "I am a cyclops! My name is Thwack! And this is my partner, Tiptin! We are…"

"Who are you!?" Tiptin cut in, while pressing to his feet.

"Pardon me!?" shouted the beaker, cupping his ear to snag sound.

"I asked, who – are – you!?"

"Oh yes! Who am I, you ask! Hoot Beaker's the name! Although, my misses has much more creative names for myself! Especially when she's upset with me! Hee, hee. She's inside with our other guests! You have taken up refuge on our boughcany!"

"What!?" Tiptin hollered to top the wailing wind.

"He says we're on his boughcany!" Thwack shouted, pointing to the drapes. "And that he has guests inside!"

Tiptin nodded. "We are so sorry if we have intruded! It's just that we had no place else to…"

"Follow me!" the beaker interrupted, parting the drapes. "This drizzle fogs up my specs!"

Even crawling on all fours, Thwack barely managed to squeeze through the natural archway that had been split into the baobab tree's enormous trunk. His bulk forced him to remain on hands and knees in the narrow shaft beyond. But at least the cramped cubicle was warm and dry, plus the feather drapes greatly muffled the storm's wailing wrath.

Hoot hung the planter from a wall hook, then used a cloth to wipe dry his specs. After pinching them back atop his beak, he folded his arms behind his back and gave the two strangers a detailed study.

"Hmmmm," he remarked. "You humanfolk sure do look a mite better than what I'd always pictured. Some entries in the Scholarship Chronicles are very vague at best. Ah, Tiptin, is it?"

"Yes, and I hail from Folkton."

Feeling left out, Thwack cut in. "And I hail from Cycity."

"Folkton and Cycity, you say?"

Both nodded.

"My, you two have journeyed far. Although, not near so far as our galfolk guest. She..."

"Galfolk?" Tiptin interjected, his tone betraying a spike in interest. "One of your guests is a galfolk?"

"Hee, hee. I suspected that might nab your focus," Hoot noted with a wink. "But I must caution you, her beauty is far exceeded by her maturity and her wit. As life is mostly just a blind quest guided by choice and chance, I would strongly advise that you choose an honourable approach with this galfolk. Otherwise, you may miss your chance."

"I simply meant that I would be happy to meet up and talk with just about any other humanfolk right about now," Tiptin explained, somewhat defensively. "Galfolk or ladfolk."

"Dear, who are you speak – ing – to?" A beautiful beaker batting brilliant blue eyes rounded a bend in the narrow shaft. Her wary stare was fixed solely upon Thwack.

Hoot took his mate by the hand. "Dearest, I'd like you to meet Tiptin, a ladfolk from Folkton. If my memory serves me well, Folkton is placed on the southern shore of The Sweet Sea – is it not?"

"It is," Tiptin confirmed, offering up a slight bow in greeting.

The beautiful beaker politely matched the ladfolk's courteous gesture, briefly straying her sights away from Thwack. "Welcome to our den hollow, Tiptin of Folkton. My name is Hweet."

"And this giant fellow is Thwack, a cyclops from Cycity. I do seem to recall that the Scholarship Chronicles show a place called Cycity plotted on the right bank of The Sweet River, an ample flight downriver from Folkton. Is it so?"

Thwack rudely ignored Hoot's query and offered Hweet his huge hand in greeting.

Although somewhat hesitant, the nervous beaker reluctantly extended her own.

"BOO!!" Thwack suddenly blurted, forming a frightening face.

"Freeeeep!" shrieked the startled beaker. She fluttered in fright as feathers filled the shaft.

"HARR!! HARR!! HARR!! HARR!! Gotcha! Wooeee! You shoulda seen your face! Your blinkers near bolted! HARR!! HARR!! HA – huh? Hey, where are you all going? Hey!"

Hoot turned about and glanced crossly over his specs. His tone went way beyond cynical as he retrieved the planter of vines. "You'll have to excuse us, Mr. Clops, if we don't share your sense of fun. We're all going to retire to our cozy little den hollow now. Much too cozy for you, I'm afraid. We would offer you some nuts dipped in bumble sweet and knit together a warm quilt from blankets just for you; however, my missus can't seem to recall where she misplaced her serving bowls and yarn. You see, she has had a most terrible fright of late. But I'm sure you'll fare just fine here in the dark all by yourself. Pleasant dreams to you, Sir."

As the three rounded the bend, a furious ladfolk turned and pointed at the puzzled cyclops. "Later," he promised, acting out an exaggerated stomp. Having made his point, he then hurried to rejoin his host and hostess.

"Hey!" Thwack hollered from the blackness. Upon trying to follow, he conked his skull. "OW!!" Next, he got himself wedged tight in a squeeze. "Hey! Hey! At least leave me the vines! Hey!

Aw, come on. It was just a fun little prank! No real harm done! Hey! Tiptin! Tiptin! TIPTIN!!"

Thwack's calls were met with stony silence...

"Oh yeah! Be that way! See if I care! I'VE GOT BUGS!!"

The highly embarrassed ladfolk tried to apologize, but Hweet wouldn't hear of it.

"We are not at all responsible for the boorish behavior of others," she explained. "If such were the case, none of us would ever nap at ease. Isn't that right, Dear?"

"Absolutely, Dearest."

The Beakers led Tiptin down a narrow shaft, through a tight corridor, and on into a large, vaulted hollow with rough-hewn walls rising from floor to ceiling. Worn, hide scrolls were rolled up and stacked neatly inside rows of cubby holes. Clearly, they were quite old and had been very well read. The uneven floor was crisscrossed with thick slats of tree bark. Two napping nests were set against one of the walls.

Tiptin noticed little of his surroundings. His sights were stuck on the most gorgeous galfolk that he had ever seen; or ever even imagined. Her striking appearance was most unusual in that her skin was fair and her hair was white. But it was her emerald eyes that most tangled his tongue. His heart shifted within his chest, and his stomach sank. A rush of warmth flowed throughout his entire body, which now seemed stuck in place like a statue. He was further captivated by her facial scars. He wondered, *'How did she come by them?'*

The galfolk lowered her head to disguise a slight smile.

"Ahem," Hweet interjected, somewhat strictly. "We certainly seem to be meeting many strangers of late. Tiptin, perhaps you might set aside your shimmering thing to munch nuts at our table and share with us news of your travels?"

Hoot couldn't resist. "If Tiptin so chooses, Dearest. We mustn't be beaky."

Hweet shot her smug mate a look. "Of course, only if you so choose."

"Oh, I don't mind," Tiptin replied, at last prying his eyes from the galfolk.

"Uh, I'm Shoenia," the galfolk blurted out, clearly not yet ripe to forego the handsome ladfolk's attentions. "I hail from Ga."

"Ga? I've never heard tell of Ga?"

"It's very far north, beyond The Saline Sea," Hoot informed him, obviously proud of his knowledge of such things.

"Oh? And are all of Ga's galfolk so – um, inspiring to behold?"

Shoenia blushed, while two jealous furballs rolled their eyes and pawtended to spit up. The pair then scurried to embrace Shoenia's legs; thereby diverting her attentions onto themselves, and sending the smitten ladfolk a blunt message: *'Back the feelings off!'*

Hoot motioned them all over to the table and, while Hweet fetched a jar of bumble sweet, Tiptin began his tale.

He started out with Xebec's conquest of Ranidae, and how he had fled Folkton to avoid the sorcerer's decrees. All but the suspicious smuzzles were intrigued by his account of how he had outwitted the boorleez in the Swallow Mountains, before plunging down into the slop of a mountain's belly. Of course, his hosts were not at all surprised by the details of his first encounter with Thwack, but his description of Spidey Smells and the gravel grinders really kept them captivated.

"... and that is how we came to be on your boughcany," Tiptin stated to finish his tale.

"Just to be clear, you and this cyclops seek to unpower the staff all by yourselves?" Shoenia asked."

"Better two try than one," Tiptin replied.

The Beakers exchanged agreeing nods.

Next, Shoenia decided to risk telling her own tale to Tiptin. She explained how her homeland came to be embroiled in a bitter conflict between humanfolk and lizarme. She noted how she had also fled into a strange place. In fact, her tale nearly paralleled his own; from them both meeting master magicians, to them both being granted items to fulfill the same purpose. They even shared the same worries over family, as well as the dumps of alone.

Tiptin's blood simmered as Shoenia told of Zebu's treachery and of how the mean magician had so callously abandoned her and her two furry friends to an early meeting with Morgue. The ladfolk wondered, *'How could anyone be so cruel?'* He secretly wished he could have been the hero who saved her.

"… so you see, Snarly thwarted our early meeting with Morgue. But sadly, my friend can aid us no more." Shoenia paused, remembering Snarly's stern warning about the objects in her skirt pouch. She had been told, *'reveal them to absolutely no one'*. "Now we must make do with just my scrapstick, my hurling dagger and a shinebulb," she said, concluding her tale.

"You also have each other," Hoot added.

"Yes, now we…" Shoenia almost concurred, before catching herself. As yet, she did not know the ladfolk, or his as yet unseen companion. She remembered Snarly's even sterner warning that, until the staff is unpowered, she is to *'trust nobody'*.

Noting her unease, the bespectacled beaker sought to sell her his take on things. "Shoenia, since you and Tiptin both seek the same thing, surely it would make more sense for the both of you to seek out and unpower this staff together? After all, two are stronger than one?"

"Five," Shoenia corrected him, while thinking to herself, *'And it depends on which five?'*

"Ah, yes. Five. We mustn't forget the rodents – uh, I mean, smuzzles. Or boorish Mr. Clops for that matter. Anyway, success together still makes much more sense to me than failure apart. Does it not make much more sense to you, Dearest?"

"It does at that, Dear."

"We could even help out by flying you to the eastern edge of The Baobabs," Hoot offered. "After the sky showers have ceased and the mucky rivers have all but dried up, of course. Couldn't we, Dearest?"

"Of course, Dear. It certainly will cut considerable time from their travels."

"Yes, it certainly will, Dearest. But now it is time to nap. Why don't you share my napping nest, Dearest? That will allow our weary guests to share yours?"

"Yes!" Tiptin blurted out. Palming mute his mouth, he blushed over his lapse of tact. After all, Hoot had wisely advised him to take an adult approach with Shoenia. Lest he should miss his chance at something special.

"Perhaps you should check on your friend?" Shoenia soberly suggested. "He has been awfully quiet for quite some time now?"

"Ha! Not necessary. He's no doubt stuffing his yap with bugs," Tiptin quipped. Then Shoenia's eyes moved him to relent. "Okay. Perhaps you are right."

"Please take one of the vine planters for light," Hoot suggested.

Tiptin grabbed hold of the sword and instantly its fibre blade pulsed to a shimmer. "Thank you, but my sword shall guide me."

"Sword, Dear?"

"A battling tool of sorts, Dearest."

"Oh."

With the sword lighting his way, the ladfolk exited the hollow, passed through the tight corridor, and strode on up the narrow shaft; where he encountered Thwack still wedged tight in the squeeze.

"Well, it's about time!" Thwack scolded, twisting his large head about to get a better look at Tiptin. Both of his arms were jammed tight to his sides. "Help get me out of this fix!"

"Ha!" Tiptin scoffed. "You're hardly in any position to be giving orders. Besides, being stuck serves you just right after scaring Hoot's kind missus like that. What is wrong with you?"

"HARR!! Did you catch the look on her face? Simply too mu… huh? Where are you going? Hey! This isn't funny anymore, Tiptin! Hey, I'm seriously stuck here!"

"At least this way you won't get into any mischief."

"Hey, come back here you puny…huh? What are you doing? Hey? Hey!"

Tiptin turned about and marched right back up to the wedged cyclops. "So, let's just see how much you like being on the catching side of a prank?"

"Ow!" Thwack yelled as Tiptin employed his fingers for flicking the tips of the helpless giant's pointy ears. "Ow! Hey! Ow! Ouch! Stop it! Ow! Hey! Ouch! No fair, I'm stuck... Ow!"

"Harr. Harr. Harr," Tiptin teased. "You should see your face."

"Ow!"

"Simply toooooo much, I tell ya. Tooooooooo much."

"Ouch! Tiptin, stop! Hey! Ow! Ow! Ow-Ow-Ow-Ow! EEEYOWW!! Stop twisting my ear! OW!! That really hurt! Oh no. No! Not nose flicks! Tiptin! C'mon, little buddy! Tiptin, no! OW!!"

Propping the sword against the wall, the ladfolk finished up tormenting his brawny victim by performing a slapping palm roll upon his shiny dome, followed up with double cheekie twists.

"EEEYOWW!!

Having made his point, the satisfied ladfolk gloated and walked away. "Harr. Harr. Harr. Harr. Harr..."

Thwack was furious. He twisted and kicked and grunted and groaned; yet he was still unable to squirm free. "I will get you for this! Do you hear me, Tiptin!? You shall pay for this! *$!@#!!"#*$!"?!*#?!*?!!!!"

Light and the ladfolk both vanished around the bend, neither being the least bit concerned over Thwack's threats; the former being indifferent to such things, and the latter having much more amorous matters on his mind.

Upon re-entering the den hollow, Tiptin noted that the vibrant vines had dimmed. Hoot and Hweet were already at nap with their dreams in one nest, while three bumps hid beneath the quilt of the other. Hide boots, a scrapstick, a shinebulb, a stalkhollow and a neatly folded tunic were placed against the wall.

Donning a smile of anticipation, the eager ladfolk sat on the quilt and removed his own boots and vest before unbinding his hairtail. His anxious fingers suddenly seemed to make even the simplest of tasks a chore. His heart pounded near to burst as he drew one leg free of his trousers. Now the other…

"Ahh!"

"Thud!"

"Ow…!?"

In painful confusion, Tiptin looked up from the floor and into denying emerald eyes. "I thought we were going to share the napping nest?" he said, shrugging shoulders with palms up.

"We are," Shoenia explained. "This nap, I shall take the nest. Next nap, you can have the nest. Rest well, Tiptin of Folkton." And with that, Shoenia rolled her back towards him, drew the warm quilt tight about her weary form, and smiled herself to sleep.

A pair of furry faces poked out at Tiptin. Each stuck out its tongue. "Pppttthhh..."

While wiping razzberry spray from his face, the humiliated ladfolk pondered over which hurt worse: the bruise from her heels, the bruise from the floor – or, the bruise to his ego?

Either way, he dared not try that again anytime soon. Stretching out on the hard and uneven floor, he mumbled, "Hmpff. Who wants to nap with two furballs anyway?"

Tiptin eventually drifted off into the dreary domain of sour dreams; waking often to stretch kinks from his sore neck and massage the aches and pains from his limbs. He wished he'd been more forgiving of Thwack, if only so that he could at least curl up on the big guy's soft, warm belly…

….zzzzzzzzzzzzzzzzzzzz….

…Tiptin's discomfort was disrupted by the sounds of others awaking. After washing up and then downing a big bowl of nuts dipped in bumble sweet, Tiptin summoned up the courage to approach the galfolk. "Shoenia, I apologize for my lack of manners at naptime. Despite your generous offer that we might take turns sharing the napping nest, I feel quite strongly that you and your smuzzles should claim it instead."

Shoenia smiled knowingly. "Do not fret over us, Tiptin of Folkton. We three have managed just fine thus far all by ourselves and without a napping nest. Although, at some point I might perhaps be persuaded to chat at length to better get to know one another. Maybe."

Tiptin was elated. *'I might have a chance to befriend her after all?'* He again recalled Hoot's advice regarding an adult approach. "Shoenia, I would be keen to talk with you. I promise that my intentions in doing so are nothing shy of noble."

"Pppttthhh…"

'Sure they are,' Shoenia thought, stifling a telling smile while glancing to see if his fingers were crossed. "We'll see, Tiptin of Folkton. I shall nap on it."

Two jealous furballs pawtended to spit up.

****

"Yesiree!" Hoot shouted down from a ledge near the ceiling, where he had been peeking out through some open shutters. After closing the shutters, he glided down to explain his excitement. "The sky showers have finally stopped, so now we can depart."

"Excellent!" Tiptin exclaimed. "We are without the luxury of time."

"Uh, but what of the forest floor? Will it not still be a river of muck?" Shoenia asked.

Hweet addressed her valid concern. "The forest floor dries most quickly here, Shoenia. Baobab roots are forever thirsty, and they can store many times their own weight in drink."

"Greedy, too," Hoot added. "They race to out-slurp one another. The ground may remain soft for a short bit, but Thwack shall fare well. As planned, we can fly the rest of you through the forest."

In next to no time, they were all ready to depart. They hastened through the tight corridor and on up the narrow shaft, where they encountered a huge, motionless form, which appeared to be wedged tight into a squeeze.

"Thwack, are you okay?" Tiptin inquired with concern. He gently patted the giant's shiny dome. "Thwack?"

Perhaps the tight squeeze squashed his breathers?" Hoot suggested.

"Thwack? Thwack?" Upon receiving no response, Tiptin knelt and lifted the cyclops' sealed lid.

"Aaaaa!" Tiptin screamed, as a fist big as a boulder yanked him through the squeeze.

Both smuzzles shed fur and clung tight to Shoenia's legs. Feathers filled the shaft.

"Schmmaaaaack!" Thwack planted a big slobbering smooch across the startled ladfolk's face. "Gotcha back! HARR!! HARR!! HARR!! Aw, I never knew ya cared, little buddy. Schmmaaaaack! HARR!! HARR!! HARR!! HARR!! Wow! Shoulda seen your faces! Tooooo much, I tell ya. Simply tooooo much. HARR!! HARR!! HA..."

The others were clearly *naaaaawwt* amused. Each gave the giant a scornful stare as they paraded past; with both smuzzles mixing in middle digit salutes.

The group all filed out onto the boughcany and made preparations for flight. Both beakers stretched their flappers to loosen up, while the competing smuzzles grappled into a heated tumble tussle over who would get to fly with Shoenia.

Two pairs of hands tore the chattering furballs apart. Sneek then gloated as Peek dangled in pout from the ladfolk's arm. Such was the contest decided.

"Hey, what about me?" Thwack voiced in protest, suddenly catching on. "I'm too heavy to carry?"

Hoot toned well beyond cynical. "Such is true, Mr. Clops. Which is why, before waking the others, I took the liberty to study up on your species. According to the Scholarship Chronicles, none of breath can match the stamina of a cyclops. Apparently none can match your atrocious manners either. I must remember to write that into my notes. Do remind me, Dearest."

"Oh, I certainly won't forget about that, Dear." Hweet replied, eyeing Thwack with open contempt.

"Therefore, Mr. Clops, you should have very little trouble keeping up with us battered old beakers. Tiptin's fibre sword and Shoenia's shinebulb shall guide you to follow us, and you do have your precious bag of bugs to nourish you. Although, the monster bugs of The Baobabs do not take kindly to bug eaters."

"M-M-Monster bugs?"

"Oh yes. Megamonster bugs, even. The forest floor is crawling with megamonster bugs. They're simply *tooooo* much." Hoot flapped aloft and clamped his talons gently about Tiptin's shoulders. "That is why the rest of us will be flying, so that they cannot surround us. You shouldn't have too much trouble though, Mr. Clops. If megamonster bugs do surround you, you can always bedazzle them with your witty sense of humor. I'm sure they'll be properly impressed. So much so that they may even forget to eat you."

"Surround me? Eat me? Megamonster bugs might surround me and...gulp...eat me?"

"It is possible, Mr. Clops. However, given your hefty bulk, you most likely need only be wary of the poisonous biter bugs. Not to fret. This late in the swarmy season they do tend to be a tad less aggressive than they are during the mating season."

"Gulp... p-poisonous biter bugs? A tad less?"

"Oh yes. Albeit, not by much. And do mind their sharp fangs as they can puncture even the toughest of skin."

"Fangs?"

"Yes, fangs. They are very long and – well, we really should be getting on now..."

Thwack was frantic. "Very long and what? Hey, and what? I asked you, and what? Hey! HEY!! VERY LONG AND WHAT!?"

"Do hurry down, Mr. Clops. You surely don't want to lose sight of our lights!"

"AND WHAT!? HEY!! WAIT UP!! THEIR FANGS ARE VERY LONG AND WHAT!?"

"That should boost his stamina," Tiptin noted with more than a hint of amusement. "Please don't lose him, though."

"What, and have him remain here in The Baobabs with us?"

Six bellies burst out in laughter.

"AND WHAT!?"

"Careful, Mr. Clops!" Hoot hollered into the blackness below. "I've spotted some movement about you!"

"WHERE!? WHERE!?"

Six bellies again burst into laughter.

"HEY!! DON'T GO!! WAIT UP!! THIS ISN'T FUNNY!! VERY LONG AND WHAT!? HEY!! AND WHAT!? AW, COME ON!! I'M SORRY!!"

Peepers still blinked from the shadows, but the strange sounds no longer shivered Tiptin's skin. In fact, he felt quite secure in Hoot's strong talons; plus there was the added lure of Shoenia's shinebulb floating up ahead of them. Yes, he definitely liked being where he was at. Albeit, he'd like being anywhere he was at, just as long as she was there. For he was smitten.

On several occasions, Hoot even exchanged pleasantries with some of the creatures behind the peepers, explaining to Tiptin afterwards who the peepers had belonged to. "That was my eldest chick's ex-mate. Young beakers sure don't tough through their troubles like we old beakers did. Such a shame. Although, sometimes I feel it may be for the best. After all, we do have the emotional health of our chicks to consider. Turmoil being turmoil, no matter who is at fault.

"And that there was old Busy Buckbiter, chief chatteryarn amongst the gliding bushytails. Always up in everyone else's business. Knows almost every rumor about everybody. Small wonder, seeing as Busy started most of them."

"Gliding bushytails?" Tiptin asked with curious intrigue.

"Yes, Tiptin. They are much like regular bushytails, but with stretchy skin joining their fore and hind limbs; thereby enabling them to glide effortlessly from tree to tree in search of nuts, and then from the trees down onto the ground to bury them. They still must climb back up though."

"So, they cannot fully fly?"

"Not that I've ever seen. Perhaps evolution hasn't quite figured out exactly what they're supposed to become yet? Hey, quick change of subject. How is it going between you and Shoenia?"

"I'm working on it."

"That bad, huh?"

"I'm certainly open to suggestions," Tiptin pled. "I really don't want to mess this up, Hoot. I might blow my chance at something very special."

"Ha! Many dream of finding true love, yet most are seldom prepared if they actually do. They either dive in much too fast and far too deep, or else they panic and take to flight."

"Isn't that the truth," Tiptin concurred.

"Hmmm? I'm certainly no expert on the *riddle gender,* however, I can't overstate the importance of your being real."

"Being real? But I am real," Tiptin responded, somewhat confused by Hoot's words?

"Are you, Tiptin?"

"Hoot, I don't quite get your meaning?"

"You must always be yourself around Shoenia, Tiptin. If you aren't being real at the beginning and she does fall in love with you, then it's not really you she loves. Hence, you won't get to keep it."

"I won't?" Tiptin asked.

"No, you won't. If you're not being real, then she will only love the imposter that you are pretending to be. Which means you will have to try and keep up your act. One can only pretend to be somebody that they are not for so long before their true self rises. Which it always does. That's why you won't get to keep her love. If you and Shoenia are meant to be together, then she will still love you despite your flaws. If not, then each of you will have lost nothing."

"Kinda like how one can only fool another for so long before they fool themself?"

"I've found that when we plot to fool others, then we have already fooled ourselves. To last, love must ruffle much deeper than feathers. For no matter how pretty our plumes may preen in our youth, time shall pluck out many quills over our flights. Therefore, you must start seeing all of Shoenia, not just the visible. You must also allow her to see whatever faults hide beneath the down. Especially those faults that you least want her to peck over.

"That is how you build a bond of love that even the trials and tragedies of life cannot break. Trust me, love is not always about dry nests and tasty rodents. There shall be torrents and want, of that much you can always be certain. Nobody, and I mean nobody, gets through this journey without suffering some real pain."

"Have you ever felt real pain, Hoot?"

"Tiptin, Hweet and I have lost three chicks during our time together. Do you know which of those three losses hurts the worst?"

"Uh, I imagine the first one?"

"No, all of them. The point is that we never really know what trials life will hurl at us. Or when? But it is life's lows that will either strengthen a bond of love, or break it? That's when feathers really feel the draft."

Only the flapping of wings sounded for a time, until Tiptin finally resumed their discussion. "Hoot, you are well learned. Tell me, why is Shoenia's skin so fair? I've never heard of humanfolk having such skin?"

"I truly don't know, Tiptin. Why is your skin dark? Why do Hweet and I have different coloured feathers?"

"I don't know?"

"Does it even matter?"

"Well…no, of course not."

"Bzzzzztt! Correct answer!"

"It is?"

"Of course. How boring life would be if we all looked exactly alike. Talk about one never-ending yawn-fest. Besides, we should never pass judgment on another based upon such trivial things. What truly matters is the spirits battling inside their heart. Hopefully their soft spirit is stronger than their hard spirit, as every being of breath is both blessed and cursed with each. If you don't like someone, at least try to get to know them better. And always give somebody who has wronged you and begs forgiveness a second chance."

"Like Thwack. He's forever frightening others."

"Tiptin, a second chance is only one past a first. Always beware those who expect a third."

"Hoot?"

"Yes?"

"You are really wise."

"Not so, I'm just well seasoned with age. Few of my thoughts are original."

"Hoot?"

"Yes?"

"What about the whoomees? I mean, should they also be given a second chance?"

"I want to say yes, Tiptin. But judging from everything I have read, trust a whoomee once and you might not get a second chance. As far as I know, they are the only exception. Although, as of yet anyway, I have never actually met a whoomee. And it is never wise to believe everything just because you read it in books."

"It isn't?"

"No, it definitely is not. Beings who speak untruths write untruths. Always try to think for yourself."

"Hoot?"

"Yes."

"I'm glad we met."

"Ditto that, my young friend. Ditto that."

In The Baobabs, none can ever say for certain who rules atop the canopy. Therefore, the group could not know how far or for how long they had traveled.

Shoenia drew energy from the titanroot sap, while Tiptin was constantly fed energy by the sword's pulse. Thwack, hollering up from somewhere below in the blackness, proved that the Scholarship Chronicles were accurate on one point. Indeed, no mortal can match the stamina of a cyclops. Although, big beakers do come close.

Finally, beams from the sun began to penetrate the thinning canopy, dancing a waltz between the diminishing tree trunks. Here the beakers touched down.

"We can go no further," Hweet informed them.

"It's our blinkers," Hoot elaborated. "Sunlight damages our sight. I flew above the canopy and looked directly at the sun only once, and now I need specs."

"Well, I told ya so," Hweet reminded him.

"Yes, Dearest. You certainly did." Hoot rolled his eyes.

"It's really unwise for anyone to stare at the sun," Shoenia informed them. "Not just those accustomed to darkness."

"See? I told ya so."

"Yes, Dearest. You did at that."

Suddenly something bulky came crashing through the bushes. The entire group turned to sight in the spectacle.

Huffing and puffing and dripping with sweat, a beefy cyclops bounded towards them. Thwack was all smiles. In one hairy fist, he gripped his club. The other held high an enormous, limp crawler.

"Well, I'll be a howlpack's chow…?"

"Wow!" Thwack exclaimed. "You weren't just chirping delicacies there, Hoot. Check out the size of these bugs!" The ecstatic giant motioned to the big bag, which was packed near to burst and slung over his back. "I bagged me a batch!"

All soured face in disgust as Thwack greedily chomped out a big chunk of crawler. "Ummmm – thendar too."

"Ah, we'll be on our way now," Hweet said. "We have grandchicks just north from here. It is long past time we paid them a visit. Do take care of yourselves."

"I so hope you will come and visit us again," Hoot offered. "After you have completed your purpose, of course."

"If, you mean?"

"No, Tiptin, I mean after. Yours is a noble purpose. Trust in your soft spirits to guide your hearts and I have no doubt that you shall prevail, for the forces of good are with all of you."

Both beakers fluttered aloft. Then, just before soaring back up into the dark, Hoot turned and winked at the ladfolk. Remember to be real, or you won't get to keep it..."

Tiptin smiled and waved to his wise friend, while Shoenia wondered what Hoot Beaker meant?

"Hey, anyone want a taste? Your choice, juicy or crunchy? HARR!! HARR!! HARR!! HARR..."

All turned away in disgust.

"Rogue," Shoenia mumbled.

"Revolting rogue," Tiptin elaborated.

Both smuzzles nodded their agreement.

The group quickly emerged from The Baobabs and waded directly into marshland. Thatches of slurpy reeds reached up from still pools, which were bounded by moist mounds matted with squooshy moss. Black ferns with white stripes squirted out stink. Scourges of skitters drilled into skin; while bothersome buzzy bugs circled about heads, expertly dodging swats and occasionally chomping out chunks of flesh.

As often as not, the group was stalked by snout-snappers, whose yellow peepers popped atop the surface of the pools. On several occasions, the sneaky creatures even tried to snack on a smuzzle. Only to swim swiftly away with large lumps between their crossed, spinning peepers; discourtesy of Shoenia's scrapstick. Or to meet Morgue belly up; discourtesy of Thwack's club.

The feisty galfolk packed a wallop worthy of one well beyond her size, and she wouldn't hesitate to protect her furry friends. Plus nobody, but *nooooobody*, was going to relieve Thwack of his big bag of bugs.

Onward they trekked, wading through pools and slogging through muck. Day after night after day after night, by both sun and by moon, under clear skies and bleak. On and on and on and...

Until finally, the soil dried firm and they entered Fern Forest. Here they saw big-footed bunnies with long, floppy ears, who hopped about munching on orange, veggie spears. There were burrowing ant bears with very long snouts; along with waddling rodents bearing quills that stuck out. They once wisely steered clear of a large sounder of snorting mad squealers with their tails coiled into knots, and avoided some tall hoppers with pouches for their tots.

There were wee whiskered squeakers that scurried past in a dash, and furry little scampers that buried nuts in a stash. They heard a choir of really hip chirpers that knew just how to groove, while large grazers with antlers clopped by on split hooves. Bucktoothed slaptails chomped down trees to build dams, and buzzing bumblers turned nectar into sap sweeter than jam. Billed chirpers built nests, and sassy cheekers dug dens; while a green croaker sat on a snapper, so they might well have been friends?

Activity of life was everywhere. Above. Below. All around. For Fern Forest was just teeming with it.

"Wait!" Thwack suddenly blurted. "I hear something coming?"

Shoenia cast a skeptical look at Tiptin.

"He does have far superior hearing to ours," Tiptin pointed out.

"What kind of sounds do you…?" Shoenia began.

"Shhhh." Thwack pressed a forefinger to his fat lips. "It sounds like many feet marching. Many heavy feet."

"From which direction?" Tiptin whispered.

"Behind us," Thwack whispered. "Probably Xebec's suck-ups patrolling his island?"

Shoenia firmed her grip on her scrapstick. "Way out here?"

"This is still Xebec's Island," Thwack reminded her.

"Yeah, but…?"

"What shall we do?" Tiptin cut in, hoping to avoid at all cost the delay and dangers of doing battle.

Thwack rubbed his chin as if in deep thought. "Hmmmm? Ah, I know. I can stride faster than boorleez can arm-swing, plus my stamina far exceeds theirs. I'll go back and act as a decoy. By the time I'm finished leading them astray, they'll be too pooped to piddle. HARR!! Get the joke? Too pooped to piddle? It's almost an oxymoron. HARR!!"

The others all thought, *'Speaking of morons…'*

"Well, get it? HARR!!"

"Shush," Shoenia scolded. "Yes, Thwack, we get it. Now, speak softly lest you give up our position."

"Oh yeah. Sorry. You four hurry along and I'll catch up later. Go on. Go. They're getting closer."

"But what if they should catch you?" Shoenia asked, her tone tinged with concern.

"Thwack can always fool them by playing *hides* and *sees*," Tiptin pointed out, making light of the situation.

"Really, Tiptin. You jest? Let's just suppose these suck-ups are not boorleez at all?" Shoenia noted. "Suppose they are cruel suck-ups instead? Like, humanfolk raiders? Or those horrible mugwump profiteers that you've spoken of? Or, what if they're not even suck-ups at all, but something much worse? More cruel. Suppose they catch Thwack. What then? Hmmm...?"

Thwack was undaunted. "You'll simply have to carry on without me. Get going before they hear us. Go. Quickly," he urged, shooing them off with his large hands.

"But…"

"Just go."

Tiptin grabbed Shoenia's arm and, together with the smuzzles, they stole in amongst the ferns.

"Thwack? Do be careful," Tiptin called out in a hushed tone.

Only the wind replied.

Tiptin and the others began sneaking cautiously about the forest. They had journeyed too far to be delayed by a bunch of bothersome boorleez. Although, Shoenia had raised a valid point: What if their stalkers weren't boorleez?

In due course, they had to stop and grant their sore feet a much-needed rest.

"Do you hear anything?" Shoenia asked.

"No, nothing. Look, the sun is retreating west towards the horizon. Soon, Night will rule, and the moon and skytwinklers will fill the sky. I do hope that Thwack can find his way back to us in the dark?"

"Tiptin, can boorleez see in the dark?" Shoenia asked. "And are you certain they are harmless?"

"No, I don't think they can see in the dark. Certainly not like felines or beakers or cyclops' are given to do, if that's what you mean? And yes, I'm quite certain they are harmless. I have not once heard of them ever hurting anyone. Any boorlee I have ever met was always kind of heart – albeit extremely annoying. Assuming that those tracking us even are boorleez?

"As you yourself have just noted, Shoenia, we don't know who is following us? Boorleez do have a keen sense of smell, yet they could not think any slower. And they really aren't a bad bunch, providing one has plenty of patience. I'd worry more about hurting their feelings than I would about them ever harming us. Of course, they could be under some sort of magic spell? Or so terrified of Xebec that it has affected their normally good nature? Fear can make us all do things we normally would not do, both good and bad. Still, even if they are boorleez, Thwack should easily evade them. They could never outdistance or outsmart him. I know of no species that can match the stamina of a cyclops."

"You worry about him, don't you?" Shoenia asked.

"Only because he fails to grasp the dangers that might hide in wait before us. This hunt for the staff may prove to be a dangerous time for him to stay stuck in his youth."

"Well, I think he's a complete louse."

Both smuzzles nodded in agreement.

"Perhaps we should all try to get to know him better. Maybe Thwack just feels..."

"Shhhh," Shoenia cautioned, dropping her voice into a whisper. "I sense a presence? Something is off…"

"AAAAARRRGGGHH!!!!"

"Yikes!" the startled pair screamed in unison, each moving to shield the other from harm.

Sneek and Peek froze in fright. Each smuzzle thought its wee ticker might tock!

"HARR!! HARR!! HARR!! HARR!! Oh, dearest Destiny! I can't believe you actually fell for that old 'we're being followed' gag! HARR!! HARR!! HARR!! What a bunch of saps, I tell ya! Ooooweeee! Simply tooooo much, I tell ya! Simply…. huh?"

Shoenia had finally swallowed her fill of the jovial joker and his reckless pranks, for now they were putting all of them at risk. With sparks spitting from her eyes, the beyond livid galfolk poked Thwack's belly hard with her scrapstick. Having thus gained his attention, she launched into a serious scolding of truth.

"You may be big and strong and carry a log, Thwack of Cycity, yet I bet you just tremble at the thought of others knowing what a lost soul you truly are. That's the real reason why you're forever putting others down and being such a smarty. Just so you'll feel a mite less miserable in your own skin; because, deep down inside, lost and lonely Mr. No Friends doesn't even like himself. Maybe you should stare into a still pond and ask yourself, would you take who you see seriously? Because nobody else here does!"

The smarty cyclops was stunned silent. His armor of attitude had just been stripped away by a galfolk barely a tad his size. His lips quivered, yet he could neither speak to nor look at her. Wet began to seep from his misty eye. Strength was sapped from his limbs and his knees began to buckle. His guts twisted to retch. Not once had he imagined that shame could actually make someone feel physically ill, or that the simple truth could cut so fast and so deep. Never had he felt so exposed. Or so alone.

"Any more of Thwack's foolishness and we all go on without him!" Shoenia railed at nobody in particular. "I mean it! From what I've seen of his character so far, we'd all be far better off without him along anyway. This is serious stuff that could cost all of us our very breath. Who needs this bunk? I know I don't. Now, come on. His antics have wasted quite enough of our precious little time."

Before scampering closer to Shoenia, both smuzzles paused briefly to kick the weeping green prankster in one of his toes.

"Weren't you a tad tough on the big guy?" Tiptin asked meekly.

"No!" Shoenia spat back. Then, upon remembering that Tiptin was not the source of her ire, she tamed her tone. "Tiptin, I like you. I truly do. But our purpose is not just some stupid game, at least not to me. If we are to unpower the staff, the three essentials for our success shall be courage, unity and trust. Thus far, your prankster pal has displayed none of those qualities. Not a one. As things are now, we would fare much better without him. In fact, I wish he'd just go away. Now, let's get on with our purpose – which clearly isn't his."

Tiptin knew he couldn't dispute Shoenia's point. Nor was he willing to risk upsetting her further than she already was. He fully understood her feelings. He too had grown weary of Thwack's attitude and antics. After all, a second chance is only one past a first. And the big guy had already been given many chances past his two.

The now sullen cyclops sulked along in the rear, without uttering so much as a peep. His mind was haunted by a shaming echo of truth. Shoenia's remark about him having no friends had cut the deepest, for he knew it to be true. And that it always had been.

Night won again. Then lost again. Attacked again. Then retreated again. Yet on and on they trekked with little rest. Up hills and down hills. Beneath sun and by moon. Amongst bracken ferns and around marshy ponds.

Thoroughly exhausted, the group at last stopped to soak their aching feet in one of the many brooks that nourished the body of Fern Forest.

"Ahhhhh…." Shoenia sighed as the clear water cooled her calloused soles. She shut her eyes and wiggled her toes.

"Ahhhhh…." Tiptin also sighed, likewise savouring the soothing sensation of cool water flowing between his toes. "I needed…. huh? Ouch!"

"Ouch!" Shoenia mimicked.

Thwack started slapping his skin, while the smuzzles chattered and swatted their paws all about.

"Charge!" a shrill voice sang out from above.

"Charge!!" responded a chorus of countless more. "*Stickem! Stickem! Stickem!*"

The group swatted and looked about in utter disbelief as a dark mass descended upon them. It was composed of a myriad of tiny flyfolk with transparent wings and tipnut helmets. Each bore a nutcap shield and wielded a thorn sword. All shouted, "*Stickem! Stickem! Stickem! Stickem!*"

"Ouch!" Shoenia shouted, attempting to catch one of the puny pests. "Ouch! Stop that! Ow! Ow! Careful, you could poke somebody in the eye with those thorns! Ow!"

"*Stickem! Stickem! Stickem!* Prick em in the ear! *Stickem! Stickem! Stickem!* Poke em in the rear! *Stickem! Stickem! Stickem! Jab em in the......?*"

"WHOOOOAAAAHH!!!!" Thwack suddenly shouted, blasting all breath from his breathers and thereby scattering the tiny flyfolk amongst the ferns.

Calm eventually returned and the army of tiny flyfolk regrouped and cautiously flittered towards the five strangers. They exchanged anxious glances, completely uncertain as to their next maneuver.

"Now then," Shoenia demanded in a terse tone while hastily pulling on her boots. She was clearly in a foul mood. "Who exactly is in command of this ornery outfit?"

The tiny flyfolk mumbled briefly amongst themselves before an especially puny warrior winged forward to act as an envoy of sorts. "The *Sheebazz* is in command," she replied.

"The Sheebazz is in command!!" echoed the chorus.

"And just where is this Commander Sheebazz?" Tiptin inquired, angrily rubbing his wee *wounds*.

"Not Commander Sheebazz. Just, 'The' Sheebazz," corrected the puny envoy.

"Just 'The' Sheebazz!!" echoed the chorus.

Tiptin was past being annoyed. "Fine. 'The' Sheebazz then. Tell us, where is 'The' Sheebazz?"

"The Sheebazz is not here," stated the puny envoy.

"The Sheebazz is not here!!" echoed the chorus.

"I get that!" Tiptin snapped. "So, where is..."

Shoenia motioned Tiptin mute. She now opted for a gentler approach, infused with patience. "But who are you? And why did you attack us?"

"We are The Weetykes," answered the puny envoy.

"The Weetykes!!" echoed the chorus.

"But why did you weetykes attack us?"

"Because we don't like strangers anymore."

"Because we don't like strangers anymore!!"

"That's not very fair," Tiptin put in. "You don't even know us."

"We would never even think to harm you," Shoenia assured them.

Thwack and the smuzzles all shook their heads to agree.

"The meany folk did," said the puny envoy.

"The meany folk did!!"

"Please, just speak one at a time." Shoenia looked to the puny envoy. "Do you have a name, young lady?"

The puny envoy looked nervously about.

"Tell her your name," encouraged one of the weetykes.

"Tell her your name!!"

"I'm Pint Little," replied the puny envoy.

"She's Pint Little!!"

"Hush. I can hear her just fine."

"Hush!! She can hear her just fine!!"

"Now, Miss Little...."

"What are your names?" Pint Little interrupted, cautiously hovering a bit closer to Shoenia.

Shoenia paused to allow for an echo that never came. "My name is Shoenia. This here is Tiptin. And these are my friends, Sneek and Peek."

"Who's the big greeny with attitude?"

"With attitude!!"

"Oh, I'm sorry. That is Thwack. He is a cyclops."

"He's even bigger than a boorlee," Pint Little observed.

"Bigger than a boorlee!!"

"*Zippit!*" Pint Little scolded. "Shoenia did say she can hear me just fine!"

"*Zippit. Shoenia did say she can hear her just fine...*" whispered the chorus.

"You know of boorleez?" Tiptin asked.

"Of course," Pint Little replied. "They come into our forest and poke holes in the roofs of our twig shelters to peek in on us. On purpose."

"On purpose!!"

"That's certainly not very nice." Shoenia looked quizzically to Tiptin.

"No, it's not," Pint Little concurred. "But it's not really their fault."

"Not their fault?" Shoenia was visibly puzzled. "You just said they damage your twig shelters on purpose and then peek into your private space. There is no excuse for either behaviour."

Pint explained. "The boorleez aren't really bad, Shoenia. They're just simple minded and nosy. Mostly they are scared of the sworcerer because he is a bully. Being bullied all of the time makes them sometimes do not nice things to others. The sworcerer tries to scare us too, because we won't do as he says. But he's not the boss of us."

"Not the boss of us!!"

Shoenia's tone was terse. "No excuse. One cannot blame another for one's own actions. If this sw – I mean, sorcerer, told these boorleez to go jump off a cliff, would they do it?"

"Uh-huh." Pint Little confirmed, nodding for effect.

"Oh? Anyway, do tell me more of this meany folk," Shoenia pressed.

"He skulked through our forest five sleeps past," Pint Little explained. "We didn't much care for his moody manner, so we swarm-bombed to *stickem!* But he knew magic. He waved his funny pink stick and made The Sheebazz slumber with sealed eyelids. We cannot open them. Now she is barely of breath." Pint Little bowed her head in sorrow. "We think The Sheebazz might meet Morgue."

"Uh, this meany folk, does he have empty eyes?"

"Uh-huh."

"And are his eyes different colours?"

"Uh-huh. Green and blue."

"Green and blue!!"

"Hush. All of you. My ears aren't plugged with wax."

"Sorry, Shoenia..."

"How is the meany folk known to you?" Pint Little asked with some suspicion. "Are you friends?"

"Certainly not," Shoenia replied with obvious disdain. "He is known as Zebu, and he is a mean and dangerous magician. He is certainly no friend of ours. I only know him from happenstance. I wish I did not."

Tiptin thought, *'It seems like this Zebu should be crowned Ruler of All Dungskulls.'*

"Where is The Sheebazz now?" Shoenia asked.

Pint Little still eyed the galfolk with some suspicion.

"Perhaps we can help her?" Tiptin offered. "At least let us try."

"Swarmhuddle!" Pint Little shouted, suddenly winging her way up into the sky.

"Swarmhuddle!!"

The dark mass lifted well clear of earshot before closing ranks into a tight scrum. Quite some time elapsed before the scrum finally dispersed and wound its way back down like a long, black whip.

Pint Little led the column, winging directly down to Shoenia. "I've been elected Proxy during The Sheebazz' slumber. Although most are staunchly opposed, I exercised my Option of Override.

"What is an Option of Override?" Tiptin inquired.

"It means that even if the majority are opposed to a proxy, the proxy can still do whatever she wants." Pint Little explained.

"Sounds like a silly rule," Tiptin noted. "Why even have a vote?"

"Then you will bring us to The Sheebazz?" Shoenia cut in, feeling quite honoured by Pint Little's trust.

"Not exactly," Pint Little glanced at Thwack. "We voted to fetch The Sheebazz to you. My peers fear for their twig shelters. You see, even a proxy must compromise or face a recall."

"Now, that sounds like a sensible rule," Tiptin noted.

"Here comes The Sheebazz!!" announced the chorus.

About a dozen weetykes, bearing a fuzzy frond, emerged from amongst some ferns. A silent form lay upon the makeshift stretcher. She was bigger than the other weetykes. Double their size, in fact. Her arms were folded across her chest, and her flesh was pasty pale. Both her eyelids were sealed tight and her breath seemed stilled.

She was clad in a regal dress, woven from fine silken thread and dyed berry blue. Colourless locks dangled from her wee head, upon which was placed the shell of a gilded nut. It's smooth surface had been painstakingly polished to a glossy sheen.

Yet despite her current plight, it was readily apparent that The Sheebazz was normally quite vibrant and lovely.

Donning expressions of hope, the weetykes gathered about the determined galfolk and started humming sweet melodies in a group effort to help out.

Shoenia tried to revive The Sheebazz by moistening her dry skin with blasts of hot breath. All to no avail. Next, she dabbed a drop of titanroot sap between The Sheebazz' cracked lips. Still no response. Chants likewise failed to work, as did pleas unto both Seed and Morgue. Even so, Shoenia simply refused to quit. She tried again and again and again, fully determined to break Zebu's spell.

Each attempt only netted more dismay than the prior attempt and less than the next. Sad and discouraged, Shoenia finally turned to Pint Little. "I'm so sorry, my tiny friends. I have done all that I can."

Pint Little smiled and kissed the dispirited galfolk's cheek. "Sorry for what, Shoenia? Never be sorry for trying to do good."

"Never be sorry for trying to do good!!"

"Wait!" Tiptin suddenly blurted.

"What?" Shoenia responded with a start.

"What!?" echoed the chorus.

"Spidey's sword." Tiptin's tone was tinged with newfound hope.

"The sword?"

"The sword!?"

"Yes!" Tiptin exclaimed. "The sword. Its fibre blade pulses with life. And it was fashioned by Spidey Smells, who is himself a master magician of the highest order. I'd wager that he is even much more skilled at magic than this Zebu will ever be."

"Try it," Shoenia prodded, her voice infused with fresh hope. "What have we to lose?"

"What have we to lose!?"

Tiptin began wavering the shimmering blade just slightly atop The Sheebazz' silent form.

"The Sheebazz stays still," Pint Little noted.

"Shhhh," Shoenia shushed. "We need to concentrate. Keep trying, Tiptin. I will offer up a chant."

The ladfolk kept wavering the shimmering blade just slightly atop The Sheebazz, while Shoenia commenced with her chant:

"OH BLADE ASHIMMER,
DO SERVE *ME* WELL,
LEND OF YOUR BREATH,
CAST OFF ZEBU'S SPELL!"

All watched with wided eyes and locked lips, but the still form did not stir.

"Try a different chant or cadence or something," Tiptin suggested.

Shoenia opted to try again....

And again....

And yet again....

And even yet again and again and again and....

...then....

"OH BLADE ASHIMMER....

DO SERVE *SEED* WELL....

PLEASE LEND OF YOUR MAGIC....

UNCAST ZEBU'S SPELL?"

No sooner had Shoenia completed her eighth chant, than the blade responded and cast a white glow over the still form. Wisps of spirit mist drifted free of the pulsating fibre and floated freely into The Sheebazz' tiny nostrils.

Almost instantly, her teeny chest inflated in breath and her pale skin bronzed. Golden hues began flowing throughout her fluttering locks as she slowly unfolded her wee arms. Her now moist lips parted a moan. Her alert eyes blinked in surprise.

"Sheebazz!! Sheebazz!! Sheebazz!!" chanted the chorus. "Sheebazz!! Sheebazz!! Sheebazz!!"

"Welcome back into the realm of the real," a smiling ladfolk stated in greeting.

"How do you feel?" Shoenia inquired, wondering if perhaps she should bow or curtsy or something?

The Sheebazz sat up and smiled at the strangers. Soft words flowed smoothly from her throat. "Like I've been revived by Seed herself. Who are you?"

Shoenia and Tiptin took turns quickly telling The Sheebazz where each of their group hailed from and what they were about. She proved to be a most polite listener, as did the rest of the elated weetykes; who were all quite intrigued by the humanfolks' tales.

"...and now we are here with you," Tiptin finished.

"And you are certain that the sworcerer's staff can be unpowered in The Saline Sea?" inquired The Sheebazz.

"Absolutely," Shoenia assured her. "Only, we may not have enough time."

"Zebu is well out in front of us," Tiptin pointed out. "And his intentions quite differ from ours."

"I have observed this pink castle," the Sheebazz informed them.

"You have?"

"Oh yes. It is a pretty place, yet the sworcerer is most glumdreary. Always surly and quite hostile to happiness."

"You have actually met Xebec?" Shoenia asked.

"No, but I have observed him from afar. His brand of scowl does carry."

"Whyever would you risk going anywhere near there?" Shoenia pressed.

"I went to voice a protest about his boorleez always poking their fingers through the roofs of our twig shelters and peeking in on our privacy. They're just being nosy and don't really mean us any harm, but we still have to repair the finger holes. However, just one glance at the sworcerer's scowly face and I knew better than to waste words on the matter. You five certainly have high hopes and pluck, Shoenia. It will take nothing short of an army to get inside those castle walls. Of that I am certain."

"But we don't have an army," Shoenia pointed out. "And even if we did, then Xebec would know well ahead that we are coming anyway. After all, an army is a very hard thing to hide."

"Hmmmm." The Sheebazz briefly pondered a thought before turning to Pint Little. "Swarmhuddle."

"Swarmhuddle!" shouted the wee proxy.

"Swarmhuddle!!" echoed the chorus.

A dark mass lifted well clear of earshot before closing ranks into a scrum. Then, with little time put to waste, the scrum dispersed and winded its way back down like a long, black whip.

The Sheebazz flew directly up to Shoenia and Tiptin. "The vote was unanimous with no declines. We weetykes are tiny and very easy to hide. Therefore, we shall be your army!"

Shoenia and Tiptin exchanged muted glances.

"You really don't owe us anything," Shoenia assured them.

The Sheebazz smiled. "Agreed. I have often felt that one of the silliest sayings ever spoken is, 'you *owe* me a favour'. But we really do want to help you. And you can certainly use our help, can you not?"

"I suppose we could use some eyes and ears inside the castle to let us know what Xebec is about? Still, it will be very dangerous. Are you certain that…"

"And to leave the staff in the care of a loony sworcerer or an evil magician is somehow less dangerous?"

Tiptin and Shoenia looked at one another and simply shrugged. Both knew that their tiny friend had just made a very valid point.

"When can your weetykes be ready to fly?" Shoenia asked.

"We are ready to fly now," replied The Sheebazz. "As you yourselves have said, there is no time to waste."

"No time to waste!!"

Thus, the original five were now joined by an army of tiny flyfolk with transparent wings and tipnut helmets; each of which bore a nutcap shield and wielded a thorn sword. Together, they flew through the forest like a dark mass. All were most eager to engage the boorleez. And *stickem!*

Ultimately, their travels brought them out of Fern Forest and they ventured into a new marshland.

This new marshland was very much the same as the last marshland. Thatches of slurpy reeds reached up from still pools, which were bounded by moist mounds matted with squooshy moss. Black ferns with white stripes squirted out stink.

Noses were often kept plugged, lest stomachs should spew. Only Thwack seemed unfazed by the stink. Not at all surprising, given that cyclops are known to have very strong stomachs; a fitting trait for any species that feeds mostly on bugs.

A brief skirmish erupted between the weetykes and some bothersome buzzy-bugs, but the well-armed weetykes won victory with ease. However, a scourge of nasty skitters proved to be a much tougher foe. Several pint-sized clashes were waged, pitting thorn swords against snout needles, before the vile suckers finally counted their losses and retreated for good.

There also appeared a new species of snout-snapper. Although they were smaller and with thinner snouts than the former, Seed had evolved to them the same sneaking skills. And, as with their larger cousins, they too tried to snack upon the smuzzles. And, as with their larger cousins, they were also sent swimming swiftly away with large lumps between their crossed, spinning peepers. Or left floating belly up.

At last, the five and their weetyke army cleared the marshlands and arrived at the coastal bluffs on the eastern coast of Xebec's Island. The refreshing seaside breeze cooled their cheeks as the weary lot sighted east across the wetrollers.

A black and white spouter with mean red eyes was lurching and lunging its way northward along the shore. Shoenia thought, *'That spouter looks familiar?'*

A shoal of porpoises performed back flips and spins, smiling with joy as they splashed back down into the wetrollers. Crabs with stemmed seers clashed claws on the beach, while ring-billed squawkers swooped low over both sea and shore.

"Shoenia!" Pint Little shouted to top the breeze. "We weetykes must remain well hidden within the bushes!"

Shoenia nodded.

"The breeze is quite strong!" Tiptin conceded.

"It's not the breeze!" Pint Little hollered into his ear, pointing at a distant squawker. "We must beware of those!"

Tiptin nodded that he understood, and then motioned for the others to follow him back in amongst the growth.

Thwack crawled along on all fours, lest he be sighted from afar. And he continued to pout by his lonesome.

While hovering near to the soil, the tiny flyfolk maintained a constant upward vigil. All held their thorn swords at the ready as they scouted the skies above for any sign of danger. They had battled shore squawkers before, and therefore knew that some of their number would surely meet Morgue.

They traveled north along the coast until the terrain became hilly and forested with tall needle trees. Yet they neither saw or heard any creatures?

'Strange?' Shoenia thought, *'It's as if none dare to dwell here?'*

And then it was right there before them! From a good vantage point in a small clearing, they took in a pink structure squatting atop a distant plateau. Xebec's castle!

"Only one valley left to cross," The Sheebazz noted with optimism. "We're almost there."

"I hear someone approaching," Thwack suddenly stated. His tone was fraught with warning.

"Yeah, sure you do, Thwack."

"We're not falling for that gag again."

"Pppttthhh..."

"No, I mean it this time. I really do hear somebody approaching us."

"Uh-huh."

"Sure you do, Thwack."

"What does it sound like?" The Sheebazz inquired with concern.

"It sounds like..."

"Ignore that fibchucker," Shoenia cut in. "He's brimmed to his brow with plant fodder."

"No, really," Thwack pleaded. "I'm telling you the truth this time."

"Yeah. Uh-huh. Sure you are, Thwack."

"Nice try, Thwack."

"Pppttthhh..."

"No, really. They're almost upon us. I'm not fib...."

"Maybe it's a parade of tuskwoolies trampling on by?" Shoenia suggested, stretching a sarcastic smirk.

"Or a gaggle of gravel grinders belching out gas?" Tiptin quipped.

"No, really...."

"Or perhaps even a crash of snouthorns doing a dance?" Shoenia giggled out.

The smuzzles chattered in screech and used their paws to imitate long beaks. Then they expanded their reach and flapped their limbs awkwardly. Lastly, they dropped to the ground and started rolling about.

"Ooooooo, good one. Maybe it is a confused flock of beakers that forgot how to fly?"

"Ha!" Tiptin kept on. "Sounds more like glowing goblins in squishy galoshes. Hee, hee."

"Or big beakers blowing bent horns?" Pint Little offered up with a grin.

Soon, even The Sheebazz could no longer resist joining in on the fun. "Perhaps it is a slime of slugs sliding across soil?"

"No," Thwack pleaded in earnest. "It's true, I tell you. Somebody or something is sneaking up on us. Really. It's true. Why won't you believe me? Honest, I'm not spinning tales this...."

"Sees! There dooz them be!" an unwelcome voice suddenly shouted.

"Ruler Xebec sez ye spozed be *prizners!*" shouted another as a hairy horde of bat-wielding boorleez arm-swung free of the surrounding bush.

"Charge!" commanded The Sheebazz.

"Charge!!" echoed her army. "*Stickem! Stickem! Stickem! Stickem!*"

"Flee!" Pint Little yelled at Shoenia. "We'll hold them off!"

"Flee to where?" came a panicky reply. "They have us completely surrounded!"

"Then fight!" shouted The Sheebazz.

Conflict erupted all across the clearing as boorleez deliberately swatted to miss at the helmeted flyfolk, who jabbed at them with thorn swords. Taking care, of course, to avoid poking any boorleez in the eyes because that really wouldn't be nice.

Thwack and three boorleez began exchanging blows with their clubs, each apologizing after every bruising bonk.

"I am so sorry. Does it hurt much?"

"Not hurts much. Ye dooz bonked me on thick skull. Guffaw!"

"Ouch!"

"Dooz pologize. Hurts?"

"HARR!! Naw, just a slight bruise. Hey guys, look up at the flying pink mooer!"

"Me not sees?"

"Me not sees?"

"Me not sees?"

Bonk! Bonk! Bonk!

"Ow!"

"Ow!"

"Ow!"

"HARR!! HARR!! HARR!!" Thwack howled as all three boorleez sprouted lumps and slumped for a nap. But the gloating cyclops was entirely unaware of a fourth boorlee sneaking up from behind. "HARR!! HARR!! HA...."

"BONK!!"

".... rr, ha.... tweet, tweet, tweet, tweet...." Thwack chirped out as he slumped to the soil.

Tiptin easily vaulted and ducked many an errant bat, sometimes somersaulting between his awkward aggressors' thighs and poking their butts with his blade. Of course, he was most careful not to actually cut anyone.

Being fully experienced at actual combat, Shoenia casually adopted the shrewd tactic of pitting one's enemies against each other. Sneaking up behind one preoccupied boorlee, she would smack his broad back with her scrapstick. When the annoyed boorlee swung about to retaliate, she would point accusingly at one of his burly budz. Instantly, the annoyed boorlee would respond by slugging the innocent and unsuspecting boorlee who, without fail, would always answer back in kind. Hence, the two boorleez would become engaged in a heated slugfest amongst themselves, while the unscathed galfolk moved on to instigate elsewhere.

As the bleedless battle wimped on, the sly weetykes started untying the boorleez' loincloths. The clearing quickly became littered with discarded buttwear. Meanwhile, some serious shrieking filled the forest as many a blushing boorlee placed one hand over their groin and hop-knuckled in haste for the foliage; lest the galfolk should see their wee thingseez!

The fight soon fizzled, as the boorleez were all either cowed behind bushes or busy clubbing each other. Hence, with the enemy thus distracted and Thwack again able to focus and think, they all prepared to make good their escape.

"KAAAPPOW!!" A blue beam of light blasted a crater in the center of the clearing, searing the very dirt itself.

Instantly, the weetykes scattered and Tiptin dove for cover behind some bushes.

"No!" Shoenia screamed as the situation unfolded.

Two boorleez stood beside the sorcerer. With saddened eyes, each dangled a smuzzle.

"No! Please, Ruler Xebec? Please don't?" Shoenia pleaded.

Xebec pointed the staff directly at Sneek. "Anyone for some roast rodent a la staff? Ha! Ha! Ha! Perhaps dipped in clops sauce?" Pointing the weapon at Thwack, the mad sorcerer took to laughing like a loony without a bin.

"Ha! Ha! Ho! Ho! Hee! Hee! Ha! Ho! Hee!"

In desperation, Shoenia resorted to outright begging. "Please, Ruler Xebec, oh greatest of sorcerers? Please spare my friends? I beg of you?"

Xebec cut to serious, donning one of the battiest stares that has ever been seen. Or ever will be. "You grovel well, galfolk. Just not well enough."

Xebec shifted his sights to Thwack. "Welcome, Mr. Ratty Shorts! I've been expecting you for quite some time. In fact...." Xebec toned his voice down into a whacko's whisper, ".... I've even enlarged my dungeon to accommodate your excessive bulk. And just in case you decide to give me any trouble, I've constructed a special stretch rack just for you – you boorish fashion fiasco! Ha! Ha! Ha! Ha! Hee! Ha! Ha! Ha! Ha! Ho! Oh, goody, goody glee drops!"

While Xebec dropped to perform his latest *horizontal* version of the Lipsbobble Boogie, Shoenia looked about at their burly captors. None were without wetted eyes, and all hung their heads in shame. At great risk to themselves, the pair holding the smuzzles gently handed them over to Shoenia.

Thwack gently rested a comforting hand on Shoenia's back.

"Disarm them!" Xebec ordered, flipping himself back up onto his feet. "Then march them straight down into the dungeon! I'll deal with them later! And they had best not get away, or it will mean a serious scolding for all of you! And worse!"

Stuffing their compassion, the boorleez encircled the trembling foursome and began marching them across the clearing.

"And catch me that ladfolk! Or else!" Xebec warned, before hop-skipping off into the bush.

Once Xebec was gone, Thwack placed the others upon his massive shoulders. There they all clung to each other for comfort.

As they marched up the valley towards the castle, the boorleez all began to sing The Boorleez Song:

"We be big boorleez,
We likes dooz noogies,
On our thick skulls!

"Noogie, noogie, noogie, noogie,
Boorlee, boorlee, boorlee, boorlee,
Noogie, boorlee, noogie, boorlee – BEASTS!!

"We not so smart,
To thinks be hard,
Cuzz we dooz be dense!

"Noogie, noogie, noogie, noogie,
Boorlee, boorlee, boorlee, boorlee,
Noogie, boorlee, noogie, boorlee – BEASTS!!"

Shoenia was somewhat surprised that such burly beasts could sing so sweetly. She was also saddened that they thought of themselves as dense. Soon, she joined in song with her captors, thinking that some good may come from it; if only to help lift everyone's spirits.

Soon, the smuzzles began clapping along to the cadence, and all of the boorleez took to smiling at Shoenia. Clearly, her joining the burly beasts in song had met with uniform approval.

Shoenia couldn't help thinking, *'These big boorleez don't seem to be mean at all?'*

They all continued singing until they came to the base of the plateau supporting Xebec's castle. There the boorleez abruptly ended their song.

"What's wrong?" Shoenia inquired. "Why have you all stopped singing?"

"Ruler Xebec not lets boorleez sings to castle," one boorlee explained.

"Him scolds us," added another.

"Or worse," included yet another.

"Worse? How so worse?" Shoenia wanted to know.

The boorleez merely hung their heads and commenced to arm-swing up the rugged path towards the castle.

Finally, they all filed across a drawbridge; the thick planks of which warped beneath their combined bulk. Then one of the boorleez rapped his hard knuckles against a thick sinkwood door.

A shutter slid open and a weaselly voice squeaked out, "Passwords?"

"Um…?"

"Come on, Taddler, ye know who we beez!"

"Passwords?" restated the weaselly voice.

"Um...?"

"Wait, me knows! Passwords be Dooz Be Us!"

Upon hearing the proper passwords, the shutter slid shut. The thick door slowly creaked open, exposing an unusually thin boorlee who was holding an iron ring with several keys.

Before entering the castle, Shoenia gave a quick look into the moat that completely encircled its foundation. Snout-snappers of many types stared up at her, as did nasty little biters with pointy teeth.

Inside the castle, it was dark, damp and dingy. Thick smoke from wall torches caused eyes to weep as the boorleez escorted their prisoners down a narrow, winding stairwell. A grimy wall, both moist and mouldy, bounded the group on one side. The other side offered up a drop straight down to the bottom.

"I'm worried about Tiptin and the others," Shoenia whispered into Thwack's ear, trying not to alarm the smuzzles.

The big guy responded by patting her knee, while Sneek and Peek each offered up hugs.

Keys jangled as the thin boorlee named Taddler fumbled to unlock an iron door. Upon swinging it fully open, he pointed and rudely commanded, "Gets in!"

"Hey!" exclaimed one of the biggest boorleez, grabbing Taddler's loincloth and lifting the unfortunate boorlee clear off the floor. "Galfolk dooz sings nice with boorleez! Ye shows her erspect!"

"Ye beddar, Taddler!" berated all of the other boorleez. "Ye shows galfolk erspect!"

Taddler dangled and wiggled to adjust the loincloth, kicking his spindly legs in mid air. His weaselly voice climbed from squeak to squeal. "Ah-ah-ah-ah – okay, me dooz pologize to galfolk. Me be muches sorry, Galfolk. Sees, Shmash, me doozed pologized. Now ye stop lifts me by gacheez. Pleeze."

"Ye dooz be plite to nice galfolk, Taddler," Shmash warned. "Ye Beddar!"

"Ye beddar!" asserted all of the other boorleez.

After lowering Taddler back down to his feet, Shmash turned to face Shoenia. "We hides fruits and nuts under rack stretches thingy. Warm quilts too. Ye not sez to Ruler Xebec that boorleez dooz helps ye, okay?"

"We won't tell him," Shoenia assured her captors.

"Ye pledges?" Shmash pressed.

"Oh yes, I promise we won't say a word. Will we, Thwack?"

Thwack and the smuzzles all shook their heads to concur that they too would keep the food and quilts secret.

"Clops not dooz be scared. Stretch thingy not work," added another boorlee.

"Me snaps spindle by oops," a beaming boorlee informed them. He clearly took much pride in his role in disabling the harsh device. "Boorleez not like Ruler Xebec's nasty hurts thingeez. All hims hurts thingeez dooz be broked and not gets fixes, never. Guffaw!"

All but one of the boorleez nodded their approval, with Taddler being the lone exception.

"We dooz pologize," Shmash stated in a sullen tone. "Ruler Xebec sez we spozed dooz puts ye six in dungeon so ye not escapes."

"Five," a second boorlee wrongly corrected him. "Them dooz be five."

"Them dooz be three," argued another, while holding up two fingers.

"Four," Shoenia corrected them all. "Thwack, set us down."

Thwack lowered Shoenia and the smuzzles to the floor.

"Boorleez dooz pologize, nice Galfolk. Ruler Xebec sez ye spozed dooz be prizners."

"My name is Shoenia," she replied. "And I know this is not your fault."

All but one of the boorleez hung their heads as Shmash ruefully shut the iron door; with Taddler, of course, being the lone boorlee out.

"Ye beddar not snitches about fruits and quilts, Taddler," warned a harsh voice from beyond the door.

"M-Me not snitches, Munch," squeaked Taddler's weaselly voice.

"Beddar not, or we not let ye plays noogies, ever!" Shmash warned. *And he wasn't bluffing!!*

Taddler was visibly distressed. "Me not snitches."

"Pledges?" demanded the harsh voice belonging to Munch.

"Pledges."

"Dooz clunk skulls to seal it...."

"Clunk."

Shoenia listened until the voices had completely faded away before turning to view the damp and dingy dungeon. She then slumped to her knees and wept alongside her furry friends.

Thwack gently scooped the sobbing trio up into his massive arms and hugged them against his warm belly. "I'm so very sorry, Shoenia. If I hadn't pranked so much, then perhaps you could have believed me and we would have eluded capture. This is all my fault."

Shoenia snuggled tightly into the big guy's warm embrace. She could feel the beat of his troubled heart. "Xebec already knew we were coming, Thwack. Besides, you're not to blame for his madness. We are not at all responsible for the poor conduct of others. If such were the case, none of us could ever nap at ease. Isn't that right, you two?"

Both smuzzles nodded their short snouts.

"Thwack?"

"Yeah?"

"Didn't your parents ever learn you the tale of the ladfolk who hollered howlpack?"

"Shoenia, my parents met Morgue when I was still a tot."

Shoenia stared up into Thwack's eye. "Then who reared you?"

"My Uncle Tipler, I guess? Well, sort of?"

Shoenia sensed Thwack's discomfort, yet elected to pry anyway. "What do you mean by, sort of?"

"Uncle Tippler didn't much like me. Or much like anyone else for that matter. Not even himself. He just wanted to guzzle his jabber juice and yell a lot. Do you know of jabber juice, Shoenia?"

"Shoenia sighed. "Oh yes. I don't much care for it."

"Me either," Thwack said. "Although, I do suppose for many it is okay to drink it. Just not for my Uncle Tipler. He wasn't a bad clops when he was in his right mind, but once he'd popped the plug from his jug nobody could ever tell what he was going to do next? Especially not him. And he popped the plug lots."

"You must have had some friends, though?"

"Naw. I was big and clumsy. All the young clops called me Cyclod. And cygals always giggled and pointed at me."

Shoenia hesitated before delving deeper. "What did you do whenever your Uncle Tipler started into his jug?"

Thwack averted his eye in shame. "I did what any young clops would do, Shoenia. I hid and pretended I was someplace else. And that I was somebody else. I made myself believe things were not as they were. Over time, dwelling in dreams became my jabber juice and I struggled to tell the so from the not so. I eventually ran away for good and became a loner. You know, Shoenia, there's a funny thing about running away..."

"What is it?" Shoenia pressed.

Thwack sighed heavily before responding. "...once we start, it can be very hard to stop."

Shoenia was unsure of what she should say next, so she decided not to press the big guy any further. She recalled Snarly's advice: *'I know you are prone to speak what you think, but from now on you must think what you speak. And especially think of to whom you do speak it. Words have power. And consequences. Which is why a wise grown-up never wastes words.'* Instead of pressing the matter even further, the maturing galfolk simply kissed Thwack on his cheek.

The vulnerable giant merely blushed.

"Do you want to know what I think, Thwack?" she asked after a bit.

"What, Shoenia?"

"I think that the real Thwack is a kind, gentle, caring guy who's terrified somebody might find out who he really is and then hurt him quite badly. I do hope to spend more time getting to know that Thwack."

Thwack blushed again. "I've never had any real friends before."

Shoenia and the smuzzles snuggled in even tighter. "Well, now you have three. Four counting Tiptin. Stop behaving like such a smarty and you'll even meet that special cygal as well. Just be real. Trust me, we gals know it when you're not being real."

Thwack patted her head. "Don't fret, Shoenia. He will save us."

"Who?"

"Tiptin, of course."

"I so hope he's safe?"

"He will come for sure. I know so because he is in love with you."

The galfolk lifted her head. "Oh? And just how would you know that?"

Thwack grinned. "Simple. Whenever he watches you, he gets that look. And he watches you aaah-lot."

"Oh?" Shoenia was intrigued. "What type of look?"

"The exact same type of look you get when you watch him," Thwack noted, while stretching his grin. "Which you also do aaah-lot."

Now it was Shoenia's turn to blush.

7
Gaffwit's Boo-Boo

A giggling figure tossed and turned on his floating mattress, slowly returning from a twisted chuckle-nap. His hands groped through both blankets and quilt, seeking the shaft of his most prized possession. But without success?

Two panicked eyes snapped alert. Instantly, Xebec jerked himself up into a frenzy and frantically yanked all cloth from the mattress, aimlessly flinging it over the side. Nothing?

Scrambling down to the floor, he checked under the mattress. Still nothing? Stricken with panic, he leapt to his feet and scanned the entire bedchamber. *'Strange? Why is my door ajar?'*

His racing mind struggled hard to recall. Yes, of course he had placed the staff down beside himself. He always did so whenever he napped. Always. And he had most definitely shut the door to his bedchamber. That he would never forget. Somebody had surely stolen the staff while he napped. *'But who would dare to do such a deed?'*

"Think. Think. Think. Hmmmmm?.... dung! GAFFWIT!!"

* * *

However, Gaffwit was no longer anywhere near the castle. Instead, the simple boorlee was out arm-swinging about the heavily forested glen at the seaside base of the plateau. His singing voice mixed with the shwooshing crash of breakers assaulting the nearby shore. "Dooz gots staff! Dooz gots staff! Me dooz be Ruler, cuzz me dooz gots staff! Dooz gots staff! Dooz gots staff! Me dooz be Ruler, cuzz me…huh??"

The carefree boorlee suddenly froze in surprise. He vigorously shook his head to refocus. No, his eyes and mind were not playing tricks on him. Mere strides away, perched atop a boulder, stood a tall and lanky grandfolk in a blue robe and a pointy red hat.

"Well, hello there. Grand bright for a stroll through the forest, don't you think?" asked the grandfolk.

"Me thinks some. Who dooz ye be?" Gaffwit inquired, cocking his head to leer low on trust. "Dooz come ye eyes not be same colour?"

"Oh, but I am your friend," replied the stranger, floating down to touch soil quite close to Gaffwit. "My eyes are as Seed made them. One cannot control what colour one's eyes are any more than one can control the shape of one's ears."

"Stops!" screamed the suspicious boorlee, taking aim with the staff. "Or me dooz blasts ye with staff!"

Zebu smiled and palmed up. "But I have no weapon. See."

"What dooz pink stick thingy be, huh?" Gaffwit asked.

Zebu glanced down at the pink wand sticking out from his pouch. "You mean this silly old thing? It's – well, it's a – but what does it really matter anyway, my dear friend? I mean you no harm."

"Me thinks ye fibs."

"I wasn't hiding on you, was I?"

"No, ye not hides."

"And I don't look cuckoo like the sorcerer, do I?"

"No. Ruler Xebec dooz be boink." To stress his point, Gaffwit wound a forefinger about his ear.

"There then. I did not try to hide on you and I am not boink. That proves I am honest and you can trust me. Might I get a closer look at that unusual – uh, stick thingy in your hand?"

"Stick thingy dooz be magic staff."

"Ohhh, a magic staff. Could I possibly hold it?"

"Uh-uh. Ye not spozed dooz hold staff."

"Why not?"

"Um, cuzz."

"Because why?"

"Cuzz me thinks ye dooz be big fibber. Staff!"

"Whoa! Careful where you point that thing, my dear friend…"

"We not be budz?"

Zebu nearly lost his composure. "Just give me the dung…. uh, I mean, just grant me a chance to eat some citrus pulpy and then I'll be on my way."

"Citrus pulpy?"

"Oh yes. Citrus pulpy tastes better than most anything. Mmmmmm..."

"Even tastes beddar dooz desserts?"

"Oh, it tastes much better than desserts. Would you care to try some?"

Gaffwit remained skeptical. "Um, dooz ye lets me sees citrus pulpy?"

"Certainly. I'll show it to you." Zebu said, reaching for his wand.

"Stops! Staff!"

"Whoa! Careful there, friend. I just need my tap tool to halve the pulpy. That's all. And would you mind pointing that staff away from me?"

"Um, okay. But ye not try dooz tricks."

"No tricks," Zebu assured the suspicious boorlee while slowly removing his wand. He dipped a wrinkled hand deep into his pouch and procured a strange oval fruit with green rind. Next, he sniffed at the rind as if to savour its aroma. "Ahhhhh, it even smells better than desserts."

"Smells beddar dooz desserts?"

"It smells much better than desserts," Zebu assured him, tapping his wand to the green skin. Immediately, the oval fruit split into two perfectly equal halves.

"Huh? How ye dooz that?"

The master magician wanted to roll his eyes. "Cycles of practice, my dear friend. Many cycles of practice." He pouched the wand to free up both of his hands, and then held out both halves for the curious boorlee to inspect.

Gaffwit leaned towards the stringy fruit. "Citrus pulpy be juicy, huh?"

"Ah, it is. And the juice is delish. Mmmmmm..."

"Citrus pulpy gots lots seeds too, huh?"

"Yes. And the seeds taste yummy like candy. Mmmmmm..."

"Seeds tastes yummy like candy?"

"Mmmmmm..." Zebu enticed, smacking his lips. "Most yummy."

"Ye sez juice tastes beddar dooz desserts?"

"I wasn't hiding on you, was I?"

"Um, no. Ye not hides."

"And I don't look boink, do I?"

"No, ye not looks boink."

"Then smell this fruit for yourself," Zebu urged, extending his arms. "After all, what can one little sniff hurt?"

"Um, me sniffs citrus pulpy cuzz ye not hides. And ye not looks boink like Ruler Xebec dooz."

Zebu smirked with laughing eyes as Gaffwit leaned lower to sniff the pulpy. Then, at the very instant when the trusting boorlee's eyes came within reach, the mean magician shoved one half of the fruit into each of his victim's eye sockets and squeezed tight the rind. The fruit's sour juice squirted out in abundance.

"Ow! Ow! Ow! Ow!" Gaffwit screamed as the juice stung into his eyes. He dropped the staff and buried his face in his palms. "Juice dooz stings eyes! Me not sees! Me not sees! Me not sees! Dooz stings eyes! Me not sees!"

Zebu chuckled as he snatched up the staff. "You boorleez certainly aren't the sharpest sticks in the woods, are you? Ha! Now whose eyes are the issue."

"Ye fibs," Gaffwit whined, trying to rub the burning pain from his watery eyes. "Not fair!"

"Fair is for losers!" Zebu snapped back as he strode away with his new prize.

"Dooz stings eyes! Pleeze helps! Me not sees! Pleeze helps! Pleeze..."

Zebu responded to Gaffwit's frantic and frightened pleas for help by taking careful aim with the staff. "Staff, amuse me!" he commanded.

"OOOWWW!!"

A shrill scream filled the forest as a terrified boorlee crashed his way through thick bush with his bare butt burnt black, struggling to sight through his pain and tears.

8

Hugs And Tagles

Unseen hands parted a peep hole in a thick bush, while spying, brown eyes cautiously studied the pink limestone castle lying directly before them. Slowly, the eyes shifted to scan along the castle's walls, noting in detail the location of each turret, rampart, arch, loop, corner and angle. Then they locked onto the curved shell of the structure's solitary tower and traced up its wall to a brattice near its peak, where an open archway suggested a possible way in?

Satisfied that they had seen all that mattered, the spying eyes pulled back and the peep hole rustled shut.

"Well?" The Sheebazz inquired, hovering before Tiptin's face. "What do you think of my scouts' reports?"

Tiptin rubbed his chin. "Hmmmmm. And your scouts are absolutely certain it was Xebec himself who flew from the castle?"

The Sheebazz frowned sarcastic. "Riding a winged beast? Black cloak and skullcap? Frail? Glumdreary? Scowl? Staring off into madness? Screaming cusses like a loony spun completely round-the-twist..."

"Okay. Okay. I'm sorry I doubted them. But why then didn't Xebec have the staff? He would never part with it. He would even bathe with it. That is, assuming one so mad as he even bathes at all?"

"Stumps me?" The Sheebazz answered, along with a shrug.

"Maybe he just forgot it?" Pint Little suggested. "His mind is quite mushy."

"Or maybe he broke it?" another weetyke proposed.

"Or broke it!!" echoed the chorus.

"Zippit!" The Sheebazz scolded. "Do you want the boorleez to find us and catch Tiptin too?"

An army of teeny helmets shook that they did not.

"No more sudden outbursts then. None. Nadda. Zero. Zilch."

"Sorry, Sheebazz..." whispered the chorus.

"No," Tiptin reasoned, "Xebec may be madder than a frothing howler, but he would never part with the staff. It has been his binding obsession for far too long. It rules over both his mind and his soul. Something has happened?"

"Like what?" The Sheebazz asked.

"That, my tiny friends, is exactly what we must find out. Hmmm...? Your scouts are positive that the only way to get me inside the castle is through that tower archway?"

"Unless you want to stroll across the drawbridge and knock on the door, it is. All of the other options were either shuttered tight or too small for you to slip through."

Tiptin looked to Pint Little. "And you are absolutely certain that you checked out every option?"

Pint Little nodded. "We scouted really good, Tiptin. Honest. We spied for all of Night's time. There are many ways we weetykes can sneak into the castle, yet there is only one way in for you."

Tiptin's tone was fraught with gratitude. "I know that you and your scouts did well, Pint Little, and at great risk to yourselves. I am most grateful for your courage. Still, I fear greatly for Shoenia and the others. Who knows what...?"

"Sheebazz! Sheebazz!"

All sights set upon an incoming weetyke with wided eyes.

"Sheebazz! Shee...."

"Zippit," cautioned The Sheebazz.

"Zippit!!" echoed the chorus.

Tiptin extended a landing palm for the excited weetyke.

"What is it, Mite Diver?" The Sheebazz inquired in a cross tone. "And where have you been?"

Being thoroughly exhausted from his frantic flight, Mite Diver sat down on the ladfolk's palm and gasped to fill his breathers. "I – I was catched prisoner by a – by a boorlee..."

"Mite was catched by a boorlee!!"

The Sheebazz stared the chorus mute as she allowed the puffing scout a chance to catch his breath before pressing for an explanation. "What do you mean you were caught by a boorlee?"

Mite Diver stood up to explain. "I was spying on some guards who were talking about 'prizners', when a sneaky boorlee catched me like this." He cupped his palms and clapped them together with a pop.

"Wow wa la…" whispered the chorus, trying to tone it down.

"But how did you escape?" Tiptin asked.

"Yes, how?" The Sheebazz pressed.

"I tricked him," Miter Diver explained, using hand gestures to demonstrate. "I told him I knew a big secret. After he promised not to tell anyone, I told him to lower his face so I could whisper it. When he did, I *stickem!*"

"Wow wa la..."

"I do hope you minded the poor boorlee's eyes?" Tiptin stated with much concern.

"Oh, I'd never *stickem* in eyes. I *stickem* in fat nose!"

"Shhhh. Speak softly, Mite Diver."

"Sorry, Sheebazz."

"Don't be sorry, just lower your voice. Now, what were the guards saying about prisoners?"

"Sheebazz, the guards said the prisoners are being kept in a place called a dungeon?"

Tiptin was visibly alarmed. "In a dungeon?"

Mite Diver nodded. "Uh-huh."

"You know the meaning of such?" The Sheebazz asked.

Tiptin nodded. "Dungeons are dark and dankly places beneath castles. Bad things happen there. We must get them out – fast."

"How?" Pint Little asked. "The moat is filled with shelled snappers and finned biters, and the only way for you to get inside is high up on that tower?"

"Hmmm?" Tiptin commenced pacing back and forth. "There must be a way?"

"Why don't we just fly you up?" Mite Diver suggested.

"Why don't we just fly you up!?" shouted the chorus.

The frustrated Sheebazz simply hung her shaking head and thought, *'I give up.'*

"Thank you, Mite Diver" Tiptin replied, fondly. "Your heart is indeed precious. Unfortunately, I am much too heavy for you to lift,"

"Not me," Mite Diver corrected him. "*We*. Sometimes after a windy storm, we weetykes combine our might to lift broken tree branches up from the forest floor."

"Yes, we do!" Pint Little concurred most excitedly.

"Shush. Softly, Pint Little. How many times do I have to tell you?"

"Sorry, Sheebazz."

Tiptin was puzzled. "Whyever would you weetykes need to lift branches up from the forest floor? "

The Sheebazz giggled. "To defend our twig shelters from boorleez, we drop branches onto their thick skulls before we swarm-bomb to *stickem*. Tee-hee"

"That's what really riles them nasty," Pint Little mused. "Especially when they get conked by a biggy. Not one near so big as Thwack's club, though. All of us weetykes together could never lift that."

"May not be a problem," Tiptin said. "I am much lighter than the big guy's club."

"Then what are we all hovering about for?" The Sheebazz noted. "Let's go."

"Let's go!!"

"Zippit!"

"Sorry, Sheebazz..."

After depositing their shields into frond sacks, the weetykes swarmed all over the nervous ladfolk. Each brandished a thorn sword in one hand, while gripping a piece of Tiptin's garments in the other. Except for The Sheebazz, and those that were tasked with transporting the sacks of shields, every single weetyke was assigned to help transport their large ally up to the tower's brattice. So many, in fact, that the ladfolk was barely noticeable save for his boots and face.

"Fly-march ho!" Pint Little ordered.

"Fly-march ho!!"

"Seriously?"

"Sorry, Sheebazz..."

With a group grunt, a dark mass rose up from amongst the bushes and advanced upon the castle. Some eyes kept watch below for boorleez, while others scanned above for squawkers.

Tiptin bated his breath and closed his eyes. Unlike his flight with Hoot through the blackness of The Baobabs, here he could clearly see the ground. Thus, he knew exactly how far he would fall.

But fall he did not, for the tiny hands gripping his garments refused to fail him. Nor did the many droning wings, which blew blasts of brisk breeze as they fluttered hard up into a climb. Not one puffing weetyke surrendered the struggle. Proving that it's not the size of *a* weetyke that matters; but the will of *the* weetykes.

Upon finally reaching their objective, the feisty flyfolk gently lowered the ladfolk down onto the tower's brattice. There they touched down for a well earned rest.

Tiptin turned to Pint Little. "When Xebec and the winged beast flew from the courtyard, which way did they go?"

"Down there," she replied, pointing to the heavily forested glen at the seaside base of the plateau.

The ladfolk frowned. "That takes in a lot of area, Pint Little. Do you know whereabouts down there?"

"Uh-uh. We chose to stick with our mission and find a way to get you into the castle. Did we do wrong, Tiptin?"

"Oh no. Not at all." Tiptin reassured her with a smile. "In fact, you and your scouts did the right thing."

"We did?"

"Of course. It should be much easier to rescue our friends with the sorcerer gone. We can deal with him later."

"I still don't understand why the sworcerer didn't have the staff?" The Sheebazz put in. "It is strange."

"Very strange," Tiptin concurred.

"Sworcerer sure was riled up real nasty," one of the weetyke scouts noted.

Tiptin was curious. "Riled up? Riled up about what?"

"He was madly mad," confirmed another. "Sworcerer kept cussing bad words and swinging his fists at the wind. But the wind won the fight."

An entire army gaffed into giggles.

"Zippit! There may very well be boorleez about. Collect your shields and prepare to wing out. Keep your swords at the point and your wits on the quick. This is no time for games and giggles. I swear by Seed that I must have done something to offend either her or Destiny. Or both? "

"Yes, Sheebazz..."

Tiptin knew that The Sheebazz was right, for time did not favour them one bit. Still, he was intrigued. "Pint, what exactly was Xebec cussing about?"

Pint Little shrugged. "I'm not too sure, really. The only words that I could make out that I can repeat are Gaffwit and Morgue. Everything else was all cussing or cuckoo gibberish." She wound a forefinger about her ear. "And I mean reeeeeal cuckoo."

"Hmmmmm, interesting." Tiptin tightened his grip on the hilt, and the fibre blade pulsed to a shimmer. "Anyway, The Sheebazz is right. We have virtually no more time to waste."

With his blade readied before him, Tiptin stepped through the archway and on into the tower. There he froze with wided eyes and tangled tongue as he took in the spinny spectacle unfolding before them.

The startled ladfolk had entered a bedchamber unlike anything he had ever seen. A solitary mattress floated above a scattered mess of bedding. Two chests with short legs and hooves, along with a spindly table, all trembled against the furthest wall, while a cheeky chair challenged the humanfolk intruder by landing him a severe shin kicking!

"Ow!" Tiptin yelped, high-stepping to escape the bruising blows. "Ow! Hey! Ow! Stop it! We don't mean to... Ouch!"

"Charge!!"

Stickem! Stickem! Stickem! Stickem!"

An army of tiny flyfolk set upon the wooden attacker, jabbing at its seat and back. Undaunted, the cheeky chair kept up its relentless assault, gradually backing its dancing victim tight into a corner.

"Ouch! Look out, troops, I'm going to chop it! Ow!"

"Look out, he's going to chop it!!"

"Aiyeee!" screamed the cheeky chair as Tiptin's first blow severed a leg. Warning flames flared forth from the fibre blade.

"YIKES!" shrieked the frightened furnishings huddled against the far wall, while the table turned and bolted for the door.

"SMASH!!"

Splinters scattered as the terrified table bashed free of the bedchamber. It galloped to the end of a short corridor, before crashing and stumbling its way down a spiraled stairwell. Two shrieking chests clopped after it, while a charred chair hobbled along beneath a fleeing mattress. Wiggly blankets and a slithering quilt took up the rear.

After all the clopping and clatter had faded off into the distance, Tiptin warily poked his head out into the corridor.

"All clear?" The Sheebazz inquired, landing upon Tiptin's shoulder.

"Can't really say in this creepy place," he remarked with a shudder.

The Sheebazz smiled and brushed some long locks from her face. "Kinda freaky, huh?"

"It is that." Tiptin stepped softly out into the corridor, and then paused briefly before sneaking over to the stairwell. He was aware of the drone of wee wings at his back.

"Should I dispatch a scout?" The Sheebazz asked.

Tiptin nodded his approval.

The Sheebazz motioned to Mite Diver, and the obedient spy zipped off down the stairwell. She spoke in a soothing tone. "Don't fret, Tiptin, we've battled big boorleez before. We will rescue your friends."

Tiptin was warmed by the courage of his tiny ally and her subjects, not a single one of which showed even the slightest inkling to flee. He wished that he could somehow put their tiny hearts into the bodies of humanfolk a hundred times their size. The thought of these wee warriors in tipnut helmets, all poised to tangle with an enormous enemy, nearly moved him to weep. And it may well have, had he not redirected his sights down the stairwell.

Only a few moments elapsed before Mite Diver zipped around a corner and back up the stairwell. His eyes were wided with worry and his tongue got tangled up in his speech.

The Sheebazz took hold of his shoulders and gently shook him towards calm. "Breath deeply and lower your voice, Mite Diver. And do unscramble your thoughts before you speak. Thus far, we have not understood a single word from your lips."

Mite Diver inhaled deeply to tone down his zeal. "Sheebazz, I saw a bunch of boorleez."

"Whisper, Mite Diver. Now, where are they?"

"Whisper!! Where are they!?" echoed the chorus.

If her glare had been words, The Sheebazz spoke harshly and articulated well beyond the creative...

'....silence....'

"They are arm-swinging up a wiggly tunnel," Mite diver explained.

"He means they're approaching through a winding corridor," The Sheebazz explained.

"Does this wiggly tunnel lead directly to this stairwell?" Tiptin inquired with noted concern.

Mite Diver shook his head and parted his arms to the max. "Uh-uh. A big hollow lies in between. Biggest hollow that..."

"Quiet," The Sheebazz interjected. "I hear voices down below?"

"Quiet..." whispered the chorus.

It was true. Approaching voices could be heard coming from around the corner at the bottom of the stairwell.

"Shmash dooz be more strong than ye, Belch."

"Uh-uh."

"Uh-huh. Him dooz be muches more strong."

"Uh-uh. Me zings things more far than Shmash dooz."

"Tiptin?" whispered The Sheebazz.

"What?"

"Perhaps we should hide out on the brattice just in case some boorleez come up here? If they find us, we might not be able to rescue the others."

Tiptin briefly pondered her suggestion, while the argument down below quickly boiled over into a shouting match.

"Dooz too!"

"Dooz not!"

"Dooz too!"

"Not!"

"Too!"

"Not!"

"Too so!"

"Not so!"

"Too! Too! Too!"

"Not! Not! Not!"

"Too so! Too so! Too so!"

"Not so! Not so! Not..."

Lowering his own voice to barely a whisper, Tiptin shared his thoughts with The Sheebazz. He put forth a simple strategy.

The Sheebazz returned him an agreeing nod, and then started using hand signals to relay orders to her army.

With his shimmering blade leading the way, the determined ladfolk started sneaking down the steps with Mite Diver, Pint Little and The Sheebazz all perched upon his shoulders. The remaining weetykes took flight behind them. All were tense, but quite willing to do battle if necessary.

The heated argument quickly erupted into a direct challenge.

"Ye proves it!"

"Me dooz proves it! We zings things!"

"What things?"

"Umm - okay, we zings Taddler!"

"Not fair! Why ye always zings me!?"

"Cuzz ye always snitches."

"Not always."

"Yes, always. Ye snitched that ole Schnozzy dooz peeks at Ruler Xebec's web thingy. Him gots scolds cuzz ye snitches!"

"And worse!"

"Me only snitches cuzz we not spozed peek at Ruler Xebec's.... huh?"

"Huh? Dooz ye sees...?"

Every boorlee dropped their jaws in confusion as an army of thorn-wielding weetykes poured into the spacious chamber. The wee warriors split ranks and encircled their surprised foe. A confident ladfolk came striding across the floor towards the boorleez, wielding a shimmering blade and carrying a trio of tiny comrades on his shoulders.

"Stops!" commanded a boorlee.

"What are you doing?" Tiptin calmly asked as some of the frightened boorleez nervously brandished their bats.

"Um, we dooz *fites?*" one of the boorleez meekly replied with marked uncertainty.

"Don't you boorleez know that fighting is wrong?" Tiptin asked. "Somebody could get hurt."

The boorleez traded muddled glances.

"But we spozed dooz fites," another boorlee stated, shrugging his broad shoulders.

"We dooz be foes," added yet another.

"Yes," Tiptin concurred, "We are indeed foes. Which is why we have taken all of you prisoner."

"Dooz come we be prizners, huh? This be Ruler Xebec's castle?"

Tiptin huffed heavily. Obviously these elite boorleez were the brightest of the breed, so he knew that he really had his work cut out for him this time. "Look, did we not see you boorleez first?"

The baffled boorleez once again traded muddled glances. Then they all shrugged and replied as one. "Ye doozed."

"And do we not have you completely surrounded?"

"Huh?"

"Dooz ladfolk sez?"

"I mean, do we not have you trapped?"

All the boorleez looked about.

"Ye dooz."

"Then have we not in fact captured you?"

Every boorlee was completely befuddled. Touching forefingers to temples, they squinted and tried very hard to think. *'????????????'* Thinking, of course, never being one of their stronger suits.

Taking advantage of the boorleez' confusion, Tiptin tactfully piled on the pressure. "And do we not have swords?"

"Ye dooz."

"And shields?"

"Ye dooz."

Plus we also have you greatly outnumbered, right?"

'????????????????????????'

"Let's just nix that question. But we are an army, are we not?"

"Um? Uh-huh. Ye dooz be."

"And are you not then trapped by our army?"

The boorleez were well beyond lost?

"Which means we have captured you, correct?"

"Um? Sez dooz captoored mean?"

"Captured means caught. Have we not caught you then?"

The boorleez still looked lost, prompting The Sheebazz to come to Tiptin's aid. "Caught means catched. Have we not catched you?"

A bunch of thick skulls nodded that they had.

"Well then, if we have catched you, does that not make you our prisoners?" the Sheebazz reasoned.

Every boorlee nodded to agree.

"Dooz."

"But proper prisoners are not supposed to carry bats, are they?" the Sheebazz asked.

The boorleez all hung their heads. Apparently being proper prisoners was just the latest thing that they couldn't *dooz* right.

"So, why are you prisoners still carrying bats?" Tiptin pressed.

"Prizners not spozed dooz carry bats," one boorlee conceded while dropping his bat to the floor.

"Dooz pologize," offered another, likewise dropping his bat. "Me dooz beddar prizner stuff."

"Me dooz beddar prizner stuff too," assured another boorlee as his bat also bonked to the floor.

Mumbling mixed with the hollow sound of wood bonking onto stone as each and every boorlee apologized profusely for his poor prizner performance and promised to 'do beddar prizner stuff'. In no time flat, bats littered the floor; hence, another bleedless battle was thankfully averted.

"Alright," Tiptin continued, "Put your hands on your heads and interlock your fingers."

"????????????????????????"

"Let's nix that as well. Just hold your hands up as high as you can reach. And I'm warning you prisoners right now, try any tricks and the weetykes will untie your loincloths!"

"Huh?"

"Me thinks ladfolk sez weetykes dooz untie boorleez gacheez?"

"Uh, yes. I meant the weetykes will untie your – er, gacheez."

"Yeah!!" tenored the chorus, thrusting their thorns in a most menacing manner. "*Stickem! Stickem! Stickem! Stickem!* Poke em in the nose, but be careful of the eyes! *Stickem! Stickem! Stickem! Stickem!* Jab em in the butt, and in between the thighs!"

The boorleez all shuddered and squeezed their knees together. Only one big boorlee dared to speak up. "Gulp. We not dooz tricks, ladfolk. Pledges."

"Pledges," concurred the others, clunking skulls to seal it.

"You there," Tiptin said, pointing to the big boorlee who had dared to speak up. "What is your name?"

"M-Me?" responded one very frightened boorlee.

"Yes, you. What is your name? Speak up."

"Me name dooz be Shmash."

"Shmash what?"

"????"

"And we'll nix that question as well. But Shmash, I do have some other questions to ask you…"

"Counts questions?" the trembling boorlee asked with noted concern. His skinny legs began to bend beneath his bulk.

"No counting questions," Tiptin assured him.

All of the boorleez exhaled a collective sigh of relief.

"These are simple questions, Shmash. They only need simple answers. Still, if you fib, The Sheebazz will command her weetykes to start scolding all of you."

"And they will do it too," The Sheebazz concurred in her strictest tone.

"Me not sez fibs!" Shmash exclaimed defensively. "Me not be fibber!"

"Uh-uh," vouched another boorlee. "Shmash not be fibber. Taddler dooz be fibber."

"Me not dooz be fibber!" Taddler railed in his own defence; while virtually every other boorlee nodded that he was.

"That dooz be fib, Taddler. Ye dooz too be fibber."

"Not! Not! Not!"

"Too. Too. Too."

"Not! Not!..."

"Enough!" Tiptin cut in. "Dearest Destiny. I sincerely apologize to Shmash. I had no cause to question your – uh, integrity."

"Huh? Dooz ye sez, ladfolk?"

"He says that he trusts you," The Sheebazz explained, while trying with limited success to stifle a smile.

Shmash beamed proud and began bragging to his jealous mates. "Ladfolk trusts me. Him sezzed."

"We *heered* him, Mr. Stinks Feets."

"Me feets not stinks!"

"Dooz!!" all shouted out at once, including the weetykes.

"Dooz not!"

"Dooz too!!"

"Dooz not!"

"Whooaa!" Frustration was fast beginning to take charge of Tiptin's tone. "We really don't have any time to waste. None at all. So, perhaps you boorleez could resume behaving like proper prisoners? Please."

"Ooops. We dooz pologize."

"We dooz beddar prizner stuff."

Tiptin sucked in a deep breath and rolled his eyes. "Okay, then. Now, where were we? Hmmmmm...? Now, I forget!"

"Questions," Pint Little reminded him.

"Do allow for their very short attention span," The Sheebazz added in a whisper. "Respect their minds, or lose yours."

Turning back to Shmash, Tiptin continued asking questions in their most simplified form. "Shmash, why did Ruler Xebec fly off without the staff?"

"Ruler Xebec seeks Gaffwit," Shmash replied, smugly gloating at the other boorleez. Clearly, he was feeling quite special at having been chosen to answer Tiptin's question.

"And just who or what is a Gaffwit?" Tiptin pressed.

"Gaffwit be Ruler Xebec's best boob," responded the boorlee named Belch.

"Uh-uh. Gaffwit not be best boob," Taddler disputed. "Him not be Ruler Xebec's best boob no more cuzz of him dooz scoffed staff."

It was readily apparent that the other boorleez had no intention of letting Shmash answer all of the questions and snatch away all of the glory.

"Belch shook his head in sympathy. "Taddler fibs muches, but him not fibs always. Me not ever heered Ruler Xebec dooz so loud screams. Gaffwit dooz gets scolds bad now. And worse."

All of the other boorleez bit their upper lips and nodded with wided eyes in support of Belch's claim.

The Sheebazz shared a puzzled stare with Tiptin before fluttering closer to the boorleez. Hovering in place before them, she took over asking the questions. "Shmash, are you saying that this Gaffwit has taken the staff?"

Shmash nodded. "Uh-huh. Him dooz scoffed staff when Ruler Xebec snoozes."

"Do you know where the sworcerer hides his webscroll?" The Sheebazz pressed.

Feeling left out again, the other boorleez began cutting into the conversation.

"Not hides. Ruler Xebec keeps web thingy in cloak always," Munch explained.

"Keeps in cloak now cuzz ole Schnozzy peeked at web thingy," Belch added.

"We not spozed touches Ruler Xebec's web thingy," Taddler warned. "Not ever."

All the other boorleez nodded to concur.

The Sheebazz was just about to ask about Shoenia and the others, when suddenly two unsuspecting kooky critters came romping into the chamber. Both critters froze and gulped down large lumps of *whoops* as they took in the situation. Then they grinned out a silent *'oh-oh'* and tried slowly backing out into the corridor from whence they had just come.

They never made it. An alert unit of weetykes swooped down to block off their route of escape. Brandishing their sharp thorns to show they meant business, the tiny flyfolk then shooed the kooky critters over to join the boorleez.

"Pleeze not hurts critters," Shmash pleaded. "Critters looks mean, but them dooz be big fradies."

"We don't want to hurt anyone," The Sheebazz assured the boorleez. "What we do want is for you to take us to see our friends. Please."

"Ye budz be kept in dungeon."

"We know that, Shmash," Tiptin said. "What we do not know is how we get down into the dungeon. So, we want you to take us there."

The boorleez swapped puzzled looks.

"What's wrong?" The Sheebazz asked.

Belch spoke up. "How we spozed dooz arm-swings to dungeon with arms reaches to sky?"

The Sheebazz smiled. "Smart catch, Belch. Since you're all being such good and proper prisoners, you may now lower your arms and put your knuckles back down on the floor."

"Ye sez we boorleez dooz be good prizners?" Shmash asked, somewhat in disbelief at their having been called good at anything.

"Yes, you boorleez are the best prisoners ever," Mite Diver assured them.

"HOORRAY!!"

"NOOGIE!! NOOGIE!! NOOGIE!! NOOGGIE!!......"

After the elated boorleez had finally finished congratulating one another with a rousing round of grats noogies for actually being the best at something, they arm-swung with purpose into the winding corridor. Each tried extra hard to be a proper *prizner*, keeping their chins up and arm-swinging in time. They certainly were a proud and delighted bunch. Even the kooky critters picked up on the positive vibe and pranced alongside the boorleez with equal pride and purpose.

Tiptin and the weetykes escorted their beaming prisoners through the long and winding corridor that gradually descended in stages. They were curious about its many scorched wall paintings; yet, they did not seek to ask who bore the blame for such senseless damage. They already knew.

Just prior to exiting into a charred courtyard, they veered off into another corridor that led them to a narrow, winding stairwell. Smoke from wall torches weeped their eyes as they coped with the slippery steps. A grimy wall, both moist and mouldy, bounded them on one side. The other side offered up a drop straight down to the bottom.

By and by, the stairwell ended and they paraded across a dirty floor until they reached an iron door.

"Where dooz keys be, Taddler?" Shmash demanded to know.

"Keys be here, Shmash," Taddler nervously replied. He then produced an iron ring and started fumbling through the keys. Finally, he stuck one into the lock, but it would not turn. "Huh?"

"What's wrong?" Pint Little inquired.

"Ha!" Taddler blurted. "Door be open. Shmash forgets dooz turn lock. Guffaw!"

"Ye gots keys, Taddler. Ye spozed dooz locks door!" Shmash protested.

"Uh-uh. Ye shutted door. Ye spozed locks."

Shmash shook his head in his own defense. "Uh-uh."

Taddler nodded. "Uh-huh."

"Uh-uh."

"Uh-huh."

"Uh-uh."

"Uh-huh."

"Uh-uh."

"Uh-h…."

"Who cares!" Tiptin shouted, wildly flailing his arms about. "Just open the dung door!"

"Not plite sez bad words," Munch pointed out.

"Please," begged one very frustrated ladfolk. "We can hold my trial later. I'll even plead guilty. But for now, please just open the door."

"Huh? Dooz him sez?"

All the boorleez exchanged puzzled looks and shrugs before Taddler moved to open the door.

"AAAAAAAAAAAAARRRGH!!!!" An enormous green bulk lunged out and overwhelmed several bewildered boorleez with one timely tackle. They all landed together in a tangled heap of thrashing limbs.

"Eeeeeeee!" wailed a kooky critter as sharp, pointy teeth chomped into its tail. Wriggling free of the grappling pile, it scurried to hide behind Mite Diver.

"Stops grabs me face, ye greeny gooberschnozz!"

"Gets off me, ye clopsy nubskull!"

"Run, Shoenia! I'll hold them off!"

"Uh, Thwack…"

"Ouch! Stops squeezes me face! Not fare!"

"Go on, Shoenia! Don't fret about me! Just save yourselves!"

"Oh, Thwaaak. Yoo-hoo. Scrap the plan."

"I got this burly bunch – all – wrapped – up...?" The giant blushed purple as he took in his surroundings. "Gulp. Hee, hee. Hi ya, Tiptin. Uh – harr?"

"Ow! Me sezzed stops squeezes me face, ye boinky clops!"

"Oh, I am terribly sorry about all that. Hee, hee. Here, have your face back. My apologies for any gouges. Harr?"

"Gets off me!"

"Certainly." Thwack released all of his victims and pressed to his feet. Still blushing purple, he simply parted his massive arms. "Whoops."

Tiptin cupped Shoenia's cheeks and stared deep into her welcoming eyes. "Are you well?"

Shoenia merely nodded and snuggled tight into his arms.

After a warm hug, Shoenia realized that every single boorlee was hanging his head in shame. Pulling free of Tiptin, she addressed the somber bunch. "Why all the long faces? You never wanted to put us in the dungeon. I know you didn't. And it was really sweet of you to hide fruit and nuts and quilts for us. And to break the stretching rack."

Shmash raised his head to expose trickles of tears trickling trails down his cheeks. "We not wants put ye in dungeon, but Ruler Xebec sez. Cuzz ye scaped, Ruler Xebec dooz to scolds boorleez."

"And worse," added the boorlee named Munch.

"Yes, I know and worse," Shoenia said. "But how and worse?"

"Him – Him…"

"He what?" Shoenia pressed. "What does that brute do to you?"

After some strong silence, Shmash finally solved the mystery. "Ruler Xebec dooz sez us names."

"He calls you names?"

Tiptin thought, *'That's it? That's the worse? Ya gotta be kidding me?'*

"What types of names?" Shoenia wanted to know.

The boorleez all hung their heads.

"What names?" Shoenia pressed.

"Dense," one put out.

"Stoopid," added another.

"Sez we dooz be loozers."

"Him sez critters dooz be erpulsive."

"Oh, Xebec does, does he? And he even calls your pets repulsive?"

The boorleez nodded their heads.

Shoenia was visibly irate. "That's not very nice. Names can really hurt, sometimes even worse than blows. And bruised skin can often times heal much faster than bruised feelings. That is why we must always think of who is saying these mean things to us. Even when it is somebody who is *spun tight in a twist*."

The boorleez cocked their heads and scrunched their brows in confusion.

Shoenia clarified, "Xebec dooz be boink."

All the boorleez eagerly nodded their agreement.

Shmash pouted behind wet eyes. "Ruler Xebec not fibs. Boorleez not dooz counts even."

"Aawwww..." sighed the chorus of weetykes.

A flood of compassion drowned Shoenia's ire. "Has anybody ever taught you how to count?"

"Taught?"

"Yes, taught. Were you not taught counting in school?"

"Skool?"

"Yes, you know, in arithmetic classes?"

"Huh?"

"Dooz she sez?"

The boorleez were clearly lost?

Warm tears of compassion seeped past Shoenia's eyelids. "You boorleez are not at all dense."

"Boorleez not be dense?" Munch asked, exchanging befuddled looks with the others.

"No," Shoenia continued. "You've just never been taught how to count is all. No wonder you think so little of yourselves. Has anyone ever given even one of you a hug?"

"Hugs?"

"Yes, hugs. Or ever tickled you?"

"Tagles?"

Shoenia was hardly surprised that the boorleez knew naught of such things. "Why, I'll wager not a one of you has ever even been kissed?"

"Ruler Xebec cusses us always," Belch noted.

"Not cussed, Belch. Kissed. Like this." Shoenia motioned for Shmash to bend down and, stretching up on her tippytoes, she planted a peck firmly on his cheek.

Shmash bit his bottom lip and blushed deepest purple, while both kooky critters shrieked and fled.

The other boorleez moved to shy away.

"No need to be scared," she explained. "Hugs can also be fun."

"Hugs?"

"Yes, watch." Shoenia embraced the still blushing boorlee.

Both smuzzles also hugged. Then the weetykes hugged. Even Thwack and Tiptin faked a sort-of-hug, while muttering real macho-like.

"Now then," Shoenia said. "You boorleez try it with each other. Go on, give each other a nice, warm hug."

Although it required several attempts for the teetering bunch to successfully wrap their arms around each other's burly bodies, they nevertheless managed to tame the tricky task.

"Hugs feels funny?" Shmash noted.

"Mmmmm... Me likes hugs," added another boorlee.

"Hugs not beddar fun dooz be noogies," Belch quickly pointed out.

But then again, what is?

"Boorleez dooz hot hugs to sheeleez in Ezu?" Taddler inquired of Shoenia, while slyly wriggling his brows.

"Only if they say it is okay first, Taddler. Nobody should be hugged if they don't want to be. Now everyone try hugging again. But this time say some nice words to each other."

"Nice words like this!" Tiptin exclaimed, suddenly most eager to *help out*. He snatched the surprised galfolk up into his arms. "I love you, Shoenia of Ga. I know this to be true because every time I think of you, I feel all nice and warm inside. And I feel all nice and warm inside all of the time. I would be so very proud to have you as my partner. Please twine your life's journey with mine?"

Although still somewhat stunned, Shoenia somehow managed a reply. "Yes, Tiptin of Folkton, I will twine my... mmmmmmmmmmmmmmmmmmmmmmm..."

"Ooooooooooooooooooooooo..." teased the boorleez and weetykes; while two jealous furballs merely rolled their eyes and pawtended to spit up.

"Thems lips be stuck maybe?" Munch eventually asked, clearly quite concerned.

"No," the Sheebazz assured him. "It's just a humanfolk thing. They should stop kissing soon enough."

"Dooz twine mean?" Belch asked.

"It means that they want to be special best budz forever," the Sheebazz explained.

Compliments now abounded throughout the dungeon as the boorleez also hugged and spoke very nice words to one another.

"Ye schnozz not be mostest gross."

"Ye not stinks yucky gross always."

"Ye face not be so muches gross like slimy wigglers."

Thwack shrugged and sighted above. "Hey, at least it's a start."

"Dooz be tagles?" Munch asked at last.

Shoenia was still aflush from Tiptin's kiss. "Well, tickles make others tingle and laugh. See?"

She seized the unprepared ladfolk and began wiggling her fingertips about his torso. The weetykes, Thwack and the smuzzles also began tickling one another. Even the kooky critters scurried back down the stairwell to take part.

Soon, the entire dungeon roared with laughter, which kept on until the thoroughly drained lot slumped to the cold floor. Every single boorlee but one agreed that, 'Tagles still not be more fun dooz noogies.'

But then again, what is?

Once all had caught their breath, Shoenia addressed the burly bunch. "You know, you boorleez could help us unpower the staff."

Almost all of the boorleez were visibly terror-stricken.

"But Ruler Xebec sez…" Taddler began.

"Guffaw! Ruler Xebec dooz be boink," Belch interrupted, crossing his eyes and sticking out his tongue for effect.

Laughter roared throughout the chamber.

"Boorleez dooz secret huddle!" Belch stated with some authority.

Tiptin thought, *'What's with all these huddles?'*

"Me helps!" Shmash exclaimed. "Me likes Shoenia."

"Oooooooooo," teased the other boorleez as they all bunched into a tight scrum, where Shmash promptly fell victim to a vigorous volley of razz noogies.

Thwack sighted to the above as the burly bunch quite loudly debated their next course of action. "Dearest Destiny, even the surreal has taken a leap into the bizarre."

"Relax, big guy," Shoenia said. "This is a very brave choice for them. Perhaps even the bravest choice that they shall ever make."

"Okay. Okay. When they inform us of their very brave choice, I will act very big surprised."

Shoenia patted the giant's massive arm. "Now, there's the Thwack I like."

"Yeah, yeah. Whatever."

"We chooses," Belch finally announced after two sidetrack debates about stinky feets and funny ears. "Shmash counts cuzz him be most *smard.*"

Shmash beamed proud at having been deemed the smartest. "We dooz votes. Votes sez we not dooz helps Shoenia gets staff?"

Only Taddler raised his arm.

"Um, votes sez we not dooz helps Shoenia gets staff be – um – one. Okay, Boorleez votes to sez we dooz dooz helps Shoenia gets staff?"

Virtually every other boorlee raised his arm, yet some time still elapsed before Shmash finally finished tallying up the votes. "Um, votes sez we dooz dooz helps Shoenia gets staff be – um – two. We dooz dooz helps Shoenia gets staff!"

"HOORRAY!!"

The loud cheer was followed, of course, by the customary round of grats noogies. Belch then broke the good news to the others.

"Wow!" Thwack blurted out. "Really? You will help? What a surprise! And the vote was just '*sooo*'... close. Talk about a real claw chomper!"

"Huh? Dooz boinky clops sez, Shoenia?"

"He says that he *erspects* you very brave boorleez for helping us to unpower the staff. Isn't that right, Thwack?"

"Uh, yeah. Sure. That's exactly what I meant. I *erspect* you boorleez."

"HOORRAY!!"

Being fully conscious of Shoenia's stern stare, Thwack gritted his teeth and just took it as he was subjected to a vigorous volley of *cheers* noogies. Clearly, all had been forgiven.

The entire group hastened back up the steps and on through the corridor. Upon exiting the castle, they wasted no time in crossing the charred courtyard. They then started down a steep path, which led to the heavily forested glen at the seaside base of the plateau.

Upon reaching the glen itself, Shoenia noticed that one of the younger boorleez was grimacing. "What is the matter?" she inquired.

"Pixx gots sliver," Belch explained.

The grimacing boorlee extended a pinky to show Shoenia the exposed shaft of a tiny splinter of wood.

"Is that from your bat?" she asked.

Pixx nodded that it was. "Me fites nasty buzzer bugs cuzz them dooz bites."

Shoenia was somewhat puzzled. "Why don't you just pull the sliver out?"

"Cuzz hurts," Pixx replied.

"Not if you pull it out fast, it won't."

"Huh? Pulls fast?"

"Sure, then it only hurts for the bat of a blink. Here, I'll pull it out for you."

As Shoenia pinched the minute object between her finger nails, the other boorleez all shuddered and turned away. For none could bear to watch.

"Ahh-ahh-ahh…."

Shoenia frowned. "At least wait until I pull on it, Pixx."

"Okay, Shoenia. Me waits for... YEOW!!" Pixx yelped as the sliver was pulled out.

"Now suck on your sore finger," Shoenia advised. "And stop picking your nose. If you bump into something your finger might get stuck up your nostril."

"Me doozed before."

"Then you should already know better."

Having tended to Pixx's *battle wound*, Shoenia hastened to rejoin Tiptin and the smuzzles at the front of the column. The Sheebazz and her army hovered closely overhead, keeping a wary watch for squawkers and chirpers. The boorleez nervously arm-swung along in the rear.

Scooching down low to help hide his bulk, Thwack stole through the forest greenery alongside the path. His pointy ears were fully perked to snag even the faintest of sounds, and his eye was peeled to catch even the slightest movement. "Psst, hey, Tiptin, I hear somebody sobbing," he whispered.

"Sure you do, Thwack. Now, be quiet."

"From which direction?" Shoenia inquired.

"It's coming from just up ahead of us," Thwack said, pointing to be more precise.

"Nice try…"

Shoenia's stern look stopped Tiptin in mid-speak. "Thwack, can you guess how far away the sobbing is?" she asked.

"It's quite close, Shoenia. I think that…"

"Sees!" Shmash suddenly interrupted, pointing through the trees to a small clearing, where a weeping boorlee sat upon a log. "There dooz be Gaffwit!?"

Upon hearing voices in the forest, Gaffwit squinted in an attempt to focus his burning eyes. Unable to see the beings behind the voices, the frightened boorlee panicked and moved to swift-swing away.

"Stops, Gaffwit! Dooz be me, Shmash! Sees!" Shmash waved his arms. "Belch dooz be here too!"

Belch emerged from the forest and swift-swung over to comfort his injured brudz. "Gaffwit, how ye hurts eyes?"

"Meeny scoffed staff," Gaffwit replied, clearly still shaken up from his ordeal.

"Who exactly stole the staff?" Tiptin inquired. "Was it Xebec?"

"Who dooz them be?" Gaffwit asked, pointing at Tiptin and Shoenia.

Belch clued his brudz in. "Hims dooz be Tiptin. Galfolk dooz be Shoenia."

"Oh. Greetz," the despondent boorlee said, while shaking his head. "Uh-uh. Ruler Xebec not scoffed staff."

"Then who did?" Shoenia pressed, already fearing the answer.

"Magic meeny doozed scoffed staff."

Shoenia's stomach sank. "Gaffwit, this magic meany, were his eyes two different colours?"

Gaffwit nodded that they were. "Uh-huh. Him tricks me. Sez citrus pulpy tastes even beddar dooz desserts. Then him stings me in eyes with juice."

"Gaffwit, listen to me," Shoenia pressed, "Which way did the magic meany…?"

"Tiptin! Shoenia!" Mite Diver shouted as he swooped down to meet them.

"What is it?" Tiptin inquired of the excited spy.

"Over there!" Mite Diver shouted, pointing towards the beach. "We spotted the magic meany on the seashore!"

"Did he have the staff?" Shoenia asked.

"Uh-huh."

Tiptin and Shoenia exchanged troubled looks.

"Just how in Morgue's maze are we ever going to take it away from him?" Tiptin asked.

"By trusting in Destiny and truly trying," Shoenia reminded him. "Mite Diver, lead us to where you last saw the magic meany. Quickly."

They followed Mite Diver free from the path and in amongst the greenery. Thwack took up the lead, stomping flat all bushy obstacles. As the group crossed over the flattened foliage, their ears soon snagged the crashing hush of nearby wetrollers assaulting the shore.

"There dooz be where magic meeny beed!" Gaffwit exclaimed, pointing at a boulder.

"Not dooz sez things, Gaffwit," Belch whispered, pinching his brudz' lips shut.

An army of weetykes was already assembled at the forest's edge, peeking out from amongst leaves and branches. None uttered so much as a peep as they scanned the nearby shore and sky, both of which were completely void of squawkers? Very strange?

The Sheebazz and Pint Little swooped down and perched on Shoenia's shoulders.

"Where is he?" Shoenia inquired.

"Pint Little says he just faded away," replied The Sheebazz.

Both humanfolk looked to Pint Little. "Faded away?"

"Uh-huh," Pint Little confirmed. "Some of us were following him along the shore, when he took a bitty bottle from his robe and popped the plug. And poof."

"And poof?" Tiptin was confused.

"Bottle makes big poof of haze. When haze clears, meany is gone? See where his tracks stop."

"Maybe Zebu floated away with the haze?" suggested The Sheebazz.

Shoenia was skeptical as her eyes traced the trail of fresh sandal prints across the sand. "Maybe? Or maybe not? I'd wager the latter."

"Where are you going?" Tiptin inquired, clutching her arm.

Shoenia tugged free from his grip. "To follow those sandal prints – and do what we were brought here to do."

"Shoenia, it is much too dangerous," the Sheebazz warned with grave concern. "The open sand provides no cover. You must keep hidden here within the growth."

"He might know that you are there?" Pint Little added.

Shoenia toned soft yet serious. "Zebu already knows that I am here. Therefore, I am no safer here than there. And neither are any of you. Destiny did not bring us all together at this exact time and place without purpose. Destiny either sides with us, or not. And in Destiny's dramas, we mortals can only play out our own parts. The outcome is never ours to choose."

Tiptin gave thought to Shoenia's words. *'Destiny must be in control,'* he reasoned. *'Who else could have brought us all together, and then guided us safely through such a labyrinth of dangers? Where did our courage come from? Or our passion? What steered our conscience? Or fueled our resolve? Something far more potent than ourselves has to be involved?'*

Looking at the fibre sword, Tiptin thought, *'Surely Spidey must have had good reason for trusting Thwack and myself to play out our parts in such a decisive drama? Just as Snarly must have had good reason for trusting in Shoenia? Could they not also have been just playing out their own parts? Of course they could!'*

"Count me in!" Tiptin exclaimed.

Thwack was likewise emboldened by Shoenia's words. He had long wanted to be a part of something that really mattered. In fact, he had often begged of Destiny to grant him just one real friend, and the generous deity had instead delivered to him many of the very best. Who was he to turn his back on the very same friends who would always have his? He asked himself, *'Would I not also be turning my back on Destiny?'*

The cyclops brandished a fist big as a boulder. "AAAAAAAAARRGH!!" Let's go maul a magician!"

Both smuzzles nattered to agree as they traded punches with the breeze.

"Stickem! Stickem! Stickem! Stickem!"

All eyes shifted to the boorleez, who trembled with fear and stared down in shame.

"It's okay that you're scared," Shoenia assured them, herself stepping free of the foliage. "You boorleez don't have to come with us out onto the beach. You're still our budz. We still love you."

Tiptin, Thwack and the smuzzles all stepped out from the forest and onto the sand, while an army of thorn-wielding flyfolk swarmed up into the sky.

"What we spozed dooz?" one boorlee inquired of Shmash.

"We dooz hides?" another asked of Belch.

Shmash and Belch exchanged confused looks, each expecting the other to take charge. Neither would.

However, one most unlikely boorlee did.

"Me not dooz bad things no more! Me helps Shoenia fites magic meeny! Me bonks magic meeny boink!"

All the other boorleez stared with wided eyes and open mouths as one of their own plucked a hard and hairy bonker bean from a palm tree and arm-swung out onto the sand. "Me no more snitches! Me no more fibs! And ye no more dooz zings me!"

"Taddler dooz be boink," remarked one boorlee, winding a forefinger about his ear.

"Me thinks too much nasty knocks noogies," concluded another.

Most boorleez nodded in agreement. Most, but not all.

"Me dooz be boink too!" Shmash announced, arm-swinging out after Taddler.

"Me dooz be boink six!" Belch declared, busting off a heavy chunk of log. "Me conks magic meeny on skull cuzz him burns me brudz' butt!"

"Stings me in eyes with juice too!" Gaffwit railed, grabbing the rest of the log. Meeny dooz nasty fites! Not fare!"

Munch was next to follow the others out onto the sand.

All of the remaining boorleez began busting up logs and plucking bonker beans. Then they too arm-swung out onto the sand. Every last one of them.

"They're actually coming," Thwack remarked in total surprise.

Shoenia smiled knowingly. "I never doubted them for a..." she began, as they neared the end of the sandal prints. But just then a shaking beneath her feet cut short her words.

Suddenly the very beach shifted its plain, knocking all but the hovering weetykes to the sand. In sheer panic, the sprawling boorleez groped at the wind. The frightened humanfolk clung together for balance, while the smuzzles bounced about like furry balls with eyes. Thwack dropped to his knees and dug deep with fingers and toes to keep from sliding off into the sea.

"Shoenia!" Mite Diver screamed out in full panic, pointing with both hands. "Look!"

Shoenia had felt the grip of angst during the initial tremors, but now it squeezed into a grasp of terror that she had known only once before; while bound by a root in The Fluorescent Forest. Knotting guts bated her breath.

A sandy form broke free from beneath the beach, and whirled up into the breeze. It spun the sand from its garments, spraying it into wided eyes and gaping mouths.

"You annoying little fool!" Zebu berated, abruptly stopping his spin. He glared daggers at Shoenia, brandishing the staff high atop his head. "Did you really think that a simple-minded galfolk such as yourself could ever pose any threat to a master magician like me?"

Shoenia desperately sought to recall Snarly's riddle, but her racing mind only thought forth blanks.

Setting himself down upon a flat slab of stone, Zebu simply waved the staff to end the quake. With a scowl most foul, he next pointed his wand at the charging cyclops and began gyrating its tip.

"Tooooo much!" Thwack yelled as his huge form was lifted clear of the beach and rotated heels over hearers. The upside-down giant began to shake up and down, pounding his shiny dome repeatedly upon the sand. "S-S-t-t-o-o-o-p-p-I-I-t-t-t-t...." he pleaded; but to no avail.

"Charge!!" shouted a dark mass as it swarm-bombed to *stickem!*

Zebu was undaunted as he began sucking in wind. Once his breathers were filled near to burst, he blasted forth an awesome gale that blew the wee warriors reeling from sight and scattered them way back in amongst the trees.

"Dung!" Shoenia cussed. "My mind is vague. I can't recall Snarly's riddle? Destiny, help me!"

"Destiny can't help you, galfolk! It is I who wield the staff!"

"Ssssssss... KAPPOW!!" A blue beam blazed forth from the staff's tip, blasting the fibre sword from Tiptin's grasp and burning his hand. The ladfolk rolled about in the sand, wincing and wailing in agony.

"Aha!" spat the magician, redirecting his weapon at the cowering smuzzles. "Tell me, Shoenia of Ga, where is your faith in Destiny now?"

"No!" Shoenia screamed, springing afoot and charging at Zebu. Sparks spit from her eyes. "You are a liar and a scoundrel, Zebu! You even betrayed Snarly! I'll...."

"You'll meet Morgue is what you'll do!" Zebu shrilled, taking aim with the staff.

"Ssssssss... KAPPOW!!"

Upon impact, the bent beam of light exploded and tore open a gaping rift in the beach. The blast sprayed sand and broken bits of shell out in all directions, and flung Shoenia heels over hearers high up into the breeze. She flopped back down hard onto the wet sand, where she lay in a still and silent lump.

Zebu was briefly curious as to why the beam had bent to strike the sand between the galfolk's feet, for the staff had always shot true before? *'Oh well. I suppose it matters not, as its purpose has been fulfilled? Shoenia of Ga is a thorn in my side no more. Soon, the tide will wash away all memory of her – forever!'*

Next, the magician turned his attention to the boorleez, who cowered in a state such as they had never shown. They huddled together and trembled with fright. Zebu noted their fear with great satisfaction as he belted out his tirade of new rules for his realm:

"I'm the baddest Ruler to ever be,
The meanest you shall ever see,
If it's trouble that you seek,
You would do well to mess with me,
" I have rules strict for all of you,
Here's a list of my decrees,
Listen up my chattel new,
For this is how it's gonna be!"

The boorleez all hung their heads as 'Ruler Zebu' began listing off all of his new decrees:

"There will be no more having friends,
no more stinky feets greets...

Each and every boorlee was deeply saddened over the loss of the kind galfolk, who had been the first to have shown them any real *'erspect'*. Therefore, Zebu's words cut much deeper than just a bunch of new rules.

"... no more being nice,
no more desserts…

"Shoenia?" Pint Little whispered, herself having evaded Zebu's gale by hiding behind Thwack. "Shoenia, please wake up. The tide is rolling in, Shoenia. Shoenia?"

Fluttering about in a near panic, the puny weetyke struggled to revive the motionless galfolk. First, she lifted each of Shoenia's eyelids. Next, she blew into her ears. Then she tried pleading. And shaking. And pummeling upon Shoenia's brow. She prayed and begged of Destiny to awaken her friend; even promising to come clean and say sorry to Mite Diver for that time when she covered his slumbering form with sticky bumble-sweet and flower petals.

All of her efforts seemed to be made in vain. Overcome with grief, Pint Little curled up in her motionless friend's hair and wept.

The smuzzles likewise tried to revive Shoenia. They frantically pawed at her still form, whimpering as they licked her cold cheeks. All to no effect. Things just seemed so final and hopeless.

However, seems sometimes isn't what is, and the miracle that Pint Little had been begging for quietly began to happen. An unseen spirit whispered in like a warming wind. *"In the proper place and at the proper time, you shall know to do the proper thing."*

"Uhhhh…" Shoenia moaned, parting her lips to draw in a breath. "Snarly?"

"Shhhh," Pint Little whispered directly into her friend's ear. "Or Zebu shall know you've cheated Morgue."

Nearby, Ruler Xebec kept adding to his list of decrees:

"... no more laughing,
no more singing,
no more sharing,
no more caring...

Shoenia blinked her eyes and shook the mush from her mind. "Stay quiet, all of you," she cautioned as she sighted in on Zebu. "See there, the scoundrel has his back to us."

"… no more swimming,
no more playing fun games…

Shoenia's mind became focused and clear, and she recalled Snarly's riddle:

"WHEN NEXT YOU MEET UPON A SHORE,
HOW SHALL FLAMES LICK CLOTH NO MORE?"

Kissing her forefinger to stress silence, Shoenia couldn't help but smile. At last, she finally understood exactly what Snarly's riddle meant. And she knew exactly what she must do.

"… no more happiness,
no more joy,
and absolutely no more of your stupid knuckle noogies!"

Most of the boorleez wailed in anguish upon hearing Zebu's final rule. But not Shmash. Having noticed Shoenia crawling through the sand towards the unsuspecting magician, the *smardest* boorlee's mind sought feverishly for a way to keep Zebu from noticing her. "Pzzzzzzt…"

"Huh?" Belch turned to Shmash, who then used his eyes to motion behind Zebu.

"We gots dooz helps Shoenia," Shmash whispered.

Belch nodded and began waving his arms to draw Zebu's attention fully onto himself.

"You there!" Zebu growled, noticing the flailing boorlee. "Why do you cut into my words!? Well, speak up!"

"Uh, me...?"

Thinking quickly, Shmash tactfully jumped in. "We gots questions."

"Questions? Questions! I think the situation is perfectly clear! I am now your Ruler, and you are all still dirt!"

"But Ruler Zebu, we boorleez be dense dirt," Taddler added, also taking note of Shoenia and tactfully playing along. "We need things sezzed much so we know rules."

"Uh-huh," Gaffwit concurred, eager to play his part. "We even be muches more dense dooz be dirt."

Zebu rolled his empty eyes. He thought, *'Sometimes creation can be so cruel.'* "Very well, then! Because you boorleez truly are denser than dirt, I will repeat my decrees just one last time! Now, listen up!"

By now, every single boorlee had clued in to what was really going on. Thus, each nodded and hung out his tongue to look extra dense in order to help fool the magic meeny.

Even the kooky critters played along. They wrapped their long tongues about their snouts, and crossed their yellow peepers.

"There will be no more having friends,
No more stinky feets greets,
no more being nice,
no more desserts ...."

Crawling up onto the slab and sneaking within easy reach of her distracted target, Shoenia carefully retrieved the flint and striker from her skirt pouch. Both of her hands trembled and her heart pounded, yet, she knew that Destiny was within her. She could feel a warm energy calming her bellybees.

She fumbled with both items, trying to strike the flint ever so gently in order to negate any sound. But no sparks spit forth. Panic crept into her mind. If she struck the flint any harder, Zebu would surely hear her. *'Now what do I do?'*

Destiny errors not with its choices, however, and Thwack, too, still had his part to play in the unfolding drama. A part for which the big guy was most aptly suited.

"HARR!! HARR!! HARR!! HARR!!" roared the upside-down cyclops, who by now had packed the sand so firm that his dome barely even touched it. The shaking had ceased, leaving him simply suspended in midair, yet, still able to make trouble. Which, of course, is exactly what he did.

Thwack smiled and blinked at Shoenia, signalling to her that he had her back. "Hey, Zebubblebrain, is that a pointy hat, or did ya just paint yer head? HARR!! HARR!! HARR!! HARR!!"

Zebu was flabbergasted. "How dare you address me like that!"

"HARR!! HARR!! HARR!! HARR!! Hey, spearhead! What do you call that scent you're wearing? Essence of Barf? HARR!! HARR!! HARR!! HARR!!"

All of the boorleez burst into laughter.

"Hey, where'd ya get them crazy eyes? Did some fiendish finners have a parts sale? HARR!! HARR!! HARR!! HARR!!"

Hysterics now ruled the entire beach. Even Shoenia grappled to gag her giggles.

"And catch a whiff of those feet! Phew. Ya oughta be more careful where ya step, Moo-pie guy! Get it – moo pie guy? Because your feet surely smell like something, and it's definitely not fragrance or flowers! HARR!! HARR!! HARR!! HARR!! HARR!!"

"Why you insolent…!?*#!!*?!!" The furious magician pointed his weapon to blast. "I'll burn you into dust, you oversized…? Huh? What is that smoky smell? Snff. Snff. Something's burning? What the...? Hey!"

Zebu began frantically slapping at the flames which were feeding on the hem of his robe. However, his actions only fanned the flames to grow ever taller and more ravenous with each and every slap. In quick time, the panicking magician found himself faced with only two options: either douse the flames immediately, or else burn and meet Morgue.

"Yeeeeeooowww!!" Zebu screamed as he sprinted full stride into the surf of The Saline Sea.

"HARR!! HARR!! HARR!! Are those streamers, or did yer skull sprout roots! "HARR!! HARR!! HARR!! HARR!! HARR!!"

Holding the staff high atop his head, Zebu waded in up to his chest. After dousing the flames, he turned and furiously fisted his vengeance at Shoenia.

But despite Zebu's fist and his fury, revenge would be denied to him on this day. Without a wisp of warning, a breaking wetroller powered in from the deep, crashing down from above and curling him under. The drowning magician fought frantically to keep hold of his precious staff; while struggling to reach the surface and draw a breath.

It was not to be. Before he could recover, the retreating surf sucked him out into the sea's chilly depths, where a waiting black and white spouter with mean, red eyes swallowed him whole. And The Staff of The Demon Chaser was forever unpowered.

"HOORRAY!!" cheered the elated boorleez, happily granting each other grats noogies, as well as hugs and tagles. One adventurous boorlee even offered out kisses.

Thwack tumbled to the sand, and the smuzzles waltzed and whirled about the beach. Pint Little blushed as Shoenia and Tiptin locked lips for a major *smoocheroozy*. While the rest of the weetykes, now fully regrouped, swarm-bombed to boogie!

And then, just as quickly as it had started, the foreboding whoop of metallic wings put an abrupt end to all the fun. All eyes stared upward as a gold and silver beast descended upon them. Aboard its back rode a ranting sorcerer with a sane-wanting stare.

Xebec pointed about with the webscroll as he leapt from his mount, already shouting commands at the boorleez. "Seize them! Seize them all! Now! As in right now!"

Every single boorlee glanced about in confusion, entirely uncertain of what to do next?

His cheeks burning with rage, the dim sorcerer began scolding the boorleez. *And worse.* "I said seize them, you dense boobs! Now! What are you stupid boorleez all waiting for!? Dearest Destiny, you losers are as repulsive as your kooky pets!"

"Remember who is saying these mean names," Shoenia reminded her friends. "You don't deserve to be bullied by anybody. Nobody does."

"*Stickem! Stickem! Stickem! Stickem!* Reeeeeeeeeeealllly *Stickem!!*"

The distracted sorcerer swatted and cussed at the tiny pests, who pricked their thorns into his flesh. Thus, he failed to notice the burly mob that was now arm-swinging across the beach towards him. That is until, as Thwack would say, it was simply '*toooooo*' late!

"Stop it!" Xebec commanded, as large, hairy hands grabbed hold of his limbs. They whisked his frail frame clear up off the ground, before rudely shaking the webscroll free from his grasp. "P-P-Put me d-down! I s-said, p-p-put me d-down! N-N-Now!"

"Dooz Xebec hard hurts noogies!" shouted a voice from the mob.

"HARD HURTS NOOGIES!! HARD HURTS NOOGIES!! HARD HURTS NOOGIES!!" chanted the boorleez. "NOOGIE!! NOOGIE!! NOOGIE!! NOOGIE!! NOOGIE!!"

"Griffin!" Xebec screamed, in both fear and anger. "Griffin!"

With its sharp talons poised to slice, the metallic beast flapped aloft. Then with its jagged beak parted to rip out flesh, it dove to defend its creator.

"Uh-uh. No you don't!" Tiptin shouted, snatching his mangled sword from the sand. Spinning his body around to increase the force, the ladfolk hurled the weapon with all of his might.

"EEEEEEEEEEEEEEE!!" squealed the griffin, as the fibre blade pierced its armor and stuck into its body. The flailing beast came crashing down upon the beach, where it quickly melted into a smoking heap of slag and ore.

Its final task complete, the sword shimmered briefly as it pulsed its last breath. Then its shimmer was snuffed, and it wilted to meet Morgue.

"Farewell," Tiptin said. He offered his fibred friend a parting wave before turning to take in the noisy ruckus now ruling the beach.

"Dooz him nasty knocks noogies too!"

"NASTY KNOCKS NOOGIES!! NASTY KNOCKS NOOGIES!! NASTY KNOCKS...."

"NOOOOOOOOOOOOOOOOOOOOOOOOOOOO00000 ...."

"NOOGIE!! NOOGIE!! NOOGIE!! NOOGIE!!" chanted the mob, while they battered Xebec's skull a bruising black and blue. "NOOGIE!! NOOGIE!! NOOGIE!! NOOGIE!! NOOGIE!!"

"Dooz zings Xebec into sea!" Taddler suggested, clearly excited that it could finally be somebody else's turn to be zingsed.

"ZINGS IN SEA!! ZINGS IN SEA!! ZINGS IN SEA!!"

Belch and Munch tore the screaming sorcerer away from the others, and then most eagerly took to swinging him to and fro by his limbs.

"Stop it! Put me down! Right this instant! I said, put me down! Now! I am your Ruler!"

"Ye zings when me dooz counts five," Shmash instructed.

Belch nodded. "We zings when Shmash dooz counts five."

"One – four – seven – umm – three – ???? What number me spozed dooz sez next?"

"Me not cares!" Taddler suddenly piped up. "Just zings him!"

"Taddler, ye thinks muches smard. We just zings him!" Shmash concurred. "Belch and Mulch, ye dooz zings on zings!"

While Belch and Mulch continued to swing the hapless sorcerer to and fro, all of the other boorleez shouted out the count:

“SWINGS!!... SWINGS!!... SWINGS!!... ZINGS!!”

“NOOOOOOOOOOOOOOOOOOO.................” A frail figure flailed frantically as it flew through the sky, before eventually plunging into the wetrollers.

Splash...

“HOORRAY!!”

Cheers resounded up and down the shore as the joyous boorleez rewarded themselves with some super-serious grats noogies. When the blissy bunch finally calmed down, Shmash called for a secret huddle. After reaching some sort of agreement, they arm-swung back across the sand and lined up before Shoenia.

Shmash was picked to explain. “Shoenia, we votes ye dooz be *‘Fishal Boorleez Budz’*. Even Taddler votes ye dooz.”

Shoenia was choked with emotion. “I am honoured to be voted an Official Boorleez Budz. You know, you are all very special to me as well. And kinda cute.”

Every single boorlee blushed.

“Aaawww...” echoed the chorus.

“Really, you are. And The Sheebazz has kindly offered to let some of her weetykes remain here for a time to help school you on how to count.”

“And dancing too? Boorleez be skools dooz dancing? Cuzz sheeleez in Ezu likes dancing.”

Shoenia smiled. “Sure, and dancing too.”

Belch bore moist cheeks. “Dooz come ye not stays with boorleez, Shoenia? Ye stops us be scolds – and worse.”

“Pleeeeeze...” begged all of the other boorleez.

The overwhelmed galfolk began to weep openly. “I would like that, Belch. Except that my home is very far from here. And I have my own family, whom I miss very much.” Shoenia paused and palmed her chest. “I shall always carry a big part of you boorleez right here within my heart.”

The boorleez briefly hung their heads in sadness. Then, one by one, they filed past their first ever ‘Fishal Boorleez Budz’, treating her as if she was one of their very own. *Then again, maybe she was? In fact, maybe there's a wee bit of Boorleez at play deep down inside most of us?*

Every boorlee bid her a verbal, *"Slong."* Plus they each included a tender *luvs* noogie, which didn't hurt her skull one little bit.

"See!" Taddler suddenly shouted, pointing slightly past the shore. "Xebec dooz swims back to beach!"

After tucking Spidey's webscroll up under one arm, Tiptin smiled and drew Shoenia in closer with the other. "First, we must return this webscroll to Spidey Smells. After that, I go wherever you go – me very own Fishal Best Budz."

"I love you, Tiptin," Shoenia replied, taking his injured hand in her own and examining his burnt fingers. "Too bad I am without the stalkhollow. Titanroot sap would surely sooth your pain."

"Just being here with you soothes my pain," he remarked, drawing her body tight against his and sealing her lips with his own.

"HARR!!" Thwack suddenly interrupted, pointing past them. "HARR!! HARR!! HARR!! HARR!! HARR!!"

Both turned about and giggled as they watched a sopping wet sorcerer fleeing along the shore, just mere strides ahead of a gaining mob of burly boorleez. Each of which arm-swung upon extremely hard knuckles, and shouted, "NOOGIE!! NOOGIE!! NOOGIE!! NOOGIE!! NOOGIE!! NOOGIE…!!"

Taleteller's Farewell

"Hi! Hi! Hi! Hi! It's me, Me. How are you, You. Don't ya just love them boorleez? Them dooz be so plite. You know, they've really come a long way throughout the eons. I understand that some of their offspring even recently obtained degrees from The Ezu School of Higher Learning – in physics!

"Yeah, right. If you buy that one, then perhaps I could interest you in purchasing one slightly abused planet? Has a few holes in its ozone, but nothing that can't be repaired by time after its current inhabitants are all fried. Albeit, lots and lots and lots of time.

"What? You already have such a planet? So sorry. I shan't burden you with another then. Or should I say, I shan't burden another with you. Uh-uh. Noper. No way. Not a chance.

"Oops! I am straying way off topic here. Where was I? Oh yes. Yes, yes, yes. So, now the boorleez are off to school. Gee, this should be interesting? Count to ten in twelve easy grades. Talk about your teacher burnout, eh?

"Giving credit where it's due, the burly bunch did ignite their intellect exactly when it mattered most. Did so. Did too. Now, even if the magic meeny has somehow survived his tour of a spouter's innards, would you erspect any magician who has been duped by a bunch of boorleez? Ha! I bet narcy ole Zebu won't be boasting about that when he's swabbing Morgue's Maze!

"The Sheebazz and her weetykes actually became quite fond of their eager students, even teaching the burly bunch how to sort-of-dance. Now, that's knuckle-bopping at its beast! Ha! While Hoot and Hweet Beaker casually went about being their same old laid-back selves.

"The boorleez became welcome wherever they went; even in Cycity and Folkton. 'Not overly bright,' others would note,

'Although, quite polite. And very kind, especially to the little ones. Always eager to shower them with tender luvs noogies'.

"Then we have the glumdreary sorcerer. Completely washed up. A loony without a bin. But with many headaches. Many, many headaches. And we are talking about screaming skullbangers here. Ha! Ha! Hee. Hee. Ho! Ho! Ha! Hee. Ho! Ugh...

"Nix the staff. Scratch the griffin. Kiss the webscroll goodbye. Castle ruined. Zero friends. Below zero erspect. None to do his bidding. Not a single possession. Shackled by karma. Gone completely round-the-twist. All in all, not a very happy – loozer. Ha!

"As for Thwack? Well, what can I tell ya! HARR!! The big guy eventually did find that special someone, and then discovered that whatever we give, in time we shall get. Yeppers. First time they met, Hoaxy sure tripped him off his feet. Literally. You see, we're talking about one faaaaaaaaar out cygal here! HONK!! HONK!! HONK!! HONK!!

"Lastly, after attempting to return the webscroll to Spidey Smells, Tiptin and Shoenia and the smuzzles eventually made there way to The Continent, only to discover that the Second Continental Conflict was still raging, as senseless conflicts are quite prone to do. But alas, that is another tale to be told another time...

"For now –I gotta go, do too, do so,
It's time to leave, I gotta blow,
On to where, I do not know?
Yet time has come for me to go,
"Got things to see, places to be,
New adventures beckon me,
Now I'm off, I'm on my way,
Off to where, I cannot say,
"So, until we meet again, if ever,
May Destiny feed and shelter you,
And keep you safe,
And bless you with a precious heart,
"Fare ye well, my special Earthkind friend –
"FARE YE MOST WELL...................."*

DOOZ BE END

Message from the Author...

Thank you for reading my book.

I hope you enjoyed this story,
Please help guide future readers by
leaving a review on Amazon.com

If you have comments or questions,
feel free to contact me at:
rennickderon@gmail.com

Read another novel by
Deron Rennick...

'The Webscroll'

Made in United States
North Haven, CT
12 December 2022

28573077R00134